The first day

I took a deep breath, smoothed my hair down, and opened the door to the classroom. The second I did, the bell pealed out so loudly, it could have been inside my brain. I froze, startled, and every single person in the room turned to look at me. I instantly knew that I had made two drastic mistakes.

First, I had not conformed to local fashion codes, which apparently called for the wearing of much color and little cloth. I had never seen so many belly buttons in one place at one time in all my life. And I'd spent plenty of summer days at the Jersey Shore, thank you very much.

Second, I was not blonde. How had I not noticed it before? Every last female in the room was blonde. There were natural blondes and peroxide blondes, highlighted blondes and frosted blondes. Golden blondes, white blondes, ash blondes. Blondes with brown eyebrows and blondes with olive skin. There was even an Asian girl in the front row with her short blonde hair pulled back in two neat ponytails.

My gaze darted around the room from blonde to blonde to blonde to blonde. A Britney-clone looked at me and snickered.

"Nice clip," she mouthed, glancing toward my fore-head. Her friend laughed into her hand. Suddenly my rhinestone barrette felt hard and cold and jagged against my scalp.

It was official. I was in hell. And John Frieda was the devil.

OTHER SPEAK BOOKS

I Was a Non-Blonde Cheerleader

Cheerleader

KIERAN SCOTT

speak

An Imprint of Penguin Group (USA) Inc.

SPEAK
Published by the Penguin Group
Penguin Group (USA) Inc., 345 Hudson Street, New York, New York 10014, U.S.A.
Penguin Group (Canada), 90 Eglinton Avenue East, Suite 700,
Toronto, Ontario, Canada M4P 2Y3 (a division of Pearson Penguin Canada Inc.)
Penguin Books Ltd, 80 Strand, London WC2R 0RL, England
Penguin Ireland, 25 St Stephen's Green, Dublin 2, Ireland
(a division of Penguin Books Ltd)
Penguin Group (Australia), 250 Camberwell Road, Camberwell, Victoria 3124, Australia
(a division of Pearson Australia Group Pty Ltd)
Penguin Books India Pvt Ltd, 11 Community Centre,
Panchsheel Park, New Delhi - 110 017, India
Penguin Group (NZ), 67 Apollo Drive, Mairangi Bay,
Albany, Auckland 1310, New Zealand (a division of Pearson New Zealand Ltd)
Penguin Books (South Africa) (Pty) Ltd, 24 Sturdee Avenue,
Rosebank, Johannesburg 2196, South Africa

Registered Offices: Penguin Books Ltd, 80 Strand, London WC2R 0RL, England

First published in the United States of America by G. P. Putnam's Sons,
a division of Penguin Young Readers Group, 2005
Published by Speak, an imprint of Penguin Group (USA) Inc., 2006

1 3 5 7 9 10 8 6 4 2

THE LIBRARY OF CONGRESS HAS CATALOGED THE G. P. PUTNAM'S SONS EDITION AS FOLLOWS:

Scott, Kieran, 1974–
I was a non-blonde cheerleader / Kieran Scott. p. cm.
Summary: As a brunette on the all-blonde cheerleading squad at her new Florida high
school, sophomore Annisa Gobrowski tries to fit in with her popular teammates without
losing the friendship of Bethany, the only other non-blonde at the school.
[1. Identity—Fiction. 2. Popularity—Fiction. 3. Cheerleading—Fiction.
4. Blondes—Fiction. 5. High schools—Fiction. 6. Schools—Fiction.
7. Florida—Fiction.] I. Title.
PZ7.S42643Iae 2005 [Fic]—dc22 2004003788
ISBN 0-399-24279-1

Speak Splashproof ISBN 978-0-14-240832-2

Text set in Garth Graphic.

Manufactured in China

For Wendy, Shira and Ally,
and for all cheerleaders, everywhere.

Special thanks to Raina Wallens and Lisa Papademetriou
for their help and faith in the early stages of this project
and their unwavering support throughout.
To Cecily von Ziegesar for introducing me to Sarah Burnes
and to Sarah for believing in this book and making it all happen.
Thanks most of all to Jennifer Bonnell for being there every step
of the way and making the whole experience so much fun.
I would also like to thank Matt Viola, Lee Scott,
Erin Scott and Ian Scott for always believing.

First day of school.

First.

Day.

Of.

School.

Hadn't I already had one of these in September? What kind of sadistic star had I been born under that I got to have two? Two versions of the most stress-inducing day of the year?

I stood outside the back door of Sand Dune High and wondered what, exactly, I was doing here. This was Florida. I was a Jersey girl. I'd only been here five days and already the top of my nose was starting to peel, and that was *with* daily applications of SPF 15. It was so warm out at 8:00 A.M. that I had already managed to sweat through my black T-shirt on the short walk to school. And according to the huge banner that was hung across the bleachers by the football field, the school mascot was a Mighty Fighting Crab. I mean, come on! The Crabs? I had already made up about ten STD jokes to keep on reserve for parties and lagging conversations.

Okay, be positive, Annisa. It's not like you haven't done this before, I told myself.

My family had moved around the Northeast all my life as my dad, Professor Gobrowski to his colleagues, tried on

English department after English department. I had started at plenty of new schools. This was nothing new.

Okay, well, maybe it was a *little* new. After all, the last move had been almost four years ago, allowing me ample time to settle in and make friends that I now missed with an ache previously unknown to my body. And I was used to brick buildings, changing leaves, slush and rain and angry bus drivers. This school was very . . . *Florida,* with its white-washed stucco walls, Spanish-tiled roof and palm tree–lined walks. But it was just a school, right? There were teachers and students and books in there. How different could it be?

I reached up to touch my signature fashion item—the rhinestone clip that always held back my short brown hair. It acted as a kind of pacifier in moments like these. A reminder that wherever I went, I was still me.

I took a deep breath. "Here goes nothing."

The noise inside hit me like a sharp wind. People darted across the hallway, a couple of guys slapped hands while a few girls bent over an open magazine. Everyone unfamiliar. Everyone nameless. How was I going to do this?

Okay, the first step is always the hardest, I told myself. So I took it. I stepped over the threshold into my new school . . . and my toe caught the lip of the step. My heart shot into my throat. I flew forward. The floor rushed up at me. And all I could think was, *Sand Dune High, here I come!*

This was going to hurt. I knew from experience.

But before I could hit the ground, a pair of strong hands grabbed my arm and I was saved from utter humiliation. A few people still snickered around me, but it was so much better than it could have been. I looked up to thank my savior and my throat totally dried up. Maybe it was just the effects of hero worship, but the phrase *humuna, humuna, humuna* comes to mind.

2

"Are you okay?" my knight in faded Abercrombie asked, releasing me.

I smoothed down the front of my T-shirt and tried not to look anyone directly in the eye. My face was burning red. "Bones intact, ego slightly bruised," I said.

"I'll have that step removed by the end of the day," he joked.

"Thanks. You can do that?"

"I have powers beyond your understanding," he replied, a mischievous glint in his bluer-than-blue eyes. "I'm Daniel Healy, by the way."

Daniel Healy was yum. He was taller than me, but not too tall. Actually, the exact perfect height for slow dancing kind of tall. He had light brown hair with obviously natural blond highlights that matched the sun-bleached wisps on his tanned arms and legs. He was wearing long denim shorts, a faded, red, short-sleeved button-down with the first few buttons open, and a single shell on a black cord around his neck. And his smile? Whoa mama.

A few lines formed above Daniel Healy's perfectly shaped nose. He looked a little bit disturbed. Unfortunately, I get that a lot. "And you are . . . ?" he asked.

Nice one, Gobrowski, I said to myself. I gave him my best self-deprecating, doofy-me laugh. "Annisa Gobrowski," I said. "Don't call me Annie or I can't be responsible for my actions."

My stomach dropped when I saw his shocked face. Misfire. Back home that usually got a laugh. Did people in Florida have trouble catching witty sarcasm? If so, I was in big trouble.

"I'll remember that," he said. "You new? Come on, I'll show you where the office is."

Somehow I made myself move down the unfamiliar hall

with its unfamiliar smells and its unfamiliar faces. People watched me curiously, like I was some new, unclassified species. I was so nervous, I was sure my knees were going to go out any second.

All around me students lined the hallway, digging in their lockers, checking their hair in compact mirrors, passing a soccer ball back and forth across the floor. Everything seemed to blur together. Would any of these people end up being my friend? Did I have anything in common with any of them? What if this school was too cliquey and no one wanted someone new to, you know, *clique* with?

"So, where did you come from, anyway?" I asked Daniel as we rounded a corner. I needed conversation to distract me from my insecure thoughts.

"I thought I was supposed to ask *you* that," he said. "Aren't you the new girl?"

I laughed. "No, I mean, just now. When you saved me from a splat worse than death."

"Oh, I followed you to school," Daniel said, causing my heart to thump. "I'm not a stalker or anything. I just live down the block from you. We should walk together sometime."

Smiling on the outside, I tried to remember if I'd done anything super embarrassing on the walk to school, like pick a wedgie or talk to myself. Oh, God! I had tried to three-pointer my banana peel into a garbage can by the bleachers and missed by a mile. Had he seen that?

"So where *did* you move here from?" Daniel asked.

"New Jersey."

"Really? Did you ever see anyone from *The Sopranos*?"

Such a boy thing to ask.

"No. And there were no attempted whackings at my old school either," I told him.

4

Daniel laughed. "Well, this is it," he said, stopping in front of a glass door marked MAIN OFFICE. "Good luck, Annisa-not-Annie."

I grinned. "Thank you so much," I said, sounding a lot more breathless than usual.

"Hey, I know I wouldn't want to walk the halls of a new school alone," he said with a sympathetic grin. "Or, you know, trip through them."

"Ha ha."

Daniel started to back his way down the hall, somehow not stumbling over the skateboards, books and hundreds of feet in his path, all of which would have definitely sent me sprawling.

"See you later!" he added, giving me a wave.

I hope so, I thought with a smile. Maybe this new school thing wouldn't be so bad.

• • •

"Excellent record, Ms. Gobrowski, just excellent. Excellent, excellent, excellent."

I sat in the vinyl chair to the left of my new guidance counselor's desk, my hands clasped tightly in my lap. He held the manila folder containing my permanent file up in front of his round face, shaking his head, but in a good way—like he was awed by my many B-plusses and occasional A's. When he lowered the file to his lap, he grinned, his rosy red cheeks growing even rosier. He reminded me of an inflated Christmas elf or one of those lawn gnomes my grandmother has all over her yard in Chicago.

"Just excellent," he said again, his eyes twinkling.

Ever hear a word so many times it starts to lose all meaning?

"Uh . . . thanks, Mr. . . ."

I trailed off, mortified. Already I couldn't remember his

5

name. "In-one-ear-out-the-other" should really be my nickname. That or "Miss Trips-a-Lot."

"Cuccinello," he said with a laugh. "Not to worry—it's a tough one."

"Cuccinello," I repeated, wondering when he was going to let me go to class. The first day was always the toughest, and I wanted to get it over with. Besides, if he kept me here much longer, I was going to be *late* for homeroom, which meant no slipping in with the rest of the crowd, which meant big attention on me, which meant—

"So, I bet you're a little nervous, huh?" Mr. Cuccinello said, tapping the edge of my file against the corner of his desk.

"Me? Nah."

"Brave girl! I like it!" Mr. Cuccinello barked. As he said the words, he sat up straight for a split second, like a firecracker going off, then settled back down again. He slipped a thin piece of paper off his desk and handed it to me. "Now, here's your schedule. You requested a music elective, so we've put you in concert choir. Are you a singer?"

"Um . . . yeah. An alto," I said.

"Great! Now, if any of your classes are too fast or too slow, or if you just plain don't like 'em, let me know. I'm here for you, Ms. Gobrowski, remember that. Here . . . for . . . you!" he said, enunciating each word with a jab of his finger in my direction.

I looked down at the unfamiliar schedule in my hand. It ran vertically down the page instead of horizontally like the ones back home. Plus, it was peppered with strange room numbers and abbreviations. I felt a lump form in my throat. I just wanted one thing to feel the same. Anything.

"You're gonna do just great here, I can feel it," Mr. Cuccinello continued. "I get a good vibe from you, Ms. Gobrowski, a good vibe. You are going to fit right in like a square peg in a square hole." He made a popping sound with his tongue and raised his bushy eyebrows. "Now get on out there and knock 'em dead!"

"Thanks, Mr. C," I said, the nickname slipping out.

"Mr. C! I like it!" he called after me. "Get a move on! The bell's gonna ring soon!"

Great. Like I needed more pressure. The halls were almost deserted and the couple of people who *were* there were running. Never a good sign. According to my schedule, I was assigned to room 214. Ms. Walters' classroom. I made a right, vaguely remembering that Daniel and I had passed a stairwell. I figured 214 had to be upstairs, yes? It was a start.

As I scurried up to the second floor, the sweat returned and I had to hike up my long denim skirt so that my ankles could make the climb. *Mental note: Factor Florida temperature and abundance of school stairs into all future wardrobe choices.* By the time I got upstairs, I was in panic mode. When would the bell ring? Was it going to ring now? No. Now? No. I felt like I was stuck in a life-size game of Mouse Trap.

I glanced left and mercifully saw room 215 at the end of the hall. I figured 214 had to be nearby . . . except it wasn't. The room numbers only went up. And when I turned a corner, I was faced with rooms 200A, 200B and 201. What was this, some kind of sick joke? It was like the set designer from the Harry Potter movies had taken some time off to build my new school. I hustled down the hallway, the numbers flying by. All the classrooms were full of students, doors closed, conversation muffled. I had yet to see a soul in the second-floor hall. I was completely and totally late.

Around yet another corner I finally found room 214. Phew. I took a deep breath, smoothed my hair down, and opened the door to the classroom. The second I did, the bell pealed out so loudly, it could have been inside my brain. I froze, startled, and every single person in the room turned to look at me. I instantly knew that I had made two drastic mistakes.

First, I had not conformed to local fashion codes, which apparently called for the wearing of much color and little cloth. I had never seen so many belly buttons in one place at one time in all my life. And I'd spent plenty of summer days at the Jersey Shore, thank you very much.

Second, I was not blonde. How had I not noticed it before? Every last female in the room was blonde. There were natural blondes and peroxide blondes, highlighted blondes and frosted blondes. Golden blondes, white blondes, ash blondes. Blondes with brown eyebrows and blondes with olive skin. There was even an Asian girl in the front row with her short blonde hair pulled back in two neat ponytails.

I was a very new, very real, clearly distasteful minority.

I couldn't move. The teacher, a rather overweight woman with a horrid paisley dress and yes, a mannish *blonde* do, didn't even come to my rescue. I had just walked into the Barbie Dream School and I was that brunette reject doll that always got left on the shelf at Toys R Us until she got marked down fifteen times and eventually sold off for ninety-nine cents.

"Well, I'll be damned," a voice said, right behind me. "There *is* a God."

I felt like I was going to be sick. I moved out of the doorway and was faced with a seriously tall girl with purple hair, black eyeliner and multiple piercings—ear and nose. She was looking down at me like I was her exact version of Mr. Wonderful come to whisk her away to an exotic desert island.

"Hi," I said.

"You are *so* sitting with me," she replied.

She grabbed my hand—hers was covered in a fishnet glove with the fingertips sliced off—and pulled me toward the back of the classroom.

"Shouldn't I—," I began, looking over my shoulder at the teacher.

"She doesn't care who you are," the girl told me. She fell into a seat with a cacophony of clangs and clanks from her various zippers and accessories. Then she practically flung me into the desk next to hers. "I, on the other hand, do," she added. Her brown eyes glistened with interest as she held out her hand again. "I'm Bethany."

"Annisa," I told her, shaking her hand. I glanced around the room and a few of my spectators rolled their eyes and looked away. Suddenly, Ms. Walters came to life and clapped her hands, telling everyone to take their seats—the morning announcements were about to start.

"You can see me after homeroom, Miss . . . ?" the teacher said, lifting her chin to see me over the crowd of shifting students.

"Gobrowski," I said. "Annisa Gobrowski."

A Britney double in a red bandanna-print halter top a few rows ahead of me snorted and leaned over to whisper something to her friend. They both laughed and cast a disdainful look in my direction before facing the front of the room.

I swallowed hard and tried to smile at Bethany. At least she was being a human.

"You have so made my year," Bethany told me as the over-

9

head speaker crackled to life. "I have been *praying* for another brunette around here since birth."

Someone on the PA said something about the Pledge of Allegiance and everyone stood up. My knees were practically knocking together, but I made it out of my chair.

"Come on. There has to be another brunette in this school somewhere," I whispered, scoffing. I pressed my wet palms into my denim skirt and wondered if that slightly offensive smell was coming from my own armpits.

"Not one that will admit to it," Bethany answered, looking at my hair out of the corner of her eye. "This is all kinds of cool."

The more she looked at me with that stunned, almost loving expression, the more tense I became. My gaze darted around the room from blonde to blonde to blonde to blonde. The Britney-clone looked at me again and snickered.

"Nice clip," she mouthed, glancing toward my forehead. Her friend laughed into her hand. Suddenly my rhinestone barrette felt hard and cold and jagged against my scalp.

It was official. I was in hell. And John Frieda was the devil.

The best piece of advice my older brother, Gabe, ever gave me was this: When starting a new school, never, ever, under any circumstances, show up to lunch early. Always be late. Hide in the bathroom, get lost in the basement, stay after class to discuss politics with your hair-in-the-ears history teacher if you have to, but get to the cafeteria late or you're doomed.

"Why?" I asked him—naïve fifth grader that I was when he imparted this wisdom.

"Because, loser, if you sit down at an empty table, it will inevitably turn out to be the regular table of the most popular, most evil, most willing to embarrass the hell out of you crowd in the entire school and they will punish you. They will punish you dead."

He said it with such seriousness, I almost peed in my Old Navy undies.

So, like a good new girl, I arrived at the Sand Dune High cafeteria after everyone was seated with their lunches. To be honest, it wasn't entirely my doing. Ms. Trager had kept me after in choir to listen to me do scales, apparently to decide whether I was a good enough singer to keep around. Finally she'd given me a curt nod and a "very nice." At least it looked like I wouldn't have to go shopping for a new elective.

Most of the tables were outside in the courtyard at the center of the school, and I had entered from the front hallway, which meant I had to walk by a sea of gabbing blonde heads to get to the line where they actually served the food. I kept my eyes trained directly in front of me and tried not to pay attention to my pounding heart. I swear everyone was staring at my head. I may as well have been wearing one of those Viking hats with the big horns that some doof is always sporting at frat parties in the movies. (Where do they *get* those things?)

Okay, you can do this, I told myself when I emerged from the lunch line a few minutes later, a rather scary mound of mangled pasta on my plate. All the kids at the first few tables were watching me, and the Britney-clone from that morning leaned over to whisper to a friend next to her—aka Britney Two. *Oh, God, please let Bethany be here.*

"Annisa!"

Bethany stood up from a table at the far side of the courtyard. I forced myself to smile and hauled ass over to her table as quickly as my shortish legs would carry me. In that sea of tan skin, colorful clothing and blonde hair, Bethany looked like home to me. An island of dark-clothed, pale-complexioned normalcy.

"So, do you want to write an article for my website, sucks-to-be-us-dot-com? I think you would be totally perfect for it." Bethany jumped right in.

"Sucks-to-be-us-dot-com?" I asked, shaking my Snapple. I felt so much less conspicuous now that I was sitting down like everyone else.

"It's a site for teenage girls that basically gives us a chance to vent about, you know, everything that sucks in our lives," Bethany said, her nose piercing twinkling in the sun. "Everything from guys to parents to SATs to the current trends in misogynistic clothing and the fact that there's nothing good on TV anymore. I like to think it keeps people from expressing their emotions in more damaging ways."

"Like suicide or liposuction," I put in.

Bethany's face lit up. "Exactly," she said, jabbing her plastic fork in my direction. "I knew I liked you."

"Sounds cool. So, you can write about anything?"

"Anything goes," Bethany said, digging into her pasta. "Except I never allow anyone to post anything that tears down another girl. I read everything over personally."

"Huh. That's good," I said. "But what would *I* have to write about?" I took a bite of my spaghetti and dropped my fork. "I'm sure cafeteria food has been covered."

"What would you have to write about?" Bethany asked, incredulous. "How about the fact that you just got plunked down in the center of spirit central? I mean, trust me, you are about to witness the most sorry display of all-American cheese in the history of mankind. This was the absolute worst time for you to move here."

I had to give it to Bethany—she wasn't trying to sugarcoat things for the new girl. She was starting to remind me of Jordan, my best friend from back home. "Tell it like it is" is her personal mantra. I missed Jordan the instant I thought of her, and struggled to focus on the conversation.

"What do you mean?" I asked, gnawing on a plain roll.

"The big rivalry game is coming up. We're talking pep rallies, face painting, spontaneous psychotic cheering." Bethany's face grew more disgusted as she spoke. "I so wish I'd gone to school here in the nineties. At least back then there was a prank war. *That* was all kinds of cool. I may have even participated."

"A prank war?"

"Yeah, you know, West Wind High would chalk their

school colors on our gym, then we'd kidnap their mascot, then they would shaving-cream our football team's cars," Bethany said. "I heard that one time our guys filled the cheerleading captain's car with rotting apples," she added, her eyes glittering. She sighed, looking off into the sky dreamily. "Those were the days."

"So what happened?"

"Oh, some guy fell off the auditorium roof and broke both his arms," Bethany said, snapping back to the present. "Doesn't it suck when one person has to spoil everyone else's fun?"

"Totally," I deadpanned. I was starting to like this girl. At least I knew she'd get my sense of humor.

"Are you gonna eat this?" she asked, pulling my spaghetti surprise toward her.

"Go crazy," I said. If her stomach could handle it, more power to her.

"So anyway, this whole spirit thing is even worse this year because the cheerleaders have some competition coming up and they're running around here like a bunch of beagle puppies on speed," Bethany explained. "I swear those rah-rahs are getting on my last nerve. They have the collective IQ of a fruit fly."

My stomach turned. Clearly Bethany was one of those anti-cheerleader people. The ones who thought it was lame and not a sport and that every girl who did it was a ditz with a hairspray dependency. Normally I would have defended them, but considering that Bethany was the only person who had talked to me for more than five minutes all day, I decided to withhold the knowledge that I was one such rah-rah. (With an impressive IQ, thank you very much.) At least I had been at my old school.

I wondered if the squad had replaced me yet. I imagined them at practice without me, laughing, debating new stunts, going over the moves in the halftime dance for the hundredth time. I could practically smell the half-sweaty, half-antiseptic scent of the wrestling gym where we worked out. Okay. Now I was getting depressed.

"I thought you were anti-tearing-other-girls-down," I said.

"That's on the site. If I tried to do it on a daily basis, I'd have permanent tongue crampage," Bethany replied. "So, what's your schedule for the rest of the day?"

I sighed and pulled my neatly folded schedule out of my bag. We had been in chemistry and Spanish together that morning and I was hoping I would luck out and have someone to hang with that afternoon too.

"I've got geometry, honors English and then gym."

"Looks like you're on your own," Bethany said as she finished off my lunch. "Just don't let the blondies get you down."

I laughed nervously. "Is there really not a single other brunette in this school?"

It wasn't possible, was it?

Bethany leveled me with a dead-on stare. "Honey, even the mice in the bio lab are blonde."

My geometry teacher, Mr. Loreng, turned out to be a spitter. Yes, a spitter. Everyone has had at least one in their lives and it's never pretty. On every *s* and *th* he let out a spray of saliva the trajectory of which must be studied by the Guinness Book of World Records. And *sp*? Forget about it. This was the reason, of course, that the only empty seats in the room were in the front row. I had failed to notice the trend, however, and had taken a desk front and center, deciding to put myself out there, be daring, show everyone that I wasn't afraid to be seen.

I was rewarded with a refreshing afternoon shower.

And the worst of it was, he seemed to *know* what he was doing and to enjoy it. I mean, what other possible explanation could there be for the fact that he called everybody "sport"?

"David, be a sport and open the back window." (I took a blob on the cheek.)

"Hey, Sport, what did you get for number ten?" (Something landed on top of my head.)

"Well, Sporto, if you haven't grasped the concept of circumference yet, I can't help you." (Forehead, cheek again and yes, right in the eye.)

To make the whole thing even more humiliating, it turned out that the Sand Dune High sophomores were four chapters ahead of my geometry class back home. I had a total grasp of squares and triangles, but Mr. Loreng was raving on about circles and spheres and he may as well have been speaking in Japanese. I was going to have to study my butt off to catch up, and geometry had never been my best subject in the first place.

I was just trying to figure out a schedule for teaching myself the missed chapters when, out of nowhere, Mr. Loreng shouted my name.

"Miss Gobrowski!"

It was like a light spring rain.

"Yes?" I said, fighting back cardiac arrest.

"Is that *gum* you're munching on, or do you fancy yourself a cow?"

Omigod, he did not just call me a cow on my first day of school in front of everyone. He was evil. My geometry teacher was pure evil. There was a round of twittering behind me. And did I mention that both the Britney-clone *and* Daniel Healy were in my class? I thought I was going to dissolve into a pool of Annisa goo on the floor.

"No . . . it's gum," I said.

"Well, we don't allow gum chewing in this class," he told me. "Kindly spit it out into your hand."

Shaking, I lifted my hand to my mouth and dropped the wad of grape Bubble Yum into my palm. The girl diagonally behind me let out a disgusted groan.

"Now please come up here and deposit your gum in the garbage can."

How about I dump you in there right on your squirrelly little head? I thought.

I stood up slowly, glaring at the teacher, and tried to do what he said with as much dignity as possible—which was

17

difficult, considering the badly stifled laughter that followed me. The gum wad hit the bottom of the pail with a nice, resounding thud. I had never been so embarrassed in my life. Or at least in the last hour or so.

Mr. Loreng smiled condescendingly as I returned to my seat. "Thank you, Sport." Spittle, spittle. And they wonder why kids today don't like math.

• • •

In English class I decided to be as invisible as possible. I took a nice, innocuous seat right in the middle of the room behind some guy who was so tall, he *had* to be the center of the basketball team. With any luck, no one would notice I was there.

The class was reading *Romeo and Juliet,* which we had covered in English last year. Sweet relief! Something I knew! As two students read through the classic balcony scene, my eyes flicked to the clock. My first day was almost over. Of course, I could only imagine the shiny new brands of torture they had devised for me in gym.

When the readers got to the point where Juliet starts talking about a rose by any other name smelling as sweet, Mrs. O'Donaghue stopped them.

"Now, what does Juliet mean by this? What is she trying to say?" the teacher asked the class.

Total silence. Five minutes to go, then gym, then I was outta here.

"Come on, people. What does Juliet mean when she says ''Tis but thy name that is my enemy'?" Mrs. O'Donaghue was starting to grow frustrated. "I know you know this."

Students around me shifted in their seats and stared down at their books, avoiding eye contact. The teacher was clearly exasperated.

Someone answer and put her out of her misery, I thought.

"Anyone?"

Finally I couldn't take it anymore. I raised my hand.

"Yes? Annisa?"

"Well, she's saying that she loves Romeo for who he is and she would love him no matter what his name was. But she's required to hate him because his last name is Montague—because the Capulets and the Montagues have been feuding for so long," I explained. "Basically she doesn't care about their feud, but she knows it's going to cause problems between her and Romeo."

Mrs. O'Donaghue smiled. "You've read this play before."

"Yeah."

"Well, class. Annisa has made some very astute observations," Mrs. O'Donaghue said, walking behind her desk. "I'd love it if some of you would take your cues from her and participate. I think it would make our time together a lot easier on all of us."

Suddenly I realized that everyone in the class was glaring at me.

Gulp.

I'd just broken another of Gabe's rules: Never show up an entire class on your first day.

The bell rang and I was out of my seat like a shot. I was blocked by a little crowd of girls near the door, one of whom was the Britney double. Up close I noticed she had the longest eyelashes I'd ever seen on a human being. In a normal time and place I would have asked what mascara she used, but right then I just wanted to escape. I turned sideways to try to squeeze by them, and as I did, the Britney-clone looked me up and down.

"Her nose is even browner than her hair," she said under her breath.

All her friends cracked up laughing, except one—a tall, athletic girl who looked very uncomfortable. I'd never seen so many bared non-bellies convulsing at the same time. My face burning, I ducked out of the room and tried to get lost in the crowded hall. Fat chance. I stuck out like a sore brunette thumb. I needed to invest in a wig, STAT.

"Annisa! Um . . . Annisa!?"

I slowed my pace and turned around. The one non-laugher was speed-walking to catch up with me. She had naturally wavy blonde hair that hung past her shoulders and was one of those people who was so beautiful, she didn't need products of any kind.

"Hey . . . I'm Mindy," she said with a tentative smile. She hugged her notebooks close to her chest. "I just wanted to say, don't pay any attention to Sage. She's just . . . like that."

As if that was any excuse. And the Britney-clone's name was *Sage*? I'm sorry, but she seemed anything *but*. I mean, "browner"? That's not even a word. Still, I sensed that Mindy was genuinely sorry, which was nice. Of all the blonde females I'd encountered, so far Mindy was the only human. Except Mrs. O'Donaghue. But hers was a dye job—I could tell.

"Thanks. That's good to know, I guess," I said.

"So . . . where're you from?" Mindy asked. She fell into step with me as I crossed the short distance to my locker. I was surprised. Apologizing was one thing. Risking being spotted talking to the brunette suck-up with the gum addiction was another. Sage was clearly a clique leader and Mindy was clearly risking her wrath by chatting with me.

I liked her instantly.

"New Jersey," I said, twirling my lock. I did the combination, but when I yanked on the door, nothing happened. Then it hit me that I had dialed in the numbers from my locker back home. My eyes suddenly burned with nostalgic tears.

"Do you miss it?" Mindy asked.

"Me? Nah!" I replied.

"I've lived here my entire life. I don't know what I'd do if I had to move and start a new school," Mindy said. "I'd probably die of nervousness."

"Come on. It's not *that* scary," I replied.

Just then the crowd in the hallway parted as two older girls strode right down the center of the corridor. I could see why everyone was scurrying out of their way. They were both perfectly put together in the way popular kids always are, and they both looked pissed. Popularity and pissiness? Never a good combination.

"You're that new girl—Annie something, right?" one of them said, stopping right in front of me. She had short blonde hair and was runway-caliber gorgeous.

Somehow I found my voice in all the surprise. "Annisa, actually."

"So your dad's the cheapskate home-wrecker, then," the other girl snapped. Her blonde hair was of the darker, longer, stick-straight variety, and her small, round face was growing redder and redder.

"Um . . . not that I know of," I replied.

Everyone was stopping to stare now. Mindy took an instinctive step away from me. Couldn't blame her. Who wanted to stand next to the new girl while she was verbally assaulted? Any stray insults might ricochet off me and stick to her.

"Well, he is," the girl said. "And I'm just here to warn you that if you want to have any kind of a life at this school, you'd better stay as far away from me as possible."

21

She started to walk off and I almost let out a relieved sigh, but then she whirled around again and the air got all caught up in my throat.

"Which room did you take, anyway?" she blurted.

I looked at the unfamiliar faces around me, but there was no one there that could help. Or that would. They were looking at me as if I'd just shelled the Sand Dune High Fighting Crab with my own two hands.

"The pink one?" I said. Not that it would be pink much longer if I had anything to say about it. Pepto-Bismol is not my color.

The girl burst into tears and her friend led her away, looking back to shoot me an admonishing glance. As if I'd done anything wrong. I was just standing there, wasn't I? I glanced at Mindy. She looked like she'd just stepped off an out-of-control Tilt-a-Whirl.

"What?" I said.

"Um . . . that was Phoebe Cook. I'm guessing you must've moved into her old house," Mindy explained. "Her and the other girl? Whitney Barnard? They're seniors and let's just say you don't want them as enemies."

Great. This day just kept getting better. "Okay, but it's not my fault that I moved into her old house."

"Oh! I know! It's just . . . there was this whole, like, scandal," Mindy said, leaning back into the lockers. "Phoebe's family was basically booted out of their house by, like, the IRS or something, and no one knows why, but she had to move in with her aunt and it's supposedly really awful over there and . . . well . . ."

Mindy trailed off and I looked down the hall in the direction Phoebe had disappeared. Seconds ago she was scary, but now my heart went out to her. I couldn't imagine what it would be like to be forced from my home in such a humiliating fashion. What had happened to her family? Unemployment? Tax fraud? Insider trading? No wonder Dad had gotten such a sweet deal on our little bungalow.

"Well, I have to get to class," Mindy said, backing away from me. "I'll see ya."

"Yeah. See ya."

Now I felt noticeably alone again. I yanked my gym bag out, slammed my locker door and turned around to find Daniel Healy walking down the hall with a group of kids. Yay! A friendly face! I started to smile at him, but then some kid with a big 'fro moved out of the way and I saw that Daniel had his arm around—gulp—*Sage*.

Ew! They were *dating?*

Daniel grinned and lifted his hand from Sage's shoulder. "Hey, Jersey!"

A nickname! My mood was swinging so fast it was gonna give me whiplash.

"Hey!" I replied.

Sage shot me a withering look of death. "You *know* her?" she hissed at Daniel. A few of her girlfriends snickered. That was it. I was bathroom bound.

I jogged back down to the English hallway and yanked open the heavy wooden door. Luckily the room was deserted, so I had a couple of minutes to collect myself. I even checked under the stall doors—no feet.

"Okay, just chill," I told myself quietly. "It's just the first day and it's almost over."

Suddenly, the stall door directly behind me slammed open and Bethany unfolded her legs. She had been sitting on top of the toilet seat, fully clothed. Doing what, I have no idea.

"Do you always talk to yourself?" she asked with a smirk.

"Only when my life is flashing before my eyes."

The bell rang and my heart jumped. The gym was clear on the other side of the school. I was going to be *so* late! I grabbed my gym bag and raced for the door. My hands full, I used the side of my body to shove it open, but it hit something. Hard.

What the—

Suddenly the hall was filled with an inhuman screech that probably had seagulls everywhere winging it home. Everything happened at once. Bethany carefully pushed open the door and gasped. Hunched over in the hallway was a bawling girl, her hands held over her nose, blood gushing out between her fingers. I was going to hurl.

"You biiiiidge!" she shouted. "You boke by dose!"

"Omigod." That was pretty much all my brain could produce at that moment.

The girl took off at a run and I looked at Bethany, who was now laughing so hard, she was actually doubled over, holding on to the metal garbage can for support.

"What? What is so funny!?" I asked, my voice sounding shrill.

"You . . . are . . . the best," she said between gasps.

"What? Why?"

"That was Tara Timothy," Bethany said, straightening up and patting me on the shoulder. I wasn't sure if it was meant to be consoling or congratulating. "The most popular girl in school."

Slowly a pit of black tar opened beneath my feet. I had to do something.

"Where're you going?" Bethany called after me as I rushed out the door.

"I really don't know!" I shouted back.

Following the sound of Tara's screeching, I ran down the

24

hall. Faces gathered in classroom windows to watch me as I flew by. I could only imagine what the gossip was going to be the next day.

"Yeah. It was the new girl. She was tearing down the hall, all wild-eyed. I heard she just got out of some special school for the brunette and criminally insane. . . ."

The nurse was one of those soft-looking older ladies with her hair piled on top of her head and a bright pink sweater pulled over her white shirt and pants. She was just ushering Tara into a back room when I burst through the door.

"Is she . . . is it . . . all right?" I asked, desperately trying to catch my breath.

"I don't know yet, sweetie, but why don't you just get yourself back to class?" the nurse said.

"But I . . . *I'm really sorry!*" I shouted as I was backed out of the office.

"Go do 'ell!" Tara shouted back.

Yeah. She wasn't happy.

The nurse smiled and told me she'd pass along my concern, then closed the door on me. For a moment, I just stood in the hall, my gym bag clutched against my heaving chest, listening to Tara's cries. They were just all too fitting a soundtrack to go with the dirge in my head.

My life at Sand Dune High was over before it had a chance to begin.

• • •

JerseyGirl531: im sure u didn't break it
Annisa: Jordan—there was blood EVERY-WHERE!
JerseyGirl531: ok look at it this way . . . now ppl know who u r!!!
Annisa: And to stay as far away from me as possible. ☹

JerseyGirl531: i sorry sweetpea! member what u always say! tomorrow is always fresh w/no mistakes in it!!!

****Annisa***: You hate when I say that!!!

JerseyGirl531: that's what i say but secretly i luv it! and remember! at least you met a cute boy!

****Annisa***: Yeah. w/a evil girlfriend.

JerseyGirl531: not 4 long! ;-) gotta go! rickys bugging me 4 food XO

****Annisa***: xoxoXO!

I sighed, imagining Jordan in her beat-up Celica heading out to Wendy's with her little brothers. Her family eats fast food four times a week because her mom works doubles at Robert Wood Johnson Hospital all the time. At least Jordan knows enough to make Ricky and Matt eat salads or they'd all be part of those childhood-obesity studies I keep hearing about.

At that moment I missed home so much, I could have cried. Why had I let myself get comfortable there? I always knew moving again was a probability. But somehow I'd pushed that fact to the back of my mind. I'd made real friends and starting thinking of New Jersey as home. Now here I was, all depressed and trying to assimilate in a place where they apparently ate peroxide for breakfast. Where I couldn't seem to do anything right.

"Tomorrow is always fresh, with no mistakes in it."

It was my favorite *Anne of Green Gables* pearl of wisdom. I'd been writing it on textbook covers, in journals and yes, in the occasional school bathroom stall since I was about eight. And it usually made me feel better. But not this time. The damage was done. All I could do was sit there and dread the following morning.

"Dinner in five!" my father shouted up the stairs.

26

I inhaled the tangy scent of my dad's chicken tacos, and turned off the computer. I'd spent an hour surfing the Web for private schools in our area. Our Lady of Peace Catholic Girls' School seemed promising what with the uniforms and the strict anti-jewelry rule to keep me from making fashion faux pas. Bet you couldn't even tell *who* was popular and powerful around there. But it didn't matter. We didn't have enough money to send me to private school, especially not with Gabe at Miami U.

Nope. Tomorrow morning, it was back to the blonde school of death.

"Annisa! Come help me put everything on the table!" my mom called.

I hauled myself up and trudged down the stairs. At least it was one of my father's nights to cook. Whenever Dad was cooking, you knew it was one of four things—chicken tacos, chicken stir-fry, roasted chicken or hamburgers. With Mom, however, you never knew what she was going to put down in front of you and whether it was still breathing. She tried sushi once. No one left the house for days.

Mom and Dad stood at the kitchen counter, transferring the tacos to a platter. Dad was wearing his standard plaid shirt and khakis combo, his brown hair shaggy all over and in desperate need of a shaping. Mom was still dressed in the sleek putty suit and white silk blouse she had worn to work that morning. Her red hair was pulled back in a loose bun and her makeup looked perfect. It was really no wonder that every upscale department store in southern Florida had courted my mother. She was a personal shopper. People always bought stuff she recommended because they thought it would give them a slim chance of someday looking like her.

"How was your day, sweetie?" my mother asked, reaching out to tuck my hair behind my ear.

27

"Remember the final battle scene in the last *Lord of the Rings* movie?" I said. "It was kind of like that. Blood, guts and all."

"Oh, it couldn't have been that bad," Dad said, clucking his tongue.

"Dad, just because everyone, like, worships you at whatever school you go to, that doesn't mean we're all so lucky," I said, grabbing the Brita pitcher out of the fridge.

My father cleared his throat and held out his hand, palm up. I blinked, thinking back to everything I had just said, and then it hit me.

"Just because everyone, like, worships you . . ."

I pressed my eyes closed, irritated with myself, then stuffed my hand in my pocket, fishing through my change from lunch. When I found a quarter, I slapped it into my father's hand.

"Thank you!" he said.

"My pleasure."

Every time I use the word *like* in a superfluous manner, my dad charges me a quarter and he never, ever misses one. I really hoped he was putting that money into my college fund. At this point he'd probably have no problem paying for the Sorbonne.

"Where's Gabe?" I asked.

"Well, the food will be done in T-minus-five seconds, so let's see," my father said, raising his watch to his glasses. "Five . . . four . . . three . . . two—"

The buzzer went off on the stove, and the kitchen door flew open at precisely the same moment. There stood my brother, his red hair lightened from the sun and grown out to just below the ear, his green eyes sparkling. He was wearing an orange-and-yellow Hawaiian shirt, baggy shorts and Tevas.

"Dudes!" he exclaimed.

"Oh, God. You're a surfer now?" I said, scrunching my face up.

"Don't knock it till ya tried it, li'l sis," he said, reaching out and tousling my hair. He dropped a massive canvas bag full of laundry onto the kitchen floor, then stepped over it to hug my mom.

"Hey, Mama! Give me some *loooove!*"

Unbelievable. He sounded like the sea turtle from *Finding Nemo*. When had this started?

"Dinner is served," my father said, by now immune to the shock of his ever-changing son. He picked up a platter of tacos, and my brother leaned in to sniff them.

"Tacos! Righteous!"

"Do they even *have* surf-worthy waves in Florida?" I asked, following the rest of the family to the table with the water pitcher.

"Totally," Gabe said.

I have to admit the surfer look actually worked for him. Much better than the grungy punk thing he had going on the last time I'd seen him. Under his freckles his skin was a bronzy tan that brought out his smile and the color of his eyes. Gabe had tried on a lot of personas over the years— prep, skater, jock, fashion victim . . . the ill-advised Spring of the Cowboy—but he'd never tried one that wouldn't attract the ladies.

"So, what's up, li'l sis? You look down," Gabe said, serving himself four tacos before anybody else had a shot.

"Bad first day," I said. "Way bad. And don't tell me to re-create myself, because it won't work. Unless you can get me a new face."

"You're talking to the guy who went from dreadlocked Phishhead to country-club argyle boy in one weekend," Gabe said. "With my help, you can be anything."

29

"Oh, I loved your country-club phase," my mother said nostalgically. I think she liked my brother's chameleon nature because it meant she got to pick out a whole new wardrobe for him every few months.

"Never know, Mama. It may come back," Gabe said with a grin.

I rolled my eyes. This was not helping me.

"I know what'll cheer you up," my father said. "Why don't you and I make an ice cream run after dinner? You never turn down an ice cream run."

I took a deep breath. This problem was too deep for ice cream.

"I saw a Ben and Jerry's truck parked outside the 7-Eleven on my way home," my dad singsonged.

Unless, of course, we were talkin' Ben & Jerry's One Sweet Whirled. It was like happiness in a carton.

"Okay," I said to my dad. "You're on."

• • •

The first thing I noticed when my dad pulled the family truckster into the convenience store parking lot was a large group of kids hanging out between two parked cars, music pounding from the speakers of a red convertible. A couple of girls in SDH cheerleading jackets leaned back against the hood, smoking cigarettes. My heart immediately thumped with foreboding.

Why me?

Dad got out and slammed the door, attracting the attention of the crowd. I jumped out and hurried after him. From the corner of my eye I saw one of the guys tip his head back to drink out of a bottle wrapped in a brown paper bag. Apparently this was not a Smart Food and Pepsi crowd.

Dad gathered some snacks while I hit the freezer and,

eureka!, found a pint of One Sweet Whirled. I pulled it out and cradled it in my arms like a baby, then, on impulse, grabbed another. Just in case tomorrow sucked too. I joined my father on line, and the guy in front of us glanced around. It was none other than Cheerful Cuccinello, the peppier-than-pepper guidance counselor. Could this day be over now? Please!?

"Why, Annisa Gobrowski! What a pleasant surprise!"

"Hey, Mr. C," I said lacklusterly.

"And you must be Mr. Gobrowski!" He straightened up, then settled in his firecracker way on the word *mister.* "I'm Annisa's guidance counselor, Tony Cuccinello."

Mr. C shifted two of four two-liter bottles of Coke he was carrying over to one arm so he could shake hands with my dad. I couldn't help wondering what anybody needed with eight liters of Coke on a Monday night.

"So, Annisa, how was your first day?" Mr. C asked as he paid at the register.

"Great," I said. "It was just great."

Mr. C grinned. "I told ya! Didn't I tell ya? You fit right in."

Right. What kind of psychedelic Coke was this guy drinking, anyway?

"Well, see ya around campus," Mr. C said, pocketing his change. He lifted his free hand in a wave as he walked out.

Five minutes later, Dad and I emerged from the store to an oddly silent parking lot. The music that had blared from the convertible on our way in had been cut dead, replaced by a palpable tension. Mr. C was talking to a group of now obviously snagged kids, his voice more serious than I would have thought possible for him. The guy who had been swilling some unknown substance had his hands behind his back and his eyes trained on the ground. Reprimanded by a teacher-type figure in front of your friends. It was never fun.

As I got into the car, I glanced over one last time and saw the two cheerleaders glaring at me. They looked like they wanted me dead, on a slab, right there in the 7-Eleven parking lot. Had they heard about what I'd supposedly done to Phoebe? Or what I'd *actually* done to Tara Timothy? I hunkered down in my seat to save myself from the heat of their gaze. What was *that* about?

"Feeling better already, aren't you?" my dad said.

"Yeah," I replied shakily. "You bet."

*

The next morning, I did what any sane, self-respecting girl would do in my situation. I got up, I put on my red polo dress and my red-and-blue Converse throwbacks and I did not dye my hair. I did, however, clip it back with a simple tortoiseshell snap barrette. The rhinestones were retired—for the moment.

It was new-outlook time. I wasn't some loser geek klutz with no life and no friends. I was Annisa Gobrowski. I was cool. I was cute. And, okay, I *was* a klutz, but I had plenty of friends. They just happened to be thousands of miles away.

When I walked out the door, I was instantly rewarded for my good attitude. Daniel Healy was waiting for me at the end of my driveway. *Waiting* for *me*.

"Hey," he said as I approached.

"Hey."

"So . . . how was your first day?"

I snorted a laugh.

"What?"

"Nothing," I said. Maybe he really hadn't heard about my many offenses. Maybe they weren't that bad. Maybe they hadn't really even happened. Or maybe this was like that movie *Groundhog Day* and I was getting to live my first day over again to get it right.

But then, of course, Daniel wouldn't have known who I was, so no such luck. Oh, well.

"It couldn't have been *that* bad," Daniel said as we turned up the street. "Sage told me you were all over it in English class."

In other words, she told you I was a brainy snob, I thought. I hated it when people were predictable.

"Right. Sage," I said.

Don't say it, don't say it, don't say it, I thought. Then I said it. Of course.

"You guys are like . . . what? Boyfriend-girlfriend?"

Sometimes I'm about as sophisticated as a straight-to-video Mary-Kate and Ashley movie.

Daniel was suddenly looking at the ground. "Yeah. Since seventh grade," he said. "She's cool. You know. Once you get to know her."

Ha! Could that statement have *been* more loaded? Obviously he knew she was *not* cool—at least not to other people—or he wouldn't feel the need to say that. So why the heck was he going out with her?

"So I, uh . . . I heard you yesterday," Daniel said. "Doing your scales?"

"You did?" I asked. "How?"

"I was coming out of one of the rehearsal rooms," he said. "You were good. I would've said something at the time, but I didn't want to, you know, in case you were embarrassed."

"Oh. What were you rehearsing?" I asked.

Daniel flushed. "Guitar. I have a free period before lunch, so I usually go practice."

"You play guitar?" I asked.

"Sort of," he said, his skin darkening even further. "I mean . . . I mess around."

"That's so cool. I'd love to hear you play sometime."

"Oh, I'm no good," Daniel said. "I don't play in front of people. Ever."

"Not even Sage?" I asked.

"Are you kidding? She'd probably laugh her ass off."

Nice, I thought. *Some girlfriend.* "Well, if you ever change your mind and want to play for someone, I'm there. I'll even tell you the truth if you suck, but I'm sure you don't."

"Thanks," Daniel said, smiling. "I'll keep that in mind. So . . . are you coming to the football game this weekend?"

"Sure, I guess," I said as we crossed the gridiron. "Are you on the team?"

Daniel gave a quick nod. "Footballwrestlingandtrack." He said it like it was all one word. Like he'd been asked about his athletic status five hundred thousand times. "But I don't know. I'm thinking about not wrestling this year."

"Really? Why?" I asked.

"I don't know why I just said that," he replied, looking stunned. "I haven't told anybody I'm thinking of quitting."

"It's not you, it's me," I said, raising my hand. "Future Therapists of America."

"What?" he asked.

"People tell me stuff. It's like I have the words *good listener* stamped on my forehead," I said. "So why are you gonna quit?"

"I don't know. . . . I'm probably not. . . . I'm just . . ." He laughed and looked at the ground. "Can we talk about something else? What about you? Are you into sports?"

Wow. Someone was a little tense about quitting wrestling. My curiosity was piqued. Was he a wrestling legacy? Would his father never speak to him again if he quit? Did he hate the sport, but couldn't leave it because it was the only chance he had of getting into college? Sometimes it was exhausting, being in my brain.

"Tennis and cheerleading," I answered.

"Really?" Daniel's eyebrows shot up. "That's too bad. They already had cheerleading tryouts."

"That's all right. There's always next year," I said. *If I'm still here.*

Daniel opened the back door for me and I managed not to trip over myself this time. As we approached my homeroom, I noticed a clump of girls talking in low voices just to the left of the door. One of them spotted me and said something through her teeth, and they all turned to glare. My heart practically stopped.

Very subtle, girls, I thought. Part of me salivated to say it out loud, but all I wanted to do was slip into the relative safety of homeroom. Whatever they were saying about me, I didn't want to know. I avoided eye contact with everyone as I sat down at a back desk. The announcements began and Bethany had yet to show up, so on top of everything else it looked like I was going to be on my own all day. After the pledge I pulled out my history textbook and pretended to be engrossed.

That was when I heard the most beautiful string of words ever to be strung together in the English language.

"A meeting will be held this afternoon in the science lecture hall for all prospective cheerleaders. Tryouts will be held for two open spots on the squad tomorrow afternoon. All sophomore, junior and senior girls are invited."

Suddenly my hands were gripping the edges of my desk and my palms were sweating. Cheerleading tryouts. Hadn't Daniel just told me they had already held them? I wondered where the two open spots had come from, but then I realized I didn't care. It was hard to believe, but it looked like my luck was changing. I had a shot at the cheerleading squad!

As the announcements continued, my brain started to

race. Bethany had said the Sand Dune squad was a competitive team. I could be on a *competition* squad. I had always wanted to compete, but no one on my team was ever interested and, to be quite honest, we sucked anyway. I mean, our stunting was abysmal and I was the only one on the team who could even execute a passable back handspring, let alone a back tuck.

This was it. This was my chance. I could be a competitive cheerleader. Not only that, I could put Gabe's theory to the test. I had been handed an opportunity to reinvent myself. The opportunity to join a team and meet people and maybe even make a few friends. Real friends.

I had been inseparable with the girls on the squad back home. We spent so much time together, we ended up knowing everything one another, even though we hung out with totally different cliques during the regular school day. When you're with the same people every afternoon and on weekends, when you have to trust them not to drop you from a stunt or kick you in the face, when it's you against the tyranny of your coaches, you form a bond that transcends mere cliques.

I was part of a team back in Jersey. And now I could have that again.

When the bell rang, I got up and followed the rest of the class into the hallway, biting my lip to keep my smile from exploding all over the place. My life at Sand Dune High was about to begin and no amount of whispers and evil looks was going to stop me.

• • •

That afternoon, I swung open the door to the science lecture hall and stepped inside. At least twenty pairs of eyes trained themselves directly on me. Then the heavy door slammed closed, knocking me farther into the room, where I staggered before grabbing a chair for dear life.

Apparently I hadn't stepped *all* the way in. Classic.

There were a few giggles and everyone looked away. Everyone but Mindy, who was waving at me from the center of the room. I held my head high and slipped into the chair next to hers. It was *so* nice to know somebody.

"You're a cheerleader?" she asked. "That's so cool!"

"Yeah. Well, I was," I said.

"I tried out last year, but I didn't make it. Obviously," she said with an embarrassed laugh. "I don't even know why I'm here."

"No! It's cool that you're trying again," I said. "Who knows? Maybe you almost made it."

"Maybe," Mindy said. "I am kind of psyched to have another chance. I mean, I *think* I did well last time."

"Not that I'm complaining, but why *do* we have another chance?" I asked. "Did a couple of the cheerleaders bite it or something?"

From the look on Mindy's face I thought a couple of cheerleaders *had* died in some freak basket-toss accident or something. I swallowed hard. I was going to have to have my foot surgically removed from my mouth.

"We're here because of the Big Scandal," Mindy said, her eyes slightly wide.

That was just how she said it. Big Scandal. Capital *B*. Capital *S*. Clearly this was some sort of huge story that everyone in the school knew about. Everyone but me. The new girl. She Who Is Not Worthy of the 411.

"They need sixteen girls to compete at regionals, and thanks to the Big Scandal, they're down to fourteen," Mindy told me. "That's why we're here."

Suddenly the door to the lecture hall opened and everyone in the room sat up a little straighter. A tiny girl in a white cheerleading uniform walked in. The skirt was straight with light blue and yellow banding across the bottom, and the top was sleeveless and exposed a chevron of her flat stomach. The same band crisscrossed her chest, and the letters *SDH* were printed across the front in yellow with light blue piping. Totally unlike our generations-old frumpy sweaters and mismatched skirts back home.

I felt a flutter of excitement in my chest. She looked just like one of those girls from the competitions on ESPN. Totally professional. This was a whole new world.

Every girl that trailed in behind her looked exactly the same, except they got progressively taller. My heart started to pound with intimidation. They lined up at the front of the room like soldiers, hands behind their backs, faces set.

These girls were serious. And I was psyched.

And then Sage walked through the door and my mouth went dry. Phoebe walked in and I sunk a bit in my seat. Whitney walked in and I started to sweat. And then, the pièce de résistance.

Tara Timothy. Nose plate, black eyes and all. Somehow, even with all the puffiness and the squinting, even with the dozens of other hopefuls in the room, Tara's beady eyes found me instantly. Time stopped. I felt like a rabid lion had just locked its carnivorous sights on my bony little self. And she was gonna pick me dry.

Run. Just run and don't look back.

How could this be happening? How could all of these girls be on the cheerleading squad? As I looked down the line, I realized that the trio who had been talking about me in front of my homeroom that morning was also there. This could have been a meeting of the We Hate Annisa Gobrowski Society.

A petite yet powerful-looking African American woman stood at the end of the line in dark blue sweats. Her bottle-blonde hair was pulled back in a braid. She stepped forward and addressed the room.

"My name is Coach Holmes and I'd like to welcome all of you," she said with a perfunctory smile. "I'm sorry that this meeting was called on such short notice, but sometimes things happen and we just have to go with the flow."

A couple of the girls eyed me. I felt like I was on trial here. What had I done?

"For future reference, however, I am not a person who likes surprises," Coach Holmes said seriously, scanning the crowd.

I swallowed hard. Clearly she was a tough coach.

"Tryouts will be held tomorrow afternoon. You will be judged on precision, projection, enthusiasm and overall presentation," Coach Holmes continued. "Every member of the Sand Dune High cheerleading squad must be able to perform a round-off back handspring back tuck, all the basic jumps, and splits both ways. If you cannot perform these moves, please do not waste our time by coming to tryouts. We have a lot of work to do and a short period to do it in. I don't say this to be callous, I say it because I am a realist and a perfectionist. I only want what's best for this team."

Mindy and I looked at each other, and she raised her eyebrows as if to say, "Been there, done that. It ain't fun."

"Now I'll turn the meeting over to our captain, who would like to say a few words." Coach Holmes turned and gestured toward the cheerleader next to her. "Tara Timothy."

Everyone in the room applauded like she was Miss Teen

USA. Tara stepped forward. I swear I could feel the heat from her purple and yellow bruises throbbing from across the room. It looked so painful. I wished I had had a chance to apologize. But every time I'd seen her all day, she'd been surrounded by friends and I had been afraid of, well, reciprocal bodily harm.

"As you all know, the West Wind High Dolphins have beaten us at regionals for the past two years running," Tara said, her voice strained and nasal. "We have a real shot this year, so I'd just like to reiterate what Coach Holmes just said. If you can't give us one hundred percent, you don't belong here."

She looked directly at me.

"So don't bother signing the list. We only want people who are willing to work and who know what it means to be a Sand Dune High Fighting Crab.

"I'll pass this around now," Tara said, handing a clipboard to the first girl in the front row. "Those of you who still believe you might have a place on this team, we'll be meeting in the gym in an hour. Be ready to work your butt off."

At that point half a dozen girls got up and walked out without signing the sheet. Part of me wanted to follow them. To just go and save myself what was sure to be a miserable afternoon. But one look at the huddle of now-whispering cheerleaders—who were, of course, throwing looks in my direction—was enough to buoy my defiant side.

I took the clipboard from the girl in front of me and wrote my name in huge capital letters. ANNISA GOBROWSKI. It took up two lines. Let them try to argue with that.

• • •

"This is no good," I said, pulling my wrinkled gym T-shirt out of my bag in the locker room. If someone had told me we

41

were going to be practicing after this meeting, I would have tried to sweat less during gym class, but as it was, I had nothing to wear.

"Wanna borrow something?" Mindy asked. She was in a one-on-one battle with a huge duffel bag that seemed reluctant to be pulled out of its locker.

"What is all this?" I asked, helping her yank it free.

Mindy shrugged in an apologetic way. "Sage warned me about tryouts last night. I couldn't figure out what to wear, so I kind of brought everything."

She unzipped the bag, revealing an array of neatly folded T-shirts, shorts and socks. I had a sudden vision of what Mindy's room must look like. All hospital corners and posters at perfect right angles.

"Take whatever you want," she said.

"Thanks," I replied with a smile, touched by her kindness. A popular blonde who didn't want me dead. Who knew it was possible?

I picked out a pair of navy blue Soffe shorts and a white T-shirt with a Fighting Crab on the back, figuring I may as well start dressing the part. Mindy wore yellow SDH shorts and a light blue tank top. I noticed that her calf muscles were totally cut and she had some defined triceps as well. She already looked like she belonged on the team.

"You almost ready?" she asked.

I was busy staring at myself in the mirror. I wished my hair was just a little bit longer so I could at least get it into a ponytail. Clearly the SDH cheerleaders were all about uniformity.

"You go ahead. I'll be out in a sec," I told her.

Once Mindy was gone, I yanked at the drawstrings in the shorts, cinching them to my waist. Then I scrounged through my backpack for another clip. I secured both sides of my hair behind my ears to keep it off my face and stared into my own eyes.

"Okay," I said firmly. "Showtime."

That was when I realized the locker room was freakishly silent. Everyone else was already out in the gym! *Nice one, Gobrowski!*

I jogged toward the door and was about to open it when it came swinging right toward me. I had to jump back to keep from getting hit in the face. When Tara walked through, I thought, for a split second, that she'd been trying to exact her revenge.

"Hey," I said nervously, ready to make an attempt at peace. "I was just—"

Tara moved into the small hallway that led to the gym, followed by Phoebe, Whitney and then Sage. I had to back up so that they could all fit. Then they stood there and blocked the door like sentries. They had to be kidding me. Were they really going to try to keep me out of practice?

"What do you think you're doing?" Tara asked.

I, for some reason, glanced at Sage. Like she was going to help me. I guess my brain went for my closest peer. But Sage just glared at me through those long eyelashes. When I saw her standing there next to Whitney like that, I suddenly realized they were sisters. Sage was like a mini-Whitney and Whitney's eyelashes were just as obscene.

"I was going to practice," I said.

"Don't bother," Tara told me. "We don't need a back-stabbing, short-haired—"

"Casper-skinned," Whitney put in.

"Home-stealing," Phoebe added.

"Brainy-klutzo," Sage finished with a smirk.

Okay. They *had* to have rehearsed that. They managed to get *all* my sins into one round-robin insult. I mean, who has that kind of time on their—wait a minute . . .

"Backstabbing?" I said. "What do you mean backstabbing?"

"Like you don't know," Phoebe scoffed.

All I could do was blink. Suddenly my face felt puffy and warm as if it were embarrassed that I was drawing a total blank.

"Come on. You *know* it was your fault that Kristen and Danielle got booted," Tara said, crossing her arms over her chest. "You probably did it on purpose because you wanted to try out."

"As if you're really gonna make it," Sage said.

"Kristen and Danielle?" I said, baffled.

"You know, the two people you got thrown off the squad after you tattled on them last night at the store?" Whitney said. "What are you, anyway, a kindergartner?"

"Okay, I have no idea what you're talking about," I said.

They all exchanged looks as if they were just at their wits' end. Well, so was I! What had I done at the 7-Eleven other than purchase an unhealthy amount of ice cream?

"Okay, I'll bite," Tara said finally. "There's this little thing called an Athlete's Contract around here, and we all have to sign it."

"In the contract it states that we will not partake of any chemical substances during the season," Whitney said. "No drugs, no *drinking*, no *smoking* . . ."

Suddenly my brain caught up with them. Those cheerleaders who were smoking in the parking lot at the 7-Eleven. Mr. Cuccinello talking to them when I left. The looks of death they shot my way. They thought I'd told Mr. C on them. They thought I knew about this Athlete's Contract and that I had gotten them thrown off the team on purpose. Did they think I was psychic or something?

They were all glaring at me—waiting for me to beg for mercy. Not likely.

"First of all, I would *never* tell on someone. You wouldn't know this, because none of you have bothered to get to know me, but that is not my style," I said, causing a couple of them to blink in surprise. "And secondly, how the heck would I know about the Athlete's Contract after one measly day in this place?"

"They gave you a student handbook, didn't they?" Tara shot back.

"Yeah, and I had so much time to read it cover to cover *and* formulate this diabolical plan of stumbling onto your friends at the 7-Eleven when Mr. Cuccinello just *happened* to be there. I somehow squeezed it right between my seven new classes, my stunning bubble-gum embarrassment and, oh, yeah, breaking your nose."

So much for apologizing. At that moment, I was *glad* I'd done it.

"Whatever," Tara said. "All I know is this was the first year we had a shot at beating the Dolphins at regionals and you blew it for us." She stepped away from the door, practically flattening Phoebe into the wall in the process. "So enter the gym at your own peril," she said with a wicked smile that made her grotesque bruises stretch. "Personally I can't wait to see you fall flat on your face."

I hesitated for a split second. A vision of Tara's foot jutting out and me tripping into the gym in a full sprawl assaulted me. But I wasn't going to let them win. I pulled open the door, lifted my feet high and strode into the gym. I was going to show them I belonged on this squad no matter how many jumps and tumbles and stunts I had to do.

I just hoped the Great Locker Room Standoff was their last-gasp effort to throw me off.

"You people call those jumping jacks? My grandpa has more energy than that, and he's hooked up to a respirator!"

"Get your feet up, Annisa! That's how you jog? God! Do they even *have* physical fitness in New Jersey, or do you just sit around eating pasta all day?"

"Spaghetti arms! Spaghetti arms! Spaghetti arms! Ugh! Why do I *bother*?"

These are just a few of the tidbits Tara Timothy screeched at us that day. We had only been through warmups and my shirt was already plastered to my back, my hair had fallen free of its clips and I was fairly certain that on my last attempt at a front hurdler I had peed in my pants just a little bit.

"Take five!" Coach Holmes called out.

We all instantly hit the floor, where the air was ten times cooler and the glossy boards felt like ice against our overheated skin. Tara, Coach and the rest of the squad all huddled at the front of the gym for a confab.

"Was it like this last year?" I said to Mindy under my breath.

Her chest was heaving up and down, but she was trying to keep it under control. "No way. It was bad, but not this bad."

"It's all thanks to you, you know," a random girl with

kinky curls told me. She rolled over onto her side and rested her cheek on her hand. "They'll do anything to keep you off this squad. Why don't you do us all a favor and just quit now?"

My mouth dropped open, but there were no words. Was this girl serious? Were they running a tougher practice just to weed *me* out?

"Don't listen to her," Mindy whispered. "She's just upset because she tries out every year and never makes it."

"All right, everyone, on your feet!" Coach Holmes shouted, clapping her hands together. "The squad is now going to demonstrate the cheer that you will be expected to perform at tryouts. Pay attention. You only have one day to get this down pat."

We scrambled up and the squad lined up in front of us, Tara Timothy front and center.

"Ready?" she shouted.

"Okay!" the team replied.

They were so loud, I swear my hair blew back.

"Fighting Crabs up in the stands, let's—hear you—shout!"

Whoa. Those were some serious moves. Did their arms ever *stop*?

"Fighting Crabs up in the stands, let's—hear you—now! All you fans yell 'Go'!"

"GO!"

My heart hit my throat. Every prospective cheerleader standing around me had just shouted "Go!" at the top of her lungs and thrown her fists into the air. Clearly they had heard this cheer before.

"All you fans yell 'Crabs'!"

"CRABS!"

This time I managed to get in there and raise my fist too. But I felt completely conspicuous. No one had this kind of spirit where I came from. Not even at games. Of course, that may have accounted for the football team's stellar 0-and-9 season last year. Or vice versa. It's a vicious cycle, really.

Suddenly the cheer became a back-and-forth. The cheerleaders shouted "Go!" We shouted "Crabs!" Back and forth three times.

"Go!"

"Crabs!"

"Go!"

"Crabs!"

"Go!"

"Crabs!"

Then the cheerleaders finished it off with "Let's go, Crabs!" And every other one of them did a standing back tuck. It was, I have to say, the coolest thing I've ever seen in my life. (Except maybe for that time I ran into Carson Daly on the street in New York City during a class field trip and he asked me what time it was.)

Anyway, the words may have been simple, but the movements had looked utterly complex. Still, as the squad broke us up into smaller groups so they could teach us the cheer, I was fairly confident. I could learn this with an entire night of practice. And maybe a few hours in the morning. . . . Oh, hell. I was going to be up all night. But who cared? If I could be on a squad that performed like that and got that kind of response, I'd forgo sleep for a week. A month even.

My little group got Whitney as a tutor. Mindy already knew the cheer from last year's tryouts, so while Whitney seemed content to ignore my existence, Mindy taught me the cheer in the corner. It wasn't so bad once it was broken down for me.

"I think you've got it," Mindy said proudly. "You pick this stuff up fast. It took me the whole week of pre-tryout practice last time."

"I'm a quick study," I said with a shrug.

Mindy's eyes darted over my shoulder, and when I followed her glance, I saw Whitney looking me up and down like I was totally conceited. Why, oh, why did I have to say something so cocky? The second Coach Holmes left the room, Whitney walked over to Tara and Phoebe and whispered something to them. I knew enough about catty girls to know that something bad was about to happen.

"Okay, everyone, let's see what you've learned!" Tara shouted.

We all gathered in front of the squad and Tara whipped out the clipboard with the sign-in sheet on it.

"Each of you will demonstrate the cheer for us and then we'll tell you what we think you need to work on," Phoebe told us.

"Let's see, let's see. Who should go first?" Tara said, running her finger down the sign-in sheet. Like she was really mulling it over. "Annisa Goborkowski?" She said my name with a laugh and completely bastardized the pronunciation. All the cheerleaders smirked at me. Well, not *all* of them. A couple kind of glanced away uncomfortably, which basically meant they thought Tara was a bitch, but would never stand up to her. Still, even if they were nonvocal, it was nice to know they weren't all cookie-cutter evil.

"It's Gobrowski," I said as I stepped out in front of everyone, my knees quaking.

"I care," Tara said sarcastically. "Let's see what you've got."

I held my head high, squeezed my butt cheeks together and stood up straight. It wasn't easy to look confident when ninety-nine percent of the people in the room were silently rooting for me to fail. But I did my best.

"Ready! Okay!

Fighting Crabs up in the stands,

let's—hear you—shout!

Fighting Crabs up in the stands,

let's—hear you—now.

All you fans yell 'Go'!"

"GO!"

I felt as if the world had come screeching to a stop. Maybe three people had responded to my cheer—Mindy and two girls on the squad who were now turning purple under the hateful admonishing gaze of Tara Timothy. I paused for a split second, but then my brain kicked in, telling me I had to keep going. They *wanted* to throw me off. I couldn't let them see they'd gotten to me.

"All you fans yell 'Crabs'!"

"CRABS!"

Mindy. Solo Mindy was yelling now. She was red from the exertion of going against everyone else, but her eyes were locked on mine. She wasn't going to back off.

"GO!"

"CRABS!"

We sounded pathetic, just the two of us in that big gym. But we kept it up.

"GO!"

"CRABS!"

"GO!"

"CRABS!"

"Let's go, Crabs!"

I finished the cheer with my arms in the air and my eyes burning with tears. I didn't even attempt the back tuck for fear I'd spaz out and break my neck. Somehow I made myself rejoin the crowd and faced the cheerleaders. Mindy slipped her arm around my back and the tears almost let fly, but I held them in.

"It was really good," Mindy said. She practically sounded like she was going to burst into tears too.

Slowly, Tara walked over until she was standing right in front of me. She looked down at her clipboard and sighed in an exaggerated way, shaking her head like she was just at a total loss. Up close, her bruising was a thousand shades of purple.

"Everything," she said finally in a pitying voice. "You need to work on just . . . everything."

• • •

Walking home, I was crying so hard, I could barely see three feet in front of me. I felt like a weak little loser, but part of me was also quite proud of the fact I'd held it in for so long. At least Tara and her friends weren't around to witness this.

How could people be so completely awful? I had only seen behavior like that in movies and on TV and I had always thought those things were ridiculous—that no one would ever treat another human being that way in real life. I mean, yeah, I'd suffered minor humiliations in middle school—that time I sat in a plate of spaghetti Johnny Mikelson had put on my chair, that summer everyone called me Underpants Gobrowski because I'd left my plaid cotton jockeys in the dressing room at the pool. But this? This was taking it to entirely new heights.

Tara and her friends were never going to accept me. They

weren't even going to try. There was no way I was setting myself up for that kind of humiliation again. Who knew what they would do to me if I showed up for tryouts? They'd probably pants me in front of the judges or dump a bucket of pig's blood on my head.

No way. Nuh-uh. Not this girl. Tara Timothy had won. I was not going back. I mean, wasn't there something kind of admirable in admitting defeat, in knowing when to give up? The thought made me sick, but I clung to it anyway. I didn't have much else to cling to at that particular moment.

I had just reached our mailbox and was already dreaming of a nice hot bath when I heard Daniel calling my name. Or, more precisely, my nickname.

"Hey, Jersey! Wait up!"

I almost ran directly into the house. When I cry, I get all blotchy and my eyes turn this psychedelic blue-green color and I was in desperate need of a tissue. But it was too late. He had seen me and if I bolted now, he would see that too. I wiped both hands across my face, sniffled hard and turned around.

Daniel was wearing a pair of football pants and a white SDH T-shirt that was hugging his body so tight, it showed the outline of every last muscle. His hair was darkened with sweat, his face was red from exertion and there was a streak of dirt across his right cheek.

"Hey!" His smile quickly faded when he saw my face. "Are you okay?"

"Oh, I'm fine," I said, trying not to stare at his chest. "I just . . . had an allergic reaction."

"To what?" Daniel asked.

Your girlfriend and her idiot squad, I thought.

"I'm not really sure," I said, inching toward my house.

53

Daniel was very, well, perfect, but I really just wanted to be alone.

"Oh. So I hear you're going out for the cheerleading squad," he said, smiling again.

"Um . . . yeah . . . well . . ."

"That's so cool! You're gonna love it."

He must have been sucking down the same psychedelic soda Mr. Cuccinello was drinking. Didn't he see there was no way I was ever going to fit in with those people?

"We do so much cool stuff with the cheerleaders," Daniel said. "The parties, the away games, the pep rallies, the team dinners, the kidnap breakfasts. You should have seen the getup Tara Timothy was wearing last year when we kidnapped her. She looked like a wannabe porn star or something."

Suddenly Daniel seemed to realize he was babbling and he snapped his mouth shut and grinned sheepishly. Meanwhile, I found myself practically salivating for the life he had described. Well, except the Tara Timothy as sex goddess part. It all sounded like so much *fun*. And added bonus? Daniel would be there for all of it.

"Anyway, it's gonna be great," he said. And I believed him.

A car horn honked and I looked up to find a convertible full of kids barreling toward us. I jumped up onto the curb, yanking Daniel with me.

"Sand Dune High *sucks*!" the driver shouted.

A bunch of green-and-white pom-poms shook out the window as everyone in the car screamed and jeered and shouted insults before they peeled away. So obnoxious.

"Freakin' West Wind," Daniel said, staring after them.

"Wow. I can see why you guys hate them so much," I said.

He shrugged. "We'll show them on the field," he said.

Then he knocked my arm with his shoulder, which pretty much sent a shiver all over my body. Twice. "And you guys will show them at regionals, right?"

"I'm not exactly on the squad," I said, looking down at my feet.

"Oh, you'll make it. I can tell," Daniel said.

"How?" I asked.

"There's just something about you, Jersey," he said.

Omigod. Was he *flirting* with me?

"I don't know. I don't think that Tara Timothy and those girls really like me that much," I said. The understatement of the year.

Daniel laughed. "Please. They're just trying to intimidate you. It's like hazing. They want to see if you can handle it."

Well, I hadn't exactly passed that test, considering I had been blubbering about two minutes ago. But Tara and her friends didn't know that. And actually, I was feeling a little better now. A lot better. See what some cute-boy interaction can do?

"So, can you?" Daniel asked.

"Can I what?" I asked back, hoping I hadn't spaced out and missed yet another direct question.

"Can you handle it?" he asked. His blue eyes were so full of confidence and ease I suddenly felt as if I was reflecting it all back at him.

"Yeah," I said. "Yeah, I think I can."

"Cool," he said. "Well, I'll see you tomorrow. Same time, same mailbox?" he said, patting the flamingo on the head.

"Sure," I told him.

I turned and walked into my house, feeling more and more confident by the second. If I could survive pre-tryout hell, why not go back for tryouts? Coach Holmes had said that a panel of teachers would be the judges, not the squad. So unless they did, in fact, pants me, what could they do? If I could just wow the judges, I could have the life Daniel had described and everything that went with it.

Including more time with Daniel.

"So . . . I don't think I'm going to try out," I told my mom, trying to sound upbeat about the decision.

We were shopping for Sand Dune–appropriate clothes, but I was too busy trying to sort my thoughts to pay attention to the splashes of color all around me. One minute I was totally confident and could imagine myself walking into that gym and blowing the competition away. The next minute I felt terrified and couldn't remember what the point was supposed to be. Even if I triumphed and made the squad, I was going to have to hang out with fifteen me-haters every day. Where was the fun in that?

"I thought you missed being on a team," my mother said. Her eyes were focused as she studied top after brightly colored top.

"Yeah, but they all hate me already. What's the point?" I asked.

Instantly the hangers stopped scraping and my mother looked up. "Who are you and what have you done with my daughter?" she asked.

"Mom—"

"Don't 'Mom' me. You are not Annisa Gobrowski," she said, coming around the clothing rack. She put her hands on the side of my face and studied me with a mock-serious expression. "The resemblance is remarkable, though. How do you pod people do it?"

I laughed and pulled away. "Enough already. I get it."

My mom smiled and gave me a hug. "Look, the Annisa I know would never let a bunch of petty girls stop her from cheerleading." She pulled back and looked me in the eye. "The Annisa I know would never let *anything* stop her from getting something she wanted."

It never ceased to amaze me how totally deep and beautiful my mother's eyes were. They made you believe pretty much anything she said. Usually.

I mean, in theory, my mother was right. I'd never backed down from a challenge before. But I'd also never felt like this before—so alone and totally ostracized. I'd never had so many people not like me—and they didn't even know me yet. The whole thing was just too overwhelming. I was having trouble working up that go-getter excitement, and I hated myself for it. What the heck was wrong with me?

I had a feeling the Annisa my mother knew had left the car somewhere back on the New Jersey Turnpike. And it looked like the Florida Annisa was going to be an utter outcast.

• • •

"Tell me it isn't true," Bethany said, grabbing me in front of our homeroom the next morning. She dragged me inside and straight to the back. "Tell me you didn't actually go over to the dark side. I let you out of my sight for five seconds—"

"Okay, ow," I said, sitting down and extracting my arm from her grip. "What's going on?"

"What's going on? What's going on, you ask? Only the total readjustment of my entire personal peer-assessment process!" Bethany ranted. "I thought I knew you! I thought we were simpatico! And then I find out that you're going to be a cheerleader!" She brought her hand to her head and swooned. "One day without me and this is what happens to you. I think I need to sit down."

I swallowed against a dry throat. "Yeah, about that. Where were you yesterday?" I asked, hoping to change the subject.

"I ditch every once in a while. Keeps the teachers guessing. And don't try to change the subject. *Cheerleading?*" She said it like it was another word for "roadkill."

"Look, I'm not trying out," I told her. "And how did you know I went to the meeting, anyway?"

"Because my dear brother Bobby, king of all that is evil in this place, is dating Tara Timothy, queen of all that is evil in this place," Bethany whispered hoarsely. "She came over to my house last night ranting about the brunette überklutz that broke her nose and is obviously trying to ruin her," Bethany said. "Wait a minute!" Her dark-rimmed eyes brightened slightly. "Is that why you're doing this? To ruin her? Because then I might be able to get behind it."

"Um . . . no. Not really," I said.

"Then I just don't get it. You're so not a rah-rah," Bethany said, studying me.

"Why? Why is it so impossible to see me as a cheerleader?" I asked.

"You met them! Do *you* think you belong there?"

Frustration started to mount in my chest. I just wanted someone to give me a straight answer. Something to make me certain I was making the right decision.

"Not necessarily, but why? Because they're blonde? In case you haven't noticed, so is this entire school."

Bethany turned in her seat to face me and lowered her voice. "They're not just blonde. They're mega-popular. And psycho-bitchy. They look down their noses at anyone in this place who tries to be just a little different."

"You mean like you," I said.

"Please. I don't care what those people think of me," she said, turning to face forward again and picking up a pen to doodle along her desk. Body language, anyone? She obviously did care. Or at least had at some point in her life.

"Okay, so I'm not a bitch and I'm not blonde, but who's to say I can't be popular?" I said.

"You're not getting it. You're not blonde, you're not a bitch, so therefore you will never be popular," Bethany said, dead serious. "At least not around here."

Wow. Was it really possible that the social lines could be that straight and narrow at this place? And if so, who was I to try to change them? I mean, normally I'm up for a challenge, but to strive against adversity just so I could be on a squad of people who hated me anyway? It hardly seemed worth it.

Apparently my gut instinct was right. I was going to stay as far away from tryouts as possible.

"Me. Friends with a cheerleader," Bethany said under her breath. "I gotta say, I just don't think it's possible."

"Well, don't worry about it," I said grumpily, trying to ignore the closed-mindedness of her statement. "It's not gonna happen."

• • •

Sage flounced right over to my desk before English class.

"So, you're not coming today, right?" she said. "Because you seem like a smart girl, so you know enough not to come."

I wondered if I could rip those eyelashes off in one strip— quick and painful, like a Band-Aid. Not that I would ever try something like that, of course. I swallowed my pride and looked her in the eye.

"No," I said. "I'm not coming."

"Good."

My hands curled into fists and my nails dug into the fleshy part of my palm as she walked to her desk. I so wanted to go over there and tell her exactly where she could shove her pom-poms.

"You're kidding, right?" Mindy said, slipping into the next desk. "You're not coming?"

I was saved from answering by the proverbial bell. Mrs. O'Donaghue started class, but we were only a few minutes in when a note landed square in the middle of my desk. I opened it, my hands shaking.

Annisa!
You HAVE to come! I need moral support!!!
XO
Mindy

I grabbed my pen and scrawled a message back.

What about Sage?

After all, I'd just gotten to this humanity-forsaken school. Mindy had other friends—people she'd known a lot longer than she'd known me. Let them be her moral support. I tossed the note back. It took Mindy a little bit longer to respond. The return note read:

Sage doesn't want me on the squad. She's too proud of herself for being the only sophomore that made it last year. If I make it, it'll be like she's not special or something.
XO
Mindy

61

I glanced back at Mindy and lifted one shoulder. I liked the girl and all, but I had made my decision.

Maybe.

It was just . . . *Sage.* Why did she have to come up to me and get my blood boiling all over again? I had been about ninety-nine percent comfortable with my decision right up until she got her little pug nose in my face. She was so smug. Wouldn't it be worth trying out just to show these people they couldn't get to me?

You know, I was starting to think that maybe I was a kind of proud person. I would love to say I could rise above it all and let their crap roll off my back, but the idea of cheering my heart out, making the squad and shoving their faces in it was growing more and more appealing.

Hey. Nobody's perfect.

Mrs. O'Donaghue picked a few people to read aloud from *Romeo and Juliet* and, thankfully, I was not one of them. As the play was recited around me, I found myself spacing in and out, trying to envision myself at tryouts. I saw myself doing the cheer, saw myself executing a back tuck and surprising the judges. I glanced across the room at Sage, who was blithely scribbling in her notebook. She thought she was so much better than me. Just imagine the look on her face if I made the squad. Just imagine how shocked they would *all* be.

"Where be these enemies?" a guy a few rows ahead of me read, knocking me back into the present. "Capulet! Montague! See what a scourge is laid upon your hate/That Heaven finds means to kill your joys with love!"

It was the Prince's big speech at the end. The part I like to call the "Neh neh neh neh *neh* neh!" speech. He gathers Romeo and Juliet's fathers together over their children's dead bodies and basically tells them they're idiots and that their feud killed their kids. I always loved this part. It was when the old farts learned their lesson, two deaths too late.

Even though Romeo and Juliet's situation was entirely different than mine, hearing that speech made me realize what a coward I was being. This wasn't about pride. It was about courage! Conviction! Standing up for myself! Was I going to stand by and let a bunch of blondes intimidate me? No! I was not! Thank you, Big Bill!

As soon as the bell rang, I got up to deliver a "Neh neh neh neh *neh* neh!" speech of my very own.

"Sage!" I called out before she could get out the door.

She turned around, surprise in her big eyes. Mindy walked up behind me.

"I changed my mind," I said firmly. "I'll see you after school."

Then I slipped right past her and headed off down the hall, my heart pounding. Okay, so it wasn't much of a speech, but for once she didn't have a loud whisper for me as I walked away. The "Neh neh neh neh *neh* neh!" had done its job.

• • •

"You do realize that just by wearing that outfit you're seriously jeopardizing the fate of your eternal soul," Bethany told me. We were standing outside the gym after school and Bethany was giving me a last-minute anti-pep talk. "Honestly, have you ever considered the concept of eternal hellfire? It doesn't sound like fun."

I was starting to think that Bethany Goow was a bit of a drama queen.

"Thanks for your concern, but I think I'm gonna be fine," I told her with a laugh.

And I would. If all those butterflies that were currently

slam-dancing in my gut would take five already. On the other side of the wooden doors, Mindy was going through her routine. I said a quick prayer to whoever might be listening that she wouldn't mess up. Best-case scenario here? Mindy and I would both make the team, thereby making my daily life slightly less heinous than it needed to be. Unfortunately there were about twenty girls trying out for two spots, so the odds were against us.

"Are you sure this isn't a joke?" Bethany said. "You're going to go in there and moon them, right? You have 'cheerleaders blow' written across your butt."

Before I could respond to that lovely visual, the cheering inside stopped. Mindy was being scored. And I was next.

Oh, God. I was going to hurl.

I heard pounding footsteps as Mindy jogged out and then the door opened. She was smiling, but somehow still looked nauseous.

"How did you do?" I asked.

"Okay, I think. You're next," Mindy responded. Then she lowered her chin and looked around at the other waiting girls. "They have half the football team in there in the stands to respond to the cheer. It's so weird."

The butterflies dispersed, leaving a hollow feeling. Half the football team? I almost wished she hadn't warned me.

"Annisa Gobrowski?" someone called out from inside.

"Break a leg," Mindy said.

"Literally!" Bethany called after me.

I rolled my eyes at her before stepping into the gym. I would just have to deal with Bethany if I made the squad. I just hoped she didn't really make me choose between her and cheerleading. I'd only known her a few days, but somehow the girl felt like home to me. I didn't want to lose her.

I jogged into the center of the gym, hands on hips, skin-busting grin in place. I made eye contact with each of the five judges, none of whom were my teachers. Coach Holmes was in the room, but no other cheerleaders were present. (Big relief.) Daniel Healy was there, however, front and center and surrounded by at least twenty guys in varsity jackets. He flashed me a thumbs-up.

"You can begin whenever you like," Coach Holmes said. And so I did.

• • •

An hour later, it was over. Everyone had done the routine and we were all sitting on the floor in the gym, waiting for the verdict. I felt oddly calm while Mindy sat next to me, chewing her nails into oblivion. I had done the best I could. And I had nailed the back tuck. Now it was just up to the numbers.

Performing for the judges was a lot easier than performing for the squad. And Daniel and the rest of the guys had at least responded to the cheer. All of them except one big, lumberjack type that I had pegged as Bethany's brother, and therefore Tara's boyfriend. He had just sat there with a bored expression. At one point, he'd even yawned.

"Okay, as far as I can tell, there are only three people who might have scored higher than us," Mindy whispered.

I looked around the room furtively, wondering if anyone had heard. It didn't matter, however. There were little clusters of whispering girls all around us, undoubtedly hypothesizing about the same thing.

"I'll bite. Who?" I asked.

"Wendy Stewart? The girl with the wavy hair and the super-white teeth?" Mindy said, tilting her head in Wendy's direction.

"Yeah. She's pretty good," I said, recalling her performance from the day before.

"Then there's Shira Citron and Ally Stevenson," Mindy said. "I think they almost made the squad last year."

"What about that girl with the thick hair and the freckles?" I asked. "She was pretty good."

"Trista McCarthy?" Mindy said, biting her lip as she pondered the possibility. "I don't know. She seems kind of without energy."

"Maybe," I said. "We're definitely above that chick in the spandex. She was all left feet."

"Christy? Yeah. I feel bad for her. I think her mom wants her to be on the squad. She'd rather be in the library, writing romance novels," Mindy said.

I glanced at Christy from across the gym. She was sitting by herself, her nose buried in a book called *Hearts Aflame*.

The sound of the gym door opening was like a nuclear bomb blast. Everyone sat up straight and there was an intake of air that could have created a black hole. Coach Holmes walked in, clipboard in hand, followed by the rest of the squad. I stared at Tara and Sage, trying to read their faces. Did they know anything?

"Okay, everyone, I want to thank you all again for your hard work," Coach Holmes said, standing at the front of the room. "Many of you had incredibly high scores, but only two of you could make the team. I'm not one for dramatics, so those two people are—"

I reached out and clasped Mindy's hand.

"Mindy McMahon and Annisa Gobrowski."

She said my name! And wait! She said Mindy's name! We both jumped up and screeched and hugged like the little cheerleaders we were. I couldn't believe it. We'd beaten the stupid odds! We'd both made the team!

Then I realized we weren't the only ones shouting.

"Her!? *She's* on the team!?" Tara Timothy screamed. "She's the one who narced on Kristen and Danielle! We wouldn't have even had to go through this whole thing if it wasn't for her!"

Mindy and I stopped jumping up and down and looked at Tara. The rest of the squad was standing back near the wall, avoiding eye contact with anyone.

"Tara, Kristen and Danielle made their own beds," Coach Holmes told her. "No one is to blame for their behavior but themselves."

"Oh, *please!*" Tara screeched, in complete tantrum mode. "The girl broke my nose. I'm gonna look like the Elephant Man for regionals because of her. And besides, she's a total klutz! She's going to bring us all down."

Okay, that was totally uncalled for. She had no right to rag on my cheerleading skills. She hadn't even *seen* them yet. And maybe I could be a klutz sometimes, but that was *sometimes.* I wasn't a walking disaster area.

"This can't be happening," Tara continued. "Can't you recount the scores?"

"Hey! Wait a minute," I broke in.

"Was I talking to you?" Tara snapped.

I felt like I had been slapped.

"No, you weren't," I said. "But you *were* talking *about* me like I'm not even here. Don't I get a chance to defend myself?"

"Girls," Coach Holmes said in a warning tone.

"I'm sorry I broke your nose, but it's not like I did it on purpose," I said, looking Tara in the eye. Then I turned to Phoebe, who was glaring at me from the wall. "And it was not my fault you had to move. It is, however, *your* fault that I have to live in a puke pink room."

Phoebe's mouth dropped open and I felt a smidge of regret, but I was on a roll.

"And you!" I said to Sage. "I don't know what I did to offend you, but you can loud-whisper about me all you want. The last thing I need is the approval of a superficial brat like you."

There was a moment of silence and I took a step back. I looked around at all the closed-off faces. Yeah, my first day had been an abysmal comedy of errors, but I hadn't done anything on purpose. I was a good person. And I didn't deserve all this.

"I'm sorry, Mindy," I said, raising my hands. "I can't do this."

Then I turned and jogged out of the gym, slamming through the back door. I ran past the football field where the guys were practicing, past the cross-country team that was finishing their cooldown. I even cranked it up a notch and sprinted past the last few mailboxes to try to flush all the voices from my head. Voices telling me to go back—that Coach would never let me back on the team if I didn't. I had to ignore them. If I didn't, I would end up spending the next few months hanging with a bunch of girls who would make my life a living hell.

No way. It was over. When I got to my house, I realized I had never once looked back.

The next morning, I left fifteen minutes early for school. There was no way I could deal with Daniel Healy. I was sure that Sage had told him all about my freak-out and had totally embellished the things I said. He probably wouldn't want to talk to me anyway and I'd have to walk to school with him walking twenty yards behind me in uncomfortable silence.

As I was crossing the football field, my cell phone rang. When I saw Jordan's name on the Caller ID, I almost cried.

"Hey!"

"Hey, babe! I just wanted to call and see if you decided what to do about this whole cheerleaders of the Antichrist thing," she said.

"I told you last night," I said, my heart feeling sick. "I'm quitting."

"You're sure?" she said.

"Yes, I'm sure," I replied.

"Okay, then. I support you," Jordan said. "I wish I was there with you. You know I'd be kicking some blonde butt by now. I've been practicing my kar-*a*-tay."

I smiled sadly. "I know. Thanks for calling, Jor."

"Anytime. Let me know what happens."

I clicked off and took a deep breath. Jordan had no idea how much that phone call had meant to me. With her behind me, even from miles away, I could face pretty much anything. I opened the back door and found Bethany waiting for me.

"Nice outfit," she said.

"Thanks," I replied. I was back in black. Black T-shirt, gray-and-black plaid skirt, black sneakers. If the people in this school didn't like the way I dressed, they could kiss my unbronzed butt.

"So, what happened?" she asked as we headed down the hall. "Are you the enemy?"

I sighed. "Yep, but it's only a temporary condition," I told her. "I'm on my way to the athletic office to officially quit."

Bethany's entire face lit up, but then she rearranged it into a concerned frown. "Oh. That's too bad."

I laughed and rolled my eyes at her. "I'll see ya later," I said, picking up the pace. I could hear her Pumas squeaking against the floor and her bracelets rattling as she jumped up and down with joy.

"No! I'm coming with you!" she said, jogging to catch up. "Just in case they try to brainwash you."

"Anyone ever tell you you're insane?" I asked.

"Not since breakfast," Bethany replied.

We headed into the gym lobby and I paused. Whitney Barnard was standing outside the door to the athletic office. When she saw us, she pushed herself away from the wall and walked over to me.

"I figured I'd find you here," she said.

"Don't bother," I told her, gripping my backpack strap. "I'm gonna go in there and quit, so you can save your breath."

"Don't quit," Whitney said. "You can't quit."

My mouth dropped open slightly and Bethany's jaw practically hit the floor.

"Look, Tara would kill me if she knew I was here, but I don't really care," Whitney said. "I wanted to tell you that I thought it was pretty cool that you even tried out after everything we put you through. Most people wouldn't have had the guts to show."

I felt like knocking the side of my head to make sure my ears were working.

"And yesterday? When you freaked out on Tara like that?" Whitney shook her head and looked at the floor. "No one on record has ever talked to Tara Timothy that way. Well, except me. It was the coolest thing I've ever seen."

Bethany and I exchanged a look. There was no finding my tongue.

"Look, Tara . . . she's really not that bad," Whitney said. "She's just a little . . . on edge right now because she really wants to win at regionals. She's basically obsessed, and this whole thing with Kristen and Danielle . . . it's giving her permanent PMS. But she'll calm down as soon as she realizes that you're exactly what this team needs."

"I am?"

"I think so. And some of the other girls do too," Whitney continued. "If we're gonna beat West Wind at regionals, we're gonna need the best cheerleaders we can get, and you and Mindy were the best. Besides, Danielle and Kristen were bad for our image. Personally, I'm glad you got them booted."

"But I didn't—"

Whitney held up her hand to stop me. "So are you in or are you out, Gobrowski?"

A little fire of hope came to life in my chest. Maybe I *could* get along with this team. At least I now knew that some of them actually wanted me there. I looked at Bethany. Her expression fell somewhere between baffled and impressed.

"Hey, if you really wanna do this, I'm behind you one hundred percent," she said.

I smiled. It was exactly what Jordan would have said.

"Okay, maybe more like ten percent," Bethany amended.

I laughed, took a deep breath and hoped I wasn't making the stupidest mistake of my life (and I've made some stupid ones—just take a look at my sixth-grade class picture).

"Okay, Barnard," I said. "I'm in."

And then, just when I thought the morning couldn't get any weirder, Whitney hugged me.

"You are not going to regret this," she said. She started to walk away, but then stopped and spun on her heel to face me. "Oh, and if my sister tries to make your life miserable, just ignore her. The girl still sleeps with a night-light." Then she winked and sauntered off.

After that, Bethany and I laughed for about an hour.

• • •

When I first walked into practice that day, I was even more nervous that I'd been before tryouts. There were at least three internal organs jockeying for position to be the first one out of my body. It didn't help matters when, the moment I entered the room, Tara stormed up to me. Her face was now a highly unattractive goldenrod-type color.

"I thought you quit," she said loudly.

"You thought wrong," I replied, somehow.

Then I walked past Whitney—who smiled covertly—and over to Mindy, who grinned unabashedly. These were my allies. Everyone else in the room might as well have been shooting me with subzero freeze rays. Where were these other girls Whitney had told me about? The ones who supposedly wanted me there?

I didn't have long to think about it. Coach Holmes came

in, and if she was surprised to see me there, she didn't show it. She warmed us up with twenty laps around the gym, a hundred jumping jacks, and as many push-ups as we could do in one minute. I checked in with a pathetic five. "Unprecedentedly sorry" was the phrase Coach used. She was wearing a tank top and had a set of Serena Williams arms. I had a feeling it was time to hit the gym.

"All right, here's what we're gonna do," Coach called out after warm-ups. "This team isn't just about regionals. We have a pep rally this Friday and a game this Saturday and our two new members need to be prepared for both."

Tara opened her mouth to protest, and it was like Coach Holmes' eyes were hooked into Tara's jaw. The second Holmes looked at Tara, her mouth snapped shut.

"I'd like a volunteer to work with Mindy and Annisa while the rest of the team practices the routine for regionals," Coach Holmes said. "A flyer would be best so that we can keep most of the formations intact. Anyone?"

I was so relieved when Whitney stepped forward, I could have kissed her. Tara did a classic soap opera betrayed look— chin pulled back, mouth open. Whitney didn't appear to notice.

"Okay, girls," Whitney said, leading us into a corner. "We've got a lot to learn, so pay attention. This is our hello cheer."

Then she launched into the most intricate cheer I'd ever seen. There was this one clap sequence where her hands were just a blur. Mindy and I looked at each other. This was not going to be a cakewalk.

For two hours we practiced with Whitney while the rest of the squad danced and cheered behind us to a tight mix of songs. Whenever we took a break, I couldn't help staring at the squad. The routine was intense. Intensely amazing. It looked just like something out of *Bring It On.* Suddenly, I had stars in my eyes. I remembered why I was here in the first place. Competition. The thrill of victory. The agony of defeat. Getting to strut my stuff on ESPN in front of thousands of crazed cheerleaders.

As a couple of girls launched into perfect scorpions, my skin felt all tingly. It was going to happen. I could feel it.

"All right, girls, take five," Coach Holmes called out at the end of one of their run-throughs. "Mindy, Annisa, can I see you?"

The rest of the team collapsed on the bleachers—everyone except Tara, Whitney and Coach Holmes. Mindy and I stood in front of them, sweaty and tired. My head was full of a zillion cheer catchphrases. "Go! Fight! Win!" "Here we go, Sand Dune, here we go!" "V-I-C-T-O-R-Y!" I could barely hear myself think with all the shouting going on in my gray matter.

"What do you think, girls?" Coach Holmes asked Tara and Whitney. She looked Mindy and me up and down. "I think Gobrowski's the flyer."

The flyer? I was going to be a flyer? My heart jumped excitedly. We barely ever got a basket toss off the ground back home, but on this squad I'd be catching more wind than a 747.

"Yeah, I guess," Tara said. "Kristen was a base and Danielle was a flyer," she explained, looking exclusively at Mindy. "Can you handle basing?"

"No problem," Mindy said.

"She did, like, thirty push-ups," I put in.

Tara looked at me like I'd just put a hex on her. "Come on," she said. "We'll throw you."

So not the words you want to hear from the mouth of your mortal enemy.

"Autumn? Chandra? I need you at the mats," Tara said.

A couple of sturdy-looking girls roused themselves from the bleachers and walked with us to a set of mats in the center of the room.

"Autumn Ross, Chandra Albohm, meet Mindy McMahon and Annisa Goborkowski," Tara said in a bored tone.

"Gobrowski," I corrected.

"Hey," Chandra said, lifting her chin slightly. She had a gravelly voice like that curly-haired chick from *American Pie.* And similar hair, actually.

"Hiya!" Autumn chirped. White-blonde ponytail. So much energy, she must've been mainlining Red Bull.

"Okay, we need to teach Mindy to base and Annisa's gonna be our flyer," Coach Holmes said. "You ever done this before, Gobrowski?"

"Yeah," I said. "A few times. Just regular basket tosses, though."

"Okay, well, we won't try anything fancy the first time. Show her the count," Coach instructed.

Autumn and Chandra locked arms in front of me. "It's one," Chandra said. "Then two and you prep to jump with your hands on our shoulders."

I put my hands on their shoulders and bent my knees.

"Then three, your feet hit our arms," Autumn said.

I jumped up and landed awkwardly on their interlocked arms. My foot slipped off Chandra's knuckles and I lost my balance and fell. Oddly, Tara caught me before I could hit the ground.

"Thanks," I said.

"I have to do that," she told me.

"Ow! Dammit!" Chandra said, shaking out her hand.

"Toughen up, Albohm," Coach scolded her. "How many times a day did you do this with Danielle?"

"Danielle knew what she was doing," Chandra whined.

My face turned ten shades of red. I looked at Mindy and she bit her lip. This was not good.

"Is this going to be our attitude?" Coach Holmes asked. I looked at the floor guiltily. Then she turned to the bleachers and shouted. "Is this gonna be our attitude? 'Cause if it is, we should stop right now."

Everyone shifted in their seats, looking at one another to see if anyone would be brave enough to answer.

"I can't hear you, people!" Coach shouted, causing my heart to slam into my ribs.

"No, Coach!" they all said in unison.

"Oh, this is pathetic!" Coach Holmes shouted. The tendons in her neck practically exploded through her skin. "I said, Is this going to be our *attitude*!?"

"No, Coach!" they all shouted at the top of their lungs.

"That's better." Coach Holmes turned back to us, her nostrils flaring. "Now you all need to wake up and realize that Kristen and Danielle are not coming back. They screwed up and they're gone. You've got new teammates now. Stop acting like a bunch of whiners and start acting like a team."

Mental note: Never get on Coach Holmes' bad side.

After that, the stunting session went pretty smoothly. I even managed a basket toss with a flip by the end of the hour, and Mindy was basing by that point. I only hit the ground three times and I'm pretty sure they didn't miss their spots on purpose. My butt, of course, had other theories.

Then it was time to show the rest of the squad what Whitney had taught us. Of course by that point I had completely spaced on half of it. I forgot the words to the Sand Dune spirit cheer, messed up the clap sequence in the hello cheer and fumbled my way through the rest of it. Still, Coach Holmes applauded for us when we were done, so everyone else did too. I guess they didn't want to make her mad again.

"Good first day, girls. Good first day," Coach said as practice broke up. "Just practice tonight and you'll be fine. Now come with me and we'll get you some uniforms."

Uniforms! I had almost forgotten about uniforms in all the bruising and battering. Mindy and I grabbed our stuff and followed after Coach. She led us up to her office above the gym. It was a tiny stucco room with bad lighting and an old metal desk, but the walls were peppered with framed photographs of smiling squads, dozens of award ribbons and a few gleaming plaques. As Coach unlocked the closet behind her desk, I walked along the wall. Coach Holmes was front and center in almost all the team photos, wearing a red-and-white uniform with a huge grin on her face and her finger held up in triumph—We're number one. There were trophies in almost all the photos.

"Wow," I said. "You've won a lot of competitions."

Coach Holmes looked over her shoulder. "Oh, yeah, I guess. But I've lost as many as I've won."

"It doesn't look like it," Mindy said.

"Take a closer look," Coach Holmes said as she came out with a few skirts and tops. "Those pictures in the middle, there's no trophy. We still had fun, though."

I smiled. It was nice to know our coach wasn't just about winning. Especially since it seemed that was all that mattered to our captain.

"Here. These should work," Coach Holmes told us, handing each of us a uniform. She added a white SDH Cheerleader

T-shirt and a pair of blue shorts with a little white megaphone on the leg to each pile. "Don't drive yourselves nuts with those cheers tonight. I'm sure you'll be fine tomorrow."

"Thanks, Coach," Mindy and I said in unison.

"So wear your uniforms to school with white ankle socks. You both have white cheerleading sneakers, right?" she asked.

"I have Sage's extra pair," Mindy said.

"Mine have red and black stripes," I said.

"Well, they'll have to do for now, but I'll order you both some new ones tonight," she said. "What size?"

"Oh . . . uh . . . five and a half," I said, surprised. "How much are they?"

"They're considered part of the uniform, so the school foots the bill," she said. "But you two are going to have to buy competition uniforms, ribbons, practice uniforms and sweats."

Holy shopping spree, Batman. Number signs floated through my head like I was some crazed Scrooge McDuck cartoon.

"Don't worry," Coach said with a laugh when she saw our faces. "We'll figure it all out over the next couple of days. Now, when you're in uniform, it's no nail polish, no jewelry, and hair goes up." She paused and looked at my forehead. "Got any good, soft headbands?" she asked.

"I'll get some," I told her.

"Good. Make sure they're light blue, white or yellow. Ask Whitney where she gets hers. She's been wearing them ever since she chopped her hair off last year."

"Okay," I said. At least the only other short-haired-girl on the team was the only other girl on the team who was talking to me. Maybe it was short-haired-girl solidarity.

"See you tomorrow," Coach said, dismissing us.

Mindy and I turned and headed for the door, clutching our uniforms to our chests. My head felt like it was bursting with information. It was exhausting. And I still had to go home and practice for hours. What was I thinking?

"Oh, and ladies?" Coach Holmes called out, for the first time showing the infectious smile that I'd seen in all her pictures. "Welcome to the squad."

"We are the Crabs! The Mighty Sand Dune Crabs! Stand up and shout for the Mighty Sand Dune Crabs!"

You know, the more times you say the word *crabs* the weirder the word starts to sound.

"Crabs," I said to myself, staring into my full-length mirror, which I had been practicing in front of for an hour. "Crabscrabscrabscrabscrabs."

My bedroom door, which was already ajar, creaked all the way open. My father stood in the hall, eyeing me warily.

"Michella!" he called. "I think all the cheerleading has finally gotten to her brain."

"Say crabs, like, ten times and you'll understand," I said.

"Twenty-five cents, please," he said, holding out his hand and smirking.

I tipped my head back. "Oh . . . *crabs.*" I shook a quarter from the South Park bank where I keep my like-quarter stash and handed it to him. Sometimes I think if I could just stop saying *like,* I could have a wardrobe that rivaled Gwyneth Paltrow's.

"So listen, UNLV called and asked me to come out and give a guest lecture," my father said as he pocketed my cash. "Your mom and I are going to Vegas!"

"Vegas, Baby! Vegas!"

My dad looked at me blankly, like he always did when I made any kind of pop-culture reference. Mom, Gabe and I had given him a DVD player last Christmas and so far all he'd watched on it were IMAX movies.

"When?" I asked.

"Sunday. We'll be gone for a little over a week," he said. "They wanted us to leave on Saturday and attend a reception, but I said no way. I was not going to miss my daughter's first game as a Fighting Crab."

"Thanks, Dad," I said with a grin.

His brow furrowed. "Crab," he said. "Crabcrabcrabcrab. . . . You're right. That's an odd word." Then he turned and walked down the hall. I heard him muttering the crab mantra until his office door closed behind him.

I returned to my reflection. Those pink walls were still glaring at me, stark and cotton candy–esque. With my parents leaving, I was going to have to put off the paint job a little while longer. Unless, of course, I did it myself. But my mother would kill me if I robbed her of the bonding artistic experience and the obligatory paint fight. I sighed. This place was never going to feel like home.

The phone rang and I dove for it. I had already called Jordan to tell her the good news about the squad and I knew it would only take her five minutes to call everyone I knew. This had to be one of the crew calling to congratulate me.

"Hello?"

"Dude! Wassup?"

It was Gabe.

"First of all, I'm not a dude. Secondly, 'wassup' was over, like, five years ago," I said, sitting down on my bed.

"You said 'like'! Twenty-five cents!" Gabe announced.

"Whatev," I replied. "What can I do for you?"

"I just called to tell you I'm coming home for a few days to chill with my li'l sis."

"You mean you heard Mom and Dad are going to Vegas

and you want to abuse our pool with your friends," I shot back.

"You know me far too well," Gabe said. "You don't mind if me and a couple of the guys crash, do ya?"

"No, as long as it's just a *couple* of guys. You are not turning our new house into party central," I said.

"Annisa! You hurt me! I would never—"

"Do I need to start listing your many offenses? Okay, how about the weekend Mom and Dad were in Boston and you had all those people over and my stereo mysteriously disappeared? Or when you were in tenth grade and you wanted the seniors to think you were cool, so you invited the entire school over and the back deck collapsed. Need I go on?"

"Don't you realize I've grown?" Gabe lamented.

"Please. It doesn't matter what personality you adopt, there's always a party animal lurking underneath," I said. "The difference is, I have to live in this house. You destroy it and I suffer the consequences."

"Okay, killjoy. No parties!" Gabe said.

"You swear?"

"I swear!"

"Great! Then I'd love to have you," I said brightly.

I hung up the phone and lay back on the bed, staring up at the stucco swirls in my ceiling. It would actually be kind of nice to have Gabe around for a few days. He has this way of making everything fun, except, of course, in those moments he feels the inexplicable need to torture me. But he was bringing home friends. And whomever he was hanging out with these days, I was sure they were beyond hot. Somehow they always are.

The phone rang again and I sat up straight and grabbed it. This time, it was Mindy. My first phone call from a new

Florida friend. I had to write this down in my journal. *October 15, 8:46 PM. I officially reclaim my blip on the social radar.*

"Are you freaking out? I'm freaking out!" she said.

"Why are you freaking out?" I asked.

"There are so many cheers! And we don't even know the pyramid yet!" Mindy said. "Sage just told me we're going to have a practice during third period to learn it. What if I mess it up?"

"Hey, if anyone's gonna mess it up, it'll be me," I told her, attempting to calm her.

"That's true," she said.

I blinked. "Hey!"

"Oh, sorry. I didn't mean that," Mindy said. "Okay, I need more practice. See ya."

"Yeah. Bye."

I sat there for a moment, my heart pounding. Tomorrow the entire student body and all the teachers and administrators were going to be watching us cheer. It would be the first time most of them laid eyes on me. If I did screw up, it was going to be the first impression to end all first impressions.

I stood up shakily and returned to the mirror. More practice seemed like a good idea.

• • •

The next morning, I could barely move. Every muscle in my body ached thanks to Coach Holmes' insane workouts and all the new stunts I'd learned. Plus, I could barely keep my eyes open after practicing half the night. I dragged myself up to school in my Sand Dune High cheerleading uniform with clashing cheerleading sneakers, wondering how I was even going to be able to lift my arms for the pep rally. Then, when I walked in the door, the weirdest thing happened—some guy said hi to me. He just walked by and said "Hi" and kept walking like he'd known me my entire life. I had never set eyes on him before.

Must've been a mistake, I thought.

Oh, yeah. He mistook you for one of the other hundreds of short brunettes walking around the school.

Then a pair of younger girls said hi to me as well. And a couple of guys in soccer jackets walked by me and said, "Whaddup, Sand Dune!" They turned and walked backward until I lifted my hand (ouch) and waved. I heard that a few more times on my way to homeroom: "Whaddup, Sand Dune!" Apparently it was some kind of battle cry.

Each time someone acknowledged my existence, I felt my chin rise a little higher. It was like now that they saw me in their uniform, I was suddenly one of them. "Dress the part, *be* the part." That was what my drama teacher Mr. Creech used to say.

Bethany lost what little color she had when she saw me in homeroom, but she still spoke to me, which was a good sign. Sage wouldn't even look in my direction. I just hoped she and the rest of the squad would keep an eye on me later when I was flying over their heads.

The third-period practice got me out of Spanish class, which was good because we were conjugating irregular verbs that I had never even heard of. The practice went fairly well. Even though I was aching, once I stretched out and started moving, the pain wasn't so bad. I didn't forget any of the words to any of the cheers, and if I missed moves, I was able to fudge them over well enough to escape notice.

In a few weeks you're going to know all this backward and forward, I told myself whenever I started to sweat. *All you gotta do is get through today.*

The pyramid was the toughest part. I was going up in a

liberty on the left side with Mindy, Chandra and Autumn basing. My right foot was supposed to land on the shoulder of this girl Kimberly, who was going up in a double-base stand in the middle. On the other side of the pyramid, Phoebe was mirroring me with her left foot landing on Kimberly's other shoulder. Until that day I had never done a liberty in my life, so I lost my balance the first couple of times. Chandra drew actual blood from her tongue from biting it, but I was grateful for her efforts. The last thing I needed was another public bashing. Mercifully, by the end of practice, I had nailed the stunt at least ten times.

"Not bad," Chandra said reluctantly. "For a spaz."

I beamed. That was high praise from a member of this team.

• • •

My post-practice high diminished that afternoon when Mr. Loreng slapped us with a pop quiz the moment we walked through the door. Thanks to practice, tryouts and shopping with Mom, I hadn't cracked a book all week and I was already behind because of the school switch. I ended up leaving half the answers blank, sweating in desperate silence while everyone else's pencils scratched around me.

"How'd you do?" Daniel asked me as we walked out of the room.

"Can you say *remedial math*?" I joked, trying to lighten the dread in my heart.

"Cheer up," he said, knocking my arm with his shoulder. "It's practically your job now."

"Yeah, I guess," I said.

"I told you you'd make the squad. You're gonna hafta learn to trust me, Jersey."

My heart flopped around like a flounder on the beach and

I smiled. There was definite sizzle in the air between us. He had to feel it too. But of course that was when Sage caught up with us and pulled him away. So much for that.

We didn't have to change for gym because the period was shortened, so Mindy and I got to spend the whole forty minutes running through the routine. By the time the bell rang and people started to file into the gym, I was nervous, but not paralyzed.

"You ready for this?" Whitney asked me as the cheerleaders gathered.

"Yeah. I think I am," I said with confidence.

As the pep rally started, the entire squad was sitting at the foot of the bleachers, legs crooked under us, poms on our laps. It was perfect for me because, while the football coach, Coach Turcott, announced the starting lineup of the football team, and the thousand or so students behind me broke the sound barrier with their cheers, I wasn't able to *see* any of them. Their sheer volume was intimidating enough.

With each name called, another guy descended from the bleachers and joined the line of players against the far wall. There were twice as many guys as my old team and most of them were twice as big as our biggest linebacker. I had a feeling these guys actually won games. What would it be like to cheer for a team that scored touchdowns?

"Let's have one last hand for your Fighting Crabs!" Coach Turcott shouted.

Bobby Goow—Bethany's brother and Tara's boyfriend, who since tryouts I'd mentally renamed Lumberjack Bob— exploded out of the line, thrusting his fists in the air and shouting, baiting the crowd. The entire place went wild. The rest of the team followed him, and before I knew it, they were piling on top of one another in the middle of the gym floor. I found myself giggling and saw that the rest of the squad was too. Why is it that guys being guys is just so darn swoon-worthy?

As the pile grew, the place went psychotic. Girls screamed. Guys lost their voices. By the time the mess was finally broken up, the crowd was like a thousand pit bulls straining at the bit. Suddenly I wasn't so sure that school spirit was a healthy thing.

"And now, your Sand Dune High School varsity cheer-leaders!"

Mindy grabbed my hand and pulled me up. Whether I was ready to face the screaming throngs or not, it was time. We all ran out to the center of the court, cheering and shaking our poms in the air. When I took my position, it hit me. The wall of expectant faces. And suddenly I knew. I knew like you know you flunked a quiz the second you hand it in. Like when you suddenly realize you missed one of the lines on a standardized test and answered every single question one line too early.

Something was going to go wrong.

"Ready!" Tara shouted.

"Okay!"

"Fighting Crabs up in the stands, let's—hear you—shout! Fighting Crabs up in the stands, let's—hear you—now! All you fans yell 'Go'!"

"GO!"

The lighting fixtures shook above our heads.

"All you fans yell 'Crabs'!"

"CRABS!"

The floor actually vibrated.

"GO!"

"CRABS!"

"GO!"

"CRABS!"

"GO!"

"CRABS!"

"LET'S GO, CRABS!"

Everyone in the bleachers freaked out, cheering and clapping. "Whaddup, Sand *Dune!*" a bunch of senior guys yelled in unison, cracking everyone up.

Back home, we would have been facing halfhearted clapping and jeers. This was actually kind of nice. And I hadn't messed up once. I found myself starting to relax as we launched into the hello cheer.

"We've got the power!"

"To take control!"

"To rock this joint!"

"To go for gold!"

"We welcome you!"

"To our school!"

Here, we started to climb. I was hopped up on adrenaline. Everything was coming together . . .

"Take it from us!"

"Sand Dune rules!"

My liberty went up perfectly on *Sand.* But on *Dune?* Well, on *Dune* the whole thing went into the crapper.

Kimberly was half a second late going up in the center. I was so focused on the crowd that I missed it, and when my foot came down on her shoulder, it wasn't where it was supposed to be. Instead, my sneaker caught the edge of her sleeve, scraped down the side of her arm and landed nowhere.

My stomach left the building. My arms flailed. I think I may have grabbed someone's ponytail on the way down.

Somehow my spotters caught me before I could crack my head open. It was all a horrifying, mortifying, bone-jarring blur. All I know for sure is that by the time the word *rules* had finished reverberating off the walls, one side of the pyramid was a tangled blue, yellow and white mass of limbs.

Please don't let anything be broken on anyone, please don't let anything be broken on anyone, I thought as I removed a foot from my face.

The entire crowd was belly laughing. As I sat up, I saw Bethany front and center, giggling. Some scrawny kid with a camera circled us, blinding me with his flash.

"Get up! Get up!" Autumn yanked me to my feet and we all jumped up and down, cheering and yelling "Go, Sand Dune!" like nothing had happened. As we jogged back to the bleachers, I managed to glance at Tara. Her nose was not, in fact, broken again. But from the look on her face, she was seriously considering breaking mine.

"Omigod, omigod, omigod, omigod," I said over and over and over again.

"It's okay," Mindy said, putting her hand on my back.

"Oh, it is *so* not okay," Tara said from her seat a few cheerleaders away.

Eeesh.

As soon as the pep rally was over, Tara pulled me aside. I took a deep breath and looked her in the eye. I felt awful, but everyone was okay. And it wasn't like no one had ever messed up a pyramid before. Right?

"Look, Goblonski, I've thought this over from every angle, and there's nothing I can do. It's two weeks to regionals and I need sixteen cheerleaders, so apparently I'm stuck with you."

"Tara, I—"

"But you had better deal with your inner klutz and do it fast," she said. "Because I am not going down at that competition. Not this year."

She walked away and the rest of the squad filed by me, rubbing at sore spots and wincing. My heart sank slowly. I barely even knew these girls and I'd already let them down.

"Come on. Time for practice," Mindy said, rubbing a crunchy blue-and-yellow pom against my back. I suppose it was supposed to be comforting, but it made me grind my teeth. I watched the hundreds of other kids filing out the doors toward their cars and buses, tasting freedom.

"Yeeha," I said flatly.

But I made a vow to myself at that very moment. From then on, all I was going to do was practice. I was going to be worthy of the Sand Dune High cheerleading squad. Even if it killed me.

"You know, I think this you-being-a-cheerleader thing could actually turn out to be a positive development," Bethany told me that evening.

We were sitting out by the pool in my backyard as the sun went down, listening to a punk rock station Bethany had programmed into every memory button on my portable stereo. Bethany was wearing a plain black tank suit and a pair of long denim cutoff shorts with an anarchy symbol painted on the butt. She was even whiter than me.

"Why? Because I nearly sent half of them to the ER today?" I asked. Every time The Big Fall replayed itself in my brain, I had to physically shake my head to keep myself from obsessing.

"No, because this could change the Sand Dune High social structure forever," Bethany said, sitting up straight.

"Oh, come on," I scoffed.

"No, I'm totally serious. You could be like Rosa Parks! Or Chrissy Hynde or . . . or Madonna!"

"Rosa Parks is rolling over in her grave right now," I said, getting up at the sound of the doorbell.

"Rosa Parks isn't dead."

"Oh. I knew that."

I walked through the kitchen and living room to the front door, fully expecting the mailman with one of my dad's

National Geographic packages. Instead, I found Daniel Healy standing on my doorstep, holding some kind of rubber ball and disc contraption that looked like it had been stolen off the set of *Star Wars*.

"Hey!" he said with a smile.

Suddenly I was hyperaware of my bikini and wondered if it was properly covering all the parts it was supposed to be covering. Had I shaved that morning? Had I shaved in the last *week*?

"Annisa?"

"Oh, hey! Sorry!" I said. "I just . . . I came from outside to inside and my eyes are . . . you know . . . adjusting, so—"

Just shut up and smile.

"Hi," I said. I smiled. Better.

"Think fast," Daniel said.

And suddenly the black-and-silver *Star Wars* relic was flying at my face. I reached up and grabbed it from the air before it could rearrange my face.

"What is it?" I asked.

"It's for you."

"Uh . . . thanks, I think," I said, tipping it back and forth in front of me.

"It's a pogo ball," Daniel told me like it was the most obvious thing in the world. He grabbed it back out of my hands and put it on the ground. From that vantage point it looked like Saturn, except it had one solid disk around the ball instead of a bunch of skinny rings. Daniel placed his feet on the disk, on either side of the ball, holding his arms out for balance. "See? You do this," he said. And then he started to bounce up and down.

Daniel Healy, the hottest guy I'd ever seen in my life, was on my front walk in his football jersey, bouncing up and down like a five-year-old, his dark blond hair flopping and flapping all over the place. From the grin on his face he was having the time of his life.

"It's for balance and coordination," he told me, still bouncing.

He jumped off the ball, landed right in front of me and picked the thing up again.

"See, Sage told me the pyramid collapse today was all your fault," he said in a tone that told me a) he didn't care and b) he thought it was silly that she'd told him at all.

"That was nice of her," I said, laughing.

"Yeah, I thought so too," he shot back, smiling a smile of private understanding.

Sigh. It was like we were soul mates locked in an epic struggle against the evil and selfish Wicked Witch of the West. Except, of course, he was dating said Witch.

"Anyway, I figured the pogo ball might help," he said, holding it out to me again. I took it and held it to my chest. Could he be any sweeter? "And a word of advice," he said, taking a few steps back down the front walk. "Don't worry about it. Everyone messes up once in a while."

"Hey!" I shouted after him when he reached the mailbox. He turned and looked at me. "Does Daniel Healy ever mess up?"

He grinned that grin that was painstakingly designed to turn me to instant mush. "Me?" he said, spreading his arms wide. "Never!"

I had to concentrate to get my feet to move me inside. I closed the door, leaned back against it and sank down to the floor, the pogo ball landing in my lap. It was a total movie moment. I love it when I have those.

"What the?"

Bethany had walked in from the backyard to find out where the heck I'd gone. She looked at me, then looked out the window. She let out this kind of guffaw, then slapped her hand over her mouth.

"You're in love with Sage Barnard's boyfriend," she said gleefully. She crouched down in front of me, her eyes gleaming, her hand over her heart. "I didn't think I could love you any more, but now I do!"

I was in too much of a dazy haze to protest her very true statement. She leaned forward and planted a big, loud, smacking kiss on my forehead before padding off toward the bathroom.

"This is great," she said, shaking her head and laughing. "I *love* this girl!"

• • •

Saturday was the first gray day since I'd been in Florida. A crap day for a football game. I thought heat and humidity could get bad back in the tristate area, but I had been whining about nothing for the past few years. The air was so thick, you could feel the water particles trying to push you back as you moved forward. It was us versus the air and the air was winning.

It made me miss those crisp fall days of the Northeast. But hey. You work with what you've got.

I arrived at the football field early to help the rest of the squad decorate the home-side bleachers. The scoreboard was lit up, and the huge plywood Fighting Crab that stood atop it looked almost eerie through the dense air. Even with all the wetness I could feel the sizzle around the football field. There was a battle about to take place and I was going to be front and center.

I grinned. This was one of the things I loved about cheerleading—being part of the whole football experience. Fall leaves or no, I was a cheerleader again. Suddenly it was all I could do to keep from jumping up and down on the red clay track that circled the field.

Only a few of the girls were there when I reached the bleachers, including Phoebe. She was sitting near the bottom of the stands, wrapping blue and yellow streamers around the railing. Drawing on my good mood, I resolved to say hello to her. I felt a little guilty over the puke-pink-room comment I'd tossed out at tryouts and I was hoping she might give me a chance to apologize. Granted, she'd been horrendously rude to me first, but someone had to be the bigger person, right? It was time to start becoming part of this team. And that was going to mean getting the rest of them to speak to me. Whatever it took.

I started up the steps and Phoebe looked up. With a huge smile I opened my mouth to say hello, and Phoebe just turned away from me. Not just her face either. She turned her entire body, making it unduly difficult for her to continue decorating. Apparently she'd rather channel her inner contortionist than talk to me.

"Look, Phoebe, I'm really sorry about the other day," I blurted. "I was hoping—"

"Didn't I tell you to stay away from me?" Phoebe said, her back still facing me.

"Yeah, but I—"

She stood up and turned to shoot me a glare. "Then *stay* away from me."

"Listen, it's not my fault that you had to move," I said, my brain racing for the right thing to say. "And . . . and I'm a good person once you get to know me—"

"Don't you get it? I don't *want* to get to know you,"

95

Phoebe shot back, her eyes filling with angry tears. "Seeing you just reminds me of all the things that suck in my life, okay? I know it's not your fault, but that's just how it is."

As she stormed off, a huge lump appeared in my throat. Wow. This girl was *really* messed up. And she *hated* me. So much for team spirit. She might be a good writer for Bethany, though.

I wandered up the bleachers and ended up decorating with Mindy and Autumn, who in her eternal positivity seemed to be the least bothered by my presence on the squad.

"Kristen and Danielle hate me," she said with a carefree smile as we taped a huge banner to the concession stand. "They call me Peppy Le Pew because, you know, I'm so hyper. I got kind of sick of it, actually, but I never really said anything because, you know, I have a forgiving spirit."

"Right," I said.

"But I'm glad you got them kicked off," she told me confidentially, reaching back to tighten her white-blonde ponytail. "I really think their negative energy was beginning to affect the squad."

"But I didn't—"

"You really do have the most beautiful aura," Autumn said, staring at the space just above my head. "A little polluted, probably from all the stress of living in such a high-paced area as New Jersey, but the ocean air should flush that right out!"

I didn't much know what to say after that. But I thought it was nice of her to care.

• • •

Spirit ran seriously high at Sand Dune High School. By the time the game started, the stands were packed with fans in blue and yellow and anticipation filled the air. My parents were in the front row, cheering and waving a pair of souvenir pom-poms. They could be so embarrassing. But hey, no one here knew who they were. Bonus!

The East Bay Buccaneers kicked off to us and the second the kicker's foot hit the ball, I felt a rush of adrenaline. *Let's see what these Fighting Crabs can do!*

Much to my shock, the rest of the Sand Dune High cheerleaders seemed to actually know what was happening on the field. Back home, our captain was constantly calling defense cheers when we were about to score (which was rare) and making us do "Move That Ball Down the Field" when the bad guys had the ball. But now I had Tara to my right, shouting things like, "Blitz! They're coming on the blitz!" and a tall, gangly girl named Felice on my left, going, "Pick up the safety! The safety!" while she jumped up and down and pointed. The best part of all was that the Crabs actually scored twice in the first quarter and allowed no points. For a winless girl like me, it was cheer nirvana.

Then I noticed that Phoebe was spending a lot of time staring into space. Every now and then she'd wander off from the formation and either Tara or Coach Holmes, who was sitting on a bench under the bleachers, would have to whisper-shout at her to get her to come back.

"What's up with Phoebe?" an extremely tan girl named Jaimee asked Felice. "She's, like, totally zomborific."

I need to write that one down.

"I heard her parents are splitting up because her mom's still tripping over her dad losing the house," Felice said.

"That was just straight-up *wrong*," Kimberly chimed in. "What kind of man disrespects his family like that?"

"I heard her new room at her aunt's house is, like, ugly and brown and it, like, smells like something, you know, died in there," Jaimee put in.

"Poor Phoebe," Felice said.

"That girl is definitely not in cheer mode today," Kimberly said, shaking her head.

Then Tara called a cheer and my eavesdropping was over. My heart felt heavy as I moved through the chant on autopilot. It was no wonder Phoebe hated me. I wished there was something I could do, but it was kind of hard to make someone feel better when they refused to even look at you.

As the second quarter wound down, I noticed a disturbance at the other end of the line. Chandra and Autumn were bickering, their arms crossed over their chests, their expressions both extremely offended. At first no one could hear what they were saying, but the argument grew more heated, and certain words started hitting the airwaves.

"How could you say—"

"I was just making an observation—"

"An observation? Omigod! That is the worst thing you could have said right now!"

"You *guys!*" Tara scolded through her teeth.

A few people in the stands started to catch on and tune in to the escalating argument. There were twitters and pointing, and then the marching band started to chant from their spot in the center of the stands.

"Cat *fight!* Cat *fight!* Cat *fight!*"

"Tara! Get control of your squad!" Coach Holmes hissed.

The game clock ticked down and the whistle blew. Tara stalked over to Chandra and Autumn. The rest of us huddled together in a group, afraid to interfere. Everyone except Phoebe, who walked over and sat down on the bench next to Coach Holmes. She stuck her legs out, crossed her arms over her chest and slumped.

"This does not look good," Whitney said as Autumn grew more and more animated.

"Nuh-uh," Erin agreed.

"What are you *doing?*" Coach Holmes whispered.

"And now, your Sand Dune High School varsity cheer-leaders!" the guy on the PA called out.

Everyone looked at one another as if they'd forgotten where they were. Then, as one, they all started shouting, cheering and jumping and ran out onto the field. Mindy and I stayed behind, having yet to learn the halftime/competition routine. We went to sit on the bench by Coach just as Phoebe was dragging herself up to join the rest of the squad on the fifty-yard line.

"This should be interesting," Coach said under her breath.

Actually, it started out just fine. It's an impressive routine with a lot of energy and some kick-ass music. At first, every-one seemed to be moving in unison, though only about five people were smiling. Then, when it came time to do the bas-ket tosses, Phoebe didn't bother to bend her knees, so she caught little air and came down two beats too soon, throw-ing everything off. Half the team recovered the beat, but the other half didn't, so for a few moves it was all a mess. Then, at the end, Autumn was supposed to shoulder-sit on Chan-dra at the front of the formation, but they couldn't get it together—the easiest stunt in the book. They both ended up standing there, looking confused, until the final beat, when they just threw their hands up into high V's.

The sky picked that very moment to open up, showering a torrent of rain down on the cheerleaders and their pyra-mid. Instead of applauding, the crowd scrambled for cover. The result was a deathly, foreboding silence. As the squad jogged off the field, Jaimee tripped into Felice and sent her sprawling into the muddy grass. She came up looking like a black-and-white cookie.

Coach Holmes covered her face with her hands.

Mindy and I exchanged a look of doom. It was awful. It was embarrassing. It was depressing. But to be honest, all I could think was, *Heck, at least I wasn't out there.* For the first time, nothing could be blamed on me.

• • •

"What *was* that?" Coach Holmes demanded, pacing back and forth in front of us as we puddled all over the auxiliary gym floor an hour later.

In the second half we'd fallen apart even more. Tara had been forced to readjust the formation to separate Chandra and Autumn, and thanks to the rain, we were sliding around and messing up all over the place. The only bright spot had been the total trouncing the football team had recorded. They'd won, 55–7.

"Who *were* those people? Because I know that wasn't my team. That wasn't the team I know and trust and respect."

She paused as if waiting for someone to say something. I swear I heard sixteen cheerleaders gulp.

"You girls know I don't care if you mess up. We all make mistakes. We all know this," Coach continued. "But when you mess up because you can't get past petty issues, when your head's not in it because you'd rather focus on your own selfish feelings, that's when I get pissed. Now, are you losing focus, team?"

"No, Coach," was the mumbled reply.

She tipped her head back to the ceiling and flopped her hands into her thighs, fed up. "I *said,* Are you losing focus, team?"

"No, Coach!"

"Good! Because this is a very bad time for you to lose focus," she continued. "We have our number-one rivals coming to our field next weekend and I want you girls to be there

100

one thousand percent. *All* of you," she said, looking at Phoebe, who hung her head. "Here's the schedule for spirit week," she said, handing out sheets of light blue paper. "Need I remind you that, as cheerleaders, you are the embodiment of spirit in this high school?"

I almost laughed. It was knee-jerk. A statement like that at my apathetic former school would have earned a nice round of chuckles. But here, everyone just looked at her somberly. Thank God that giggle hadn't made it past my throat.

"You have a lot of responsibilities this week. Now, I want to see you all get your butts in gear, you hear me?"

"Yes, Coach!" we all shouted. I was starting to get the hang of how to answer her.

"All right then, you're dismissed."

Phoebe ran off in tears after being singled out. Autumn grabbed her bag and flounced off, pointedly turning her back on Chandra. Whitney and Tara fell into heated conversation as they followed after Phoebe.

I glanced at Coach, who was shaking her head as she packed up her gear. Somehow I got the feeling that things were going to get worse before they got better.

• • •

That night, my brother showed up with Hottie Number One (Joe Wu) and Hottie Number Two (Tucker Freeman). Florida surf boys were cu-*ute*. They threw their duffel bags in Gabe's yet-to-be-unpacked bedroom, then jumped in the pool fully clothed. (Shucks.) I was supposed to study and practice, but somehow Tucker managed to cajole me out of my room and into the water. Though I did put on my bathing suit first.

After drying off, I called Jordan to tell her all about the

insanity of the day. I was gabbing on the phone with her as I came back downstairs for a late-night snack of leftover pizza. (Gabe's friends had ordered three with everything.)

"I thought you said this squad was good," Jordan said after I related my tale of woe. "They're making *us* sound like nationals material."

"I know! And yesterday they were all over *me* for messing up. Like they would *never,*" I replied, pressing the phone into my shoulder so I could open the fridge. "You should have heard the coach. She was all—"

. I stopped midsentence. The guys were conversing in the living room.

"She was all what?" Jordan asked.

"Shhh. Hot boys talking," I said, tiptoeing down the hall.

"Ooooh. What're they saying?"

"Hang on," I whispered. I paused outside the living room, where the guys were battering each other on Xbox, and held my breath.

"You never told me your sister was so smokin', G!" Joe said.

"I'm going to pretend you didn't say that," Gabe responded.

"She did look fine in that bathing suit, dude," Tucker put in.

I grinned and scurried noiselessly back to the kitchen. "Jor?" I said, giggling into the phone. "I think I'm cheering up."

"Amazing what a few hot guys can do for ya," Jordan replied.

CHEERLEADERS GO DOWN IN FLAMES!
Not one, but TWO surprise pile-ons
make for a bizarre pep rally.

This was the headline on the school paper, *The Weekly Catch,* on Monday afternoon. It was accompanied by a highly unflattering picture of me with my cheerleading skirt flipped up to waist level and Autumn's foot pressed into my stunned face. I stared at it as I walked down the hall to geometry class, trying to ignore the blatant whispering that had been following me everywhere since lunch, when the papers had been distributed.

"Okay, Annisa! You can wake up now!" I said through my teeth. If the last week had been a dream, this seemed like the perfect moment for the alarm to go off.

"Nice hat," someone said sarcastically as they passed me by.

I reached up with one hand and touched the black knit beanie cap I'd worn to mark Hat Day, the first theme day of spirit week. Almost everyone in the school was wearing a hat, but most of them were baseball caps of the SDH variety. There were a few exceptions—the occasional cowboy hat, a visor or two, but mine was the only heavy black number.

Tomorrow was Plaid Day. I wondered if everyone in this

town owned blue-and-yellow plaid shirts. But that prospect wasn't nearly as scary as Face Paint Day, which would happen on Friday. *That* was going to be interesting.

"Annisa!" Bethany called out, stopping me before I could turn into class. She was, of course, hatless. "Sorry I missed lunch. I was in the computer lab." She looked down at the paper in my hands and winced. "So you've seen it, huh?"

"You know, I've never looked at my half-naked body from quite that angle before," I said, trying to joke through my nausea.

"Look at it this way. Any guy who asks you out now, there are no expectations," Bethany said with a shrug.

"Why, because he already knows I'm a loser?"

"No. Because he's already seen up your skirt."

I smirked even as my stomach turned. "You know, I don't think you've quite mastered the concept of the bright side."

"Gimme this," Bethany said. She snatched the paper away from me, crumpled it in one hand and launched it over her shoulder, where it hit a passing freshman in the head.

"Ow," he said.

"Whiner," Bethany replied without even looking at him. "So listen, I'm like *this close* to launching sucks-to-be-us 2.0. You wanna come over after practice today and help me test the site?"

I smiled. A night hanging with Bethany would probably be the perfect antidote to whatever torture was going to be brought my way at cheerleading practice. Plus, I felt a skitter of excitement run through me at the thought of going over to a new friend's house.

"I'm in," I said, just as the warning bell rang.

"Great. We'll burn a few school newspapers in effigy," she said.

"Sounds like a plan."

Bethany smiled encouragingly before she walked away. As she headed down the hall, I saw her snatching newspapers away from random people, all of whom protested, but none of whom tried to take them back. I laughed and walked into class. It had taken about two seconds for Bethany to make me feel better.

"Quizzes, get your quizzes," Mr. Loreng said, handing out papers as we filed into the classroom. My stomach twisted up in knots. I'd totally forgotten about the quiz!

"Ms. Gobrowski," he said, pursing his lips as he handed me my paper.

There was a huge D at the top of the page. A big, fat D. I dropped into a desk and shoved the paper into my bag before Sage could see it and comment. A D. My first grade from a Sand Dune teacher was a D. I'd never gotten a D in my life.

"Good Monday morning, class!" Mr. Loreng said once we were all seated toward the back of the room. "I hope you're all bright eyed and bushy tailed today, because *today* we're going to talk about your quarterly exam!"

Everyone around me groaned and sunk in their seats. Mr. Loreng, who was sporting a fisherman's cap with actual lures sticking out of it, grinned wickedly.

"The exam will take place in class one week from Tuesday. This gives you exactly eight nights of studying to prepare—"

"But Mr. Loreng, it's spirit week," Sage blurted out from the seat behind mine.

I swear I saw little pitchforks appear in Loreng's eyes. "I hate to be the one to remind you, Miss Barnard, but you're here to study, not to run around committing acts of *hari-kari* in the name of football dominance."

Everyone averted their eyes and shifted in their seats. I

got the feeling that no teacher had ever put the perfect Sage in her place before. This was serious.

"Now, if you underachieved on the quiz I just handed back, this is your chance to prove yourself," Loreng continued.

He handed out sheets filled with topics to study for the exam. They may as well have been written in a foreign language. I hadn't even *heard* of some of this stuff. And it said we were going to have to do five proofs. I hate proofs. They're so annoying and pointless. Why do I have to prove a concept if countless mathematicians and sophomore students before me already have? Isn't there such a thing as having too much proof?

"We are so dead," Sage said under her breath.

"Tell me about it," I replied.

For once, she said nothing snotty in return. We were in this one together.

• • •

"Goobooski! God! Where is your head today!?" Tara shouted at me that afternoon.

"We know it's not up her skirt," Chandra said, causing a round of scoffs and laughter.

"I'm sorry, you guys," I said, red from exertion and embarrassment. "I just have brain freeze on this section for some reason."

We had spent the entire practice working on the routine for regionals, and Mindy and I were playing a serious game of catch-up. While everyone else was tired and sweaty, we looked like we'd just run the New York City Marathon. My bod was just not used to this much exercise. Practice had already run over by half an hour and I'd just missed my count for the final lift—again.

"All right, girls, let's call it a day," Coach Holmes said, stepping forward. "Everyone's tired and you've worked hard. We'll get this part down tomorrow."

"But Coach," Tara began. "We just have to—"

"I'm going back to my office for a few minutes. Why don't you lead the squad through cooldown?" Coach Holmes said in a no-nonsense tone.

Tara nodded. "Okay," she said, though I could tell she was biting her tongue. The second the gym door slammed behind Coach Holmes, Tara reeled on us, her mouth set in a straight line.

"Everyone sit," she said.

"I thought we were going to cool down," Felice protested. "You know if you wait too long to stretch after a workout—"

"Felice," Tara snapped.

"Fine," Felice said quickly, and she hit the floor with the rest of us.

"Look, I don't know what all of you are thinking, but we are never going to get through this week with these kinds of attitudes," Tara began, standing in front of us. "This was the worst practice I've ever seen. No one has any energy, we're not hitting our moves. And it's not just Goberkowski either."

I blinked. Had she actually just sort of let me off the hook? Or simply singled me out again?

"No one here looks like they care one way or another how we perform at regionals," Tara continued. "Now, I know *I* want to win. What I need to know is whether you guys even want to be bothered competing."

A tense silence filled the air. A couple of the girls stared at the floor, clenching and unclenching their jaws as if they were debating whether or not to talk back. In the end, no one said a word. Tara was just too intimidating. I was start-ing to think she wasn't exactly leadership material. Well, maybe in the Marines.

"Okay, how about this," Tara said finally, breaking the silence to bits. "Do any of you have any suggestions about what we can do to pull this squad together? Because right now, this is not a team, it's a joke."

It came to me out of nowhere. It was like a file cabinet had opened in the back of my mind and started spewing out data I had filed away. My heart fluttered with excitement. It was perfect. It would show them that I knew about their tra-ditions, that I wanted to be part of the team, that I was will-ing to take risks. And it could be fun too. Wicked fun.

I looked around. No one seemed to be on the verge of say-ing anything. I raised my hand tentatively.

Tara rolled her eyes. "This should be good."

Okay, she was getting on my last nerve.

"What is it, Annisa?" Whitney asked, sounding interested.

Tara tilted her head and shifted her feet, surprised that Whitney had gotten my back. But she didn't say anything. Everyone just waited.

I looked from Mindy to Autumn to Whitney and smiled conspiratorially. "Two words," I said. "Prank. War."

The squad jumped up, cheering and shouting. Suddenly I was thrust onto their shoulders and lifted into the air as they all shouted, "Hip, hip, hooray! Three cheers for Annisa!!!"

Okay, not quite. But they did slowly begin to stir. A few girls who had been lounging defiantly sat up straight. Glances were exchanged, smiles began to appear. This was it. We all felt it. It was the plan of a lifetime. And it was mine!

"It's perfect," Whitney said. "It covers all the bases. It's a classic spirit week activity, it'll rally the school—"

"We get to trash the Dolphins," Jaimee put in.

"And it'll be kick-ass fun," Chandra said. Was it just me, or was she eyeing me with new respect?

"All in favor?" Tara said.

Everyone raised their hands. I couldn't have stopped grinning if the ceiling had fallen in on me right then and there. Was this the beginning of the end of the team-wide freeze-out?

"All right," Tara said, sitting down with the rest of us. "I say we start tonight. Now all we need is a plan. . . ."

• • •

Bethany's room was exactly how I imagined it would be. Actually, that's not really true. It was exactly how I imagined it would be times ten.

The walls were black. The blinds were dark purple. There were curtains of all colors, textures and patterns bunched onto curtain rods all around them. She had a queen-sized four-poster canopy bed strung with even more curtains and sporting at least twenty dark velvet and silk pillows. The wall behind her bed was papered with concert posters from Ozzfest, Lollapalooza, Korn, MxPx, Limp Bizkit, the Flaming Lips and a few bands I'd never even heard of. There was also a huge poster of Britney Spears with the eyes gouged out and some unsavory details added in with black marker.

"I got my dad to order us a pizza," Bethany said as she swiped a tangle of clothes off an old wooden chair and pulled it over to her desk so I could sit with her. "Hope you like onions and peppers."

"I'll just pick them off," I said.

"So, what'd you do at practice today?" Bethany asked. "Did they make you wax your legs yet?"

"Actually, you're not going to believe this," I said, sitting down next to her. "We are going to reinstate prank war!"

Bethany's hand dropped onto the keyboard. "Don't mess with me."

"I'm not! I'm totally serious. I'm even the one who suggested it."

"And those graham crackers went along with it? Did you slip hallucinogens in their Gatorade or something?" Bethany asked.

"Um . . . no," I said, laughing.

"Do you even realize what this means?" she said. "Annisa, you're not just changing things, you're a full-on revolutionary."

I blushed. "It's not *that* big a deal. . . ."

"Are you kidding? Getting Tara Timothy and the blah-rah squad to do anything even remotely interesting is definitely a radical act," Bethany said. "We're talking about a group of people who consider Justin Timberlake to be a crossover artist, who . . . who think that wearing blue nail polish is subversive. Annisa, these people have eaten the same salad with the same nonfat dressing and the same bottle of water every single day at lunch since the sixth grade. They do not do daring."

"Wow," I said. "Then go me."

"You're freakin' right," Bethany said with a nod. "Go you."

• • •

Later that night, it was war time. We all gathered in the high school parking lot and piled into cars. It took about fifteen minutes to get from Sand Dune High to West Wind—a sprawling gray structure with a green dolphin statue right smack in the middle of its front lawn. Whitney pulled her Beemer into the circular drive and parked right near the exit. She turned around and looked at me, Autumn and Mindy, who were mushed into the backseat.

110

"I'm parking here just in case we need to make a quick getaway," she said with a wink. "My car will not get caught, got it, ladies?"

"Got it," we all answered.

Whitney was pretty cool to have around.

Tara, Jaimee, Whitney and Erin popped their trunks open. Inside of each were dozens of rolls of blue and yellow streamers, bags and bags of balloons and a few huge scrolls of white paper that turned out to be painted NET THE DOLPHINS banners.

"They banned these a couple of years back when the environmental club caused a big drama over how un-PC they were," Whitney explained as we rolled them out on the ground. "Now at least we can put them to good use again."

"Rookies are on balloon duty," Tara said, tossing a couple of bags of balloons at Mindy and me. "Get blowing."

I took a deep breath and looked at Mindy. "Sure. Happy to help," I said.

"You know, I'm beginning to think that Tara Timothy isn't such a nice person," Mindy said as we sat down on the steps of the school.

I grinned. "Sarcasm from Mindy McMahon! That's new."

"I have a dark side," Mindy said, completely without irony.

We got to work blowing up the balloons while Tara, Chandra, Sage and Autumn got into shoulder sits and stands and started stringing streamers through every tree on campus. Felice and Erin put Jaimee up in a double-base extension so she could hang one of the banners from the awning that covered the front doorway while a few of the other girls went to hang one up on the gym wall.

"Where's Phoebe?" I asked, scanning the rest of the team.

"Tara said she wasn't feeling well," Mindy said with a shrug.

"Car!" Whitney shouted, diving behind the dolphin statue. Mindy and I scrambled into the bushes and Jaimee just froze, unable to dismount in time. The car blew by, blasting Bruce Springsteen and breaking the speed limit by at least fifteen miles an hour. We all climbed carefully out of our hiding places.

"Maybe I'll just keep watch," Whitney suggested.

"Sounds like a plan," Tara replied.

Mindy looked really pale as we took our seats again.

"Are you okay?" I asked.

"Yeah, I just . . . if we get caught—"

"We're not gonna get caught," I said.

"I know, it's just . . . my parents will *kill* me," Mindy said, fiddling with a limp balloon.

"Come on. We're just messing around," I said.

"Yeah, well, Matt and Mary McMahon's daughter does not mess around," Mindy said. "Matt and Mary McMahon's daughter doesn't really do much of anything."

I got that sensation around my heart that you get when there's a lot more to what someone's saying than they're letting on. I didn't know Mindy that well yet, so I didn't want to pry. Instead, I put my hand on her back and said, "You know, the faster we blow these suckers up, the faster we'll get the heck out of here."

Mindy cracked a grin. "Good point."

After we'd blown up a couple dozen balloons and were feeling the dizziness, we handed them up to the other girls to tape around the banners. Soon Tara and the rest of the squad joined us, having tastefully decorated the trees, and we all stepped back to take a look at our work.

"Well? What do we think?" Tara asked.

It looked good—the three banners, the balloons, the sagging streamers. But it wasn't exactly a battle cry. It was more like a battle nudge.

"We need more," we all said in relative unison.

That was when we stopped being careful, and went a little crazy. Maureen, Karianna and Michelle, a few of the juniors on the team, took over active balloon duty. Mindy, Jaimee, Autumn and I grabbed a few rolls of streamers and ran around the parking lot, twisting them around the handicapped signs, the guardrails and the fence that lined the far side. We did a job on the bushes by the front door as well, practically suffocating them with our colors. The rest of the team hit the football field, using whatever we had to cover their home-side bleachers with Sand Dune High colors. Whitney, meanwhile, took on the dolphin statue as her own personal project.

By the end of the night we were standing in front of the school, just tossing rolls of streamers into the trees Mischief Night style, laughing, squealing and dancing to the stereo that blasted from Whitney's car. We even stopped hiding whenever someone drove by. We were having too much fun to care.

"You know, Gobrowski, this is one of the best ideas you've ever had," Erin told me as I sat on her shoulders to toss the last of the blue streamers.

"You don't even know me," I said with a laugh.

"Don't argue with me, I'm trying to be nice," Erin replied with a grin.

"All right! That's the last of it!" I shouted once the streamer was gone.

We all cheered. The place looked like a party store had exploded on its roof. Blue and yellow streamers and balloons hung from every possible corner. There were balloons everywhere. The West Wind High Dolphin stood there, in all its glory, with a wig of blue and yellow streamer hair and a pair of impressively-sized yellow balloon breasts.

I could just imagine the faces on the West Wind students when they showed up for school in the morning. It was going to be classic. It was too bad we couldn't be there to see it.

"Well, girls, I think we've done it," Tara said.

"A picture for posterity?" Whitney suggested, whipping out a digital camera from her jacket pocket.

We all gathered in front of the dolphin statue, huddled together and grinned for the camera. As Mindy slung her arm over my shoulder and Felice pulled me closer to her side, I felt as if I had arrived. The Florida Annisa was finally here.

"Now, everyone say, 'Sand Dune Rules'!" Whitney said.

"Sand Dune Rules!"

The flash went off and Whitney came over to show us the picture on the little digital screen. I was so happy, I could have busted out in a cheer right then. There I was, undeniably frozen in time, a member of the Fighting Crabs cheerleading squad.

"Those unbelievable bastards," Tara said.

"How? How did they do it? How did they know?" Sage asked.

"It's, like, a tapestry," Jaimee put in.

"I think you mean *travesty*," Felice corrected her.

"They must've been up all night," Mindy said. "This had to have taken hours."

"Sho'nuff," Kimberly said.

I had never seen so much toilet paper in one place. It was everywhere. It covered the tree trunks and draped from the palms. It was wrapped around the school sign with a bow like a present. It decorated the columns and beams like maypoles. It was even taped to the front doors, spelling out SAND DUNE SUCKS!

"Somebody must've driven by West Wind last night," Whitney said.

"Very creative for a last-minute retaliation," I said as the crowd in front of the school grew and grew.

We all stood there, students, janitors and a spare few faculty members, a colorful sea of plaid shirts, plaid skirts, plaid scarves and plaid pants, looking up at the TP fluttering in the breeze. If an alien had landed in the parking lot at that moment in search of intelligent life, he would have fired up his booster jets and turned right back around.

"Ladies," Tara said, her eyes narrowed. "This is war."

"All right! Show's over, people! Get inside and get to homeroom unless you all want to be sitting in detention this afternoon!"

"Who's that guy?" I asked, eyeing the handsome older man who was wrangling up the onlookers. He had broad shoulders, lightly tanned skin and beach-blond hair. In his blue linen suit and plaid tie he looked like a displaced surfer.

"That would be Principal Wharton," Whitney said as we all started up the steps together. "More commonly known as Buzzkill."

"Let's go, people," Principal Wharton called out, clapping his hands for emphasis. "It's just a little toilet paper. Not all that interesting." When he noticed the squad moving together, he hustled over to us and held out his arms. "Whoa, whoa, whoa! Not so fast."

"But Principal Wharton, you told us all to get to class," Whitney said coyly, her eyes wide and innocent. "I would hate to be late for homeroom."

It was all I could do to keep from laughing.

"I'm impressed with your dedication, Miss Barnard, but there's something we all need to discuss," Principal Wharton replied. "Tara, I want to see you, your squad and the members of the varsity football team in the auditorium as soon as the first-period bell rings." He looked at all of us with his dark blue eyes as if he was looking right through us. "Spread the word. It's time for a little chat."

Then he turned and ushered a few more stragglers through the doors.

"Do you think he knows?" Mindy asked nervously.

"No! How could he?" Tara replied.

My heart thumped. Getting suspended during my second

week of school would not go over well with Mom and Dad. Even if it was all in the name of good fun.

"See what I mean?" Whitney said under her breath as Wharton held the door open for us. "Buzzkill."

• • •

Half an hour later, I was seated in the third row of the auditorium next to Mindy, who was nervously picking at the plastic cover on one of her binders. The cheerleaders took up most of the front rows, while the football team gathered behind us. Principal Wharton, Coach Holmes and Coach Turcott all stood at the front of the room. They didn't look happy, but it was kinda difficult to take them seriously, what with Turcott sporting a red plaid jacket and Coach Holmes in pink-and-yellow plaid capris.

"I'm just going to cut right to the chase," Principal Wharton began.

The back door of the auditorium slammed as Daniel Healy stepped tentatively into the room.

"Please join us, Daniel," Principal Wharton said sternly.

Daniel jogged down the aisle and dropped into the seat right next to me. Not next to the football players, not next to Sage, but next to me.

"I want you all to know that I will not tolerate a prank war," Principal Wharton announced.

Daniel rested his elbow on the armrest. The sleeve of his colorful madras shirt grazed my upper arm. There was a tiny little scar near his pinky. Hmm . . . what was that about?

"I already know that persons in this very room decimated West Wind High last night, but I'm not here to ask you exactly who was involved," Buzzkill continued. "Not yet. I am willing to give you a pass on that one. It was an error in judgment and I can forgive it. Once."

117

Daniel shifted in his seat. His knee brushed mine. Oh, God. Was it possible to sweat to death?

"But if I hear of anything going on over at West Wind, I mean if they have one book go missing, one kid get food poisoning . . . if one blade of grass dies on their football field, I will find out who did it and those persons will suffer the consequences."

Wow. This guy had missed his calling. Can you say *prison warden*? But I guess Warden Wharton would be a mouthful.

"If anything else happens here, I want you to report it immediately and do not retaliate, understood?"

Yeah, right, I thought.

His question was met with that silence that all school disciplinarians take to mean that their message has struck the appropriate fear in the hearts of their charges. Meanwhile, I saw Tara and Lumberjack Bob exchange a look and I knew. There was no fear in them. If anything, we had just been issued a new challenge. We started this war and we were going to see it through. Buzzkill be damned.

"You're dismissed," Buzzkill said.

"So, Jersey, how's the pogo ball treating you?" Daniel asked as we all gathered our things.

"I think I'm gonna end up in the emergency room," I said. "I tried it for five minutes the other night and almost took out my dad's entire presidential plate collection."

"Your dad has a presidential plate collection?" Daniel asked.

"There's no excuse for him," I said.

Daniel paused at the top of the aisle and my pulse seized up with anticipation. He had that look on his face that he was about to say something. Something that he wasn't sure how to say. Like a question, maybe? Or maybe an invitation of some kind? Ooh! Maybe he'd decided to give me a little private concert!

What? I thought. *What? What?* WHAT?

"So, I—"

"Hey, baby!"

Sage appeared out of nowhere, her blonde hair flying as she practically tackled Daniel away from me. She slung her arms around his neck and planted a huge kiss on his lips. Daniel looked surprised for a moment, but then wrapped his arms around her and hugged her back.

"Walk me to class?" Sage cajoled, looking at me out of the corner of her eye.

Then she basically dragged Daniel away, her arm through his. Daniel tripped forward, turned slightly and gave me a little wave. I waved back, all nonchalant. But the second their backs were turned, my eyes narrowed. One of these days I was really going to have to save him from her clutches. I know that in classic fiction it's usually the guy who swoops in and saves the girl, but in this scenario it was more than clear—Daniel was definitely the one in need of a knight in shining armor.

• • •

"Okay, according to Bobby, the best defense is a good offense *and* a good defense . . . whatever that means," Whitney said as she stopped her car in my driveway that night. Sage was in the front seat with her while Mindy, Autumn and I had, once again, been relegated to the back. "So we're going to go to West Wind to execute Operation Bleach while the guys hang back at the school to keep watch."

"Okay. I'll be right back," I said, climbing out of the car. I was about to slam the door when I saw that Mindy, Autumn and Sage were following. "What, you're coming?"

"I want to see your house," Sage said.

"Us too," Autumn said.

"Why?" I asked Sage.

"Morbid curiosity?" she said. "I want to see what you've done with the place since rendering Phoebe homeless."

Would it be *wrong* to scratch her eyes out? "Fine," I said. "Let's go."

As we stepped into the kitchen, the floor crunched under our feet. Pork rinds and peanut shells. Yum. The place was a complete wreck. There were empty beer cans on every surface and a pile of pizza boxes stacked up against the overflowing garbage can.

Gabe was so dead. If I ever had time to get around to killing him.

"Do you not have parents?" Sage said.

"My brother's home," I told her. "He's like a walking landfill."

We walked through the kitchen toward the stairs, but had to pass the living room on the way there. Gabe, Tucker and Joe were all sacked out on the couch, bags of Doritos and Fritos surrounding them and spilling out onto the floor. Some Russell Crowe movie played on the TV, but the guys weren't paying attention. They were too busy conducting a freakishly loud belching contest.

Ick. I was *so* over college guys. Even if they did think I was hot.

"Hey Gabe-rot!" I shouted.

"Hey Annoy-sa!" he shouted back without turning around. He punctuated his greeting with a burp.

I started up the stairs and was halfway to my room when I realized that only Mindy had followed me. Apparently Sage and Autumn had been too intrigued by the so-called men in the living room.

Good deal. Maybe Tucker or Joe will sweep Sage off her feet and make her forget all about Daniel Healy, I thought.

"Dude! Is it true that if chicks eat a lot of red meat, they can make their boobs grow?" I heard Joe ask loudly.

Okay. Maybe not.

• • •

Operation Bleach turned out to be sixteen girls with buckets of white paint attempting to paint twenty-foot-tall letters into the grass of the West Wind High football field. Apparently it was something Buzzkill had said that had inspired the idea—his warning about one dead blade of grass. There were going to be a lot more than one.

Mindy, Sage, Chandra, Kimberly and I worked on the *H* of *SDH,* holding towels over our mouths with one hand to block the fumes while clumsily splashing paint everywhere. I did my best to just breathe through my mouth so I could have both hands on my bucket. The last thing I wanted to do was ruin my favorite black Lycra pants. If only someone had warned me. I would've worn something more expendable.

"So, your brother goes to Miami U., huh?" Sage asked through her towel.

"Yep," I said. *Why are you talking to me?*

"What is he, a sophomore?"

"Yep."

"How long is he home?"

Okay, that's it.

"Why do you care?" I asked her.

"Just trying to make conversation," Sage replied. "Sheesh! Forget it!"

I couldn't believe it. How big of a moron did Sage think I was? Everything she'd ever said to me up until now had been obnoxious and hurtful. Now, on the very night she'd met my brother, who for reasons completely baffling to me was some kind of chick magnet, she suddenly wanted to be my best friend? She was more transparent than a roll of Saran Wrap.

I wanted to puke, and not from the intense paint stench that was assaulting my nasal passages. Sage wanted Gabe-rot. Not Tucker, not Joe, but Gabe. It was all too gross to contemplate. So of course my brain couldn't *stop* contemplating it.

Sage and Gabe-rot sittin' in a tree, K-I-S-S-I-N-G!

We worked in silence for a few minutes while I fumed. How could she grill me about Gabe when she was already dating Mr. Perfect? If only Daniel were here to hear all this instead of sitting back at SDH, oblivious.

"So are you and Gabe, like, close?" Sage asked.

Ugh!

"Very close," I said, tilting my head to one side. "Incestuous, actually. He's a *fabulous* kisser."

"Eeeeeeew!" Sage cried. "Omigod! You are such a total freak!"

"Sage! Keep it down!" Whitney hissed.

"Did you hear what she just said?" Sage squeaked.

"We're almost done!" Tara told her. "Just finish up so we can get out of here!"

"You have issues, Annisa Gobrowski," Sage said as we came to the end of our leg of the *H*.

"And don't *you* have a boyfriend?" I shot back.

"Yeah, I do. One you should stay away from," she told me.

My face heated up. "Fine. Then you stay away from my brother."

Sage narrowed her eyes, held her bucket of paint up with two thumbs and then dropped it on the ground right at my feet. Before I could jump back, paint had splattered all over my pants and sneakers. A couple of droplets even hit me in the face.

"Ooops!" she said, opening her mouth in an exaggerated O. "Too bad."

Then she turned on her heel and walked off, heading for the parking lot. I was so stunned, I couldn't even move, though in my mind's eye I let out a barbaric screech and tackled her right into the white S.

"Are you all right? I can't believe she did that," Mindy said, coming to my aid with a tissue from her bag.

"I'm fine," I said.

Though I couldn't have said the same for my black Lycra pants. I wiped off my face and glared after Sage the Psycho. It just didn't make sense. What could a guy like Daniel possibly see in a girl like her?

Back in my Room of Pink Shame, I found a note sitting on my computer keyboard.

> **A—**
> **I thought I was supposed to meet you here, but I guess not. You'll be making this up to me tomorrow. Latah.**
> **—B**
> **P.S. LOVE the pink.**

Bethany. How had I totally spaced that I'd told Bethany she could come over and work on the site that night? She must have been so mad at me. Stupid prank war. My stellar idea was coming back to bite me in the ass in more ways than one.

I walked down to Gabe's room, where I could hear him and his friends engaged in a heated debate. I shoved the door open without knocking. Gabe was lying on his bed, tossing a Nerf basketball into the air while Tucker and Jon played spit with a deck of Miller Lite playing cards on the floor.

"Did you guys see Bethany when she came over?" I asked, holding up the note.

"You mean High-Strung Girl? Yeah. We saw her," Gabe replied with a laugh.

"Oh, God. Did you torture her?" I asked, a newfound fear

taking over. Bethany stranded in the house with a bunch of surf boys. It was probably her idea of a waking nightmare.

"Hey, all I did was offer her a brew, dude," Gabe replied.

"She was all, 'Thanks, but I need all my brain cells just now.' That babe needs to *relax*."

"How long did she wait?" I asked.

"Not long," Gabe replied. "Like I said, the girl was high . . . *strung*."

He launched the ball at me and I caught it before it could hit my face. "Are you going to clean up the kitchen anytime soon?"

Gabe made a fake-concentration face. "Umm . . . I don't believe that's on my current schedule, no." His friends cracked up laughing.

"Gabe, come on. You promised," I said, sounding whiny.

"I promised no parties. I never promised I would clean," Gabe said. "And come on, it's not that bad."

"There's something growing on the floor."

"All right, fine, *Mom*. I'll do it in the morning."

I narrowed my eyes. "Don't you guys ever have, like, classes?"

They all looked at each other and laughed again. I rolled my eyes and turned to go. Back in my room, I read over the note once more. Tomorrow? How was I going to swing that? Not only was I sure that I would have more wacky hijinks to pursue with the squad, but I had that geometry test to study for. It was already eleven and I was exhausted. When was I going to study?

All I wanted to do was go to bed, but as I stared longingly at my sheets, suddenly a little angel-me appeared on my right shoulder. *"Annisa! You have to study!"* she trilled in my ear. *"No time like the present!"*

125

With a heavy sigh I slipped out of my paint-spattered pants, bunched them up and shoved them into the garbage can. Sage-related anger flared up in my chest again, but I had to ignore it. There was nothing I could do about it now, and if I sat there and obsessed, I'd never get any work done. I changed into my PJs and, pushing all thoughts of Bethany, Daniel, Sage and Gabe aside, cracked my geometry book. I could deal with the social drama tomorrow.

• • •

A double toot of a car horn ripped me from a sound slumber. I raised my head, vaguely aware of that whirring sound a car makes when it backs up. Something was stuck to my face. I batted it away in a half-asleep, there's-a-bug-on-me panic and saw that it was just a piece of notebook paper fluttering to the floor. Blinking in confusion, I realized I had fallen asleep at my desk with my head in my geometry notebook. Lovely.

I glanced at the clock and fast-forwarded into panic mode. It was already 8:00 A.M. I had fifteen minutes to get to homeroom.

I scrambled out of my clothes and into a pair of gray sweats and a white T-shirt, then hid my scraggly hair under my Yankees baseball cap. In the bathroom I threw some cold water on my face, doubled up on the layers of deodorant and brushed my teeth. I looked like death warmed over, but there was nothing I could do about it now. I had to get to class.

I jogged downstairs with my backpack and froze in my tracks. There, standing in the center of my kitchen in nothing but a pair of baby-doll pajamas and furry pink slippers, was none other than Sage Barnard. And she was feeding my brother a powdered jelly from a box of Dunkin' Donuts. My brother in all his Tasmanian Devil–boxered glory.

126

"Is *that* what you wear to bed?" Sage asked me, her face scrunched up in disgust. I had totally spaced on the fact that it was Pajama Day.

"Expecting a camera crew from *Playboy*?" I shot back. I grabbed a chocolate donut as I headed out the door, not even bothering to acknowledge my brother. There was no way I wanted to be around to witness whatever was going to happen next.

I couldn't believe it! How could Sage possibly have the gall to show up at my house after what she'd done to me last night? And in that outfit with my brother! Didn't she know she had a boyfriend?

I was shoving half the donut in my mouth when I noticed Daniel waiting for me at the edge of the driveway. He was wearing a wife-beater and striped pajama pants with flip-flops. Just looking at his shoulder muscles made my fingertips tingle. I was so not worthy.

I swallowed, wiped the back of my hand across my mouth and prayed that crease I'd noticed on the side of my face was gone. Daniel's eyes flicked over my outfit.

"Nice pj's, Jersey," he said.

"Eh, these? They're nothing special," I said, the sight of Sage's exposed thighs flashing through my mind.

"Hey, was that Whitney I saw driving away from your house a couple of minutes ago?" he asked as we started to walk.

I blinked and it all came to me in a haze. The double horn honk. The backing-up car. Whitney must have been dropping her sister at my house and had honked before driving away.

"Um . . . yeah," I said.

"What was she doing over here?" Daniel asked.

Dropping your semi-clothed girlfriend at my house so she

127

could hand-feed my semi-clothed brother? I thought. *Come on!
Say it! Didn't you just decide that somebody has to put her in
her place?*

"She stopped by to drop off something I left in her car last
night," I heard myself say.

*What? Hellooooo? Who's in charge of the voice box around
here?*

"That was cool of her," Daniel said, totally oblivious.

What was wrong with me? Why didn't I open my mouth
and say, "Actually, right now your girlfriend is hanging all
over my brother, and if you want to go back and see, I'd be
more than happy to show you the way"? If he saw what I'd
seen, he and Sage would definitely break up. And if Sage and
Daniel broke up, he'd be free to date other people. Namely,
me. So why couldn't I say it?

*Because you're a wuss and a goody-goody and you know it's
not your news to relate,* the little angel on my shoulder trilled.
You're just not a vindictive person, Annisa.

What I *really* needed was a devil to show up and take care
of business—knock that angel off her high horse and start
running the Annisa Gobrowski Show. Why, oh, why could I
never conjure a devil?

• • •

When we got to school, the usually bustling back hall was
deserted. Daniel and I paused in the doorway and looked at
each other.

"It's way too quiet in here," I said.

"Something's up," he replied.

He let the door slam behind us and we double-timed it
down to the front hall. My heart was pounding with anticipation. Had West Wind struck back somehow?

Moments later, we skidded into the packed lobby and

found our answer. The huge cloth banner that draped from one end of the lobby to the other usually read, HOME OF THE FIGHTING CRABS! Now it read, WE'VE ALL GOT CRABS!

Daniel and I both laughed and then slapped our hands over our mouths as at least fifty pairs of indignant eyes turned our way.

"Sorry!" I whispered.

"Oh my God, how did they do it? It's perfect," Daniel whispered to me, pulling me away from the pack.

"I know! The letters exactly match!" I replied under my breath.

"And how did they get into the school? We were here half the night," Daniel said.

"We are going to have to get them back for this one," I said. "Big-time."

"No doubt," Daniel replied.

"I couldn't agree more," a third voice entered the conversation.

A near clone of Daniel walked toward us with Lumberjack Bob and Tara Timothy trailing behind them. All of them looked sickened and glowery. Suddenly a somber mood descended upon us even though we were surrounded by terry-cloth robes and fuzzy bunny slippers. It was amazing how very seriously everyone seemed to take this whole prank-war thing. It was like I'd initiated a Navy Seal operation, not a spirit week event.

"Annisa, this is my brother, Christopher," Daniel said, gesturing toward his clone with an open palm. "He's the starting quarterback. Christopher, Annisa."

"So you're the one who started this whole thing," Christopher said, eyeing me.

"Uh . . . yeah. I guess," I replied.

129

"Nice," Christopher said. "That's a lot of school spirit for a transfer."

Hey, I was just looking to fit in, I thought. But I had a feeling that statement might refute this newfound Crab cred I seemed to be garnering, so I kept my mouth shut.

"Look, we're going to have an emergency meeting at Goow's house tonight to figure out how to retaliate," Christopher said. "Spread the word to the cheerleaders and the team, but keep it as quiet as possible. Buzzkill's on the warpath."

He moved his eyes toward the front of the room, where Mr. Wharton stood fuming and red, directing the janitors as they removed the offending banner.

"Got it?" Christopher said.

"Yeah, got it," Daniel replied.

I said nothing, and Christopher, Tara and Bobby sauntered away.

"Looks like we're going to be spending a lot more time together," Daniel joked.

I smiled back, but inside I was all in turmoil. How was I supposed to practice, go to an emergency prank war meeting, help Bethany with her website *and* study for the geometry test?

I was beginning to regret ever opening my big mouth about the prank war. I'd barely been here a week and already my life was getting way out of control—all because I'd wanted the squad to think I was cool.

When was I going to learn to think before I blabbed?

• • •

That day at lunch, I sat in the sun at the table Bethany and I had claimed the week before and waited. She had been late to homeroom, so I had yet to have a chance to apologize to her for the major infraction of the night before, and I didn't like this sinking feeling that she was walking around out there, mad at me. Toward the end of the period, when my carrot sticks were long gone and the sun was starting to grill me like a side of salmon, a shadow fell over my book. I looked up to find Bethany hovering over me. She was wearing a pair of dark pajama pants and a black tank top.

"You're participating in spirit week?" I asked.

"Even I can't pass up the opportunity to wear my pj's to school," she replied. She didn't sit. Not a good sign.

"Listen, I'm really sorry about last night," I told her.

"Whatev," she said, looking away.

"No, seriously, I'm *really* sorry. I swear I'll come over tonight and we'll work on the site. As long as we can study a little too. I'm totally screwed in geometry."

"You swear you're coming?" she asked.

"I *swear*," I replied.

"Cool," she said with a smile. Relief rushed through me like a cold drink on a hot day. "So who were those losers at your house? They were all kinds of defective."

I laughed. "Most girls *love* my brother!"

"That guy was your brother?" She whistled low and long. "You must've come out of the deep end of that particular gene pool."

"Hello? Look at *your* brother!" I said. "He's totally Cro-Mag."

"I know! I used to call him Me-Bobby-You-Jane until my mother threatened to take my computer away."

The bell rang and we made our way inside. I felt about a million times better already. I had been stressing about nothing. Bethany wasn't irreparably mad at me. Why did I always blow everything out of proportion in my mind? Did my brain *like* to stress over nothing?

"So, did you see the banner this morning?" I asked.

"Who didn't?" Bethany said.

"Did you hear what *we* did to *them*?" I asked, eager to share last night's prank-war exploits and put a positive spin on the whole sucky experience.

"Something about wiping out their football field with paint?" Bethany said absently. She chewed on the inside of her cheek, forcing her lips into a sideways pucker.

"Yeah, you should have seen it. We were there for, like, *hours,* and—"

"I've got to hit my locker before class," Bethany said, stopping so suddenly, I was already five feet ahead of her. "I'll see you tonight."

Then she turned and disappeared into the melee of the hallway.

"Uh . . . okay!" I shouted back, though I'm sure she could no longer hear me.

I walked toward my next class, hoping I would suddenly develop the ability to make myself disappear. If anyone called on me that afternoon, I was toast. Not only hadn't I had time to study for geometry, but all my other homework was piling up as well.

I managed to make it through geometry unscathed as Loreng was in some kind of lecture-happy trance. (Few breaths taken + many words = *mucho* spittle.) On the way to English I racked my brain, trying to recall the assignment, but it was like that part of my mind was blocked. I couldn't remember a *thing* about the last class. Disturbing.

"Hello, everyone! I hope you've all read the first act of *Othello!*" Mrs. O'Donaghue said as we filed into her classroom. "I expect a lively discussion full of unparalleled insight and fresh, new ideas!"

132

Mindy and I looked at each other, then sunk into our seats. All I knew about Othello was that he was a pissed-off Moor who killed his white wife. And that Mekhi Phifer played him in the movie. This underachieving was so not like me.

That was it. As of right then, the prank war was over for Annisa Gobrowski. I was sure whatever the team decided to do could be done without my help. I was going to help Bethany tonight, then chain myself to my desk to study. All I needed were a couple of good sessions with my books and I would be right back on track.

At least I hoped so.

• • •

"Thank God you're here! The Idiot Squad and their Y-chromosome counterparts have taken over my living room!" Bethany said when she opened the door for me that night. Then her eyes fell on Mindy, who had walked over with me, and it was like someone had used a candle snuffer on Bethany's spirit. Her entire body slumped as she opened the door wider.

"Oh. Hey," she said.

"Hi," Mindy replied, tentatively stepping over the threshold. We could hear the sound of raised and raucous voices coming from the back of the house, and Mindy looked at me with a question in her eyes.

"Go ahead. I'll be right there," I said.

Mindy scurried off and Bethany closed the front door with a bang, then crossed her arms tightly over her chest.

"So you're here for the meeting?" she said.

"I'm just gonna make an appearance, then I'll come right upstairs," I told her.

"I don't know. You guys might be doing something *really*

important after this, like rigging all the West Wind High toilets to flush at once."

"Bethany—"

"No! Forget it! I should have known this would happen," Bethany said. "I knew you would get sucked in!"

"I'm not sucked in!" I replied. "I just want to go for a little while—"

"I have to get out of here," Bethany said, grabbing her book bag off the bottom of the stairs that led to the second floor. "There's too much testosterone and hairspray in the air."

"Bethany—"

She stalked out of the house and grabbed a dirt bike off the front lawn. I shouted after her, but she just ignored me and kept pedaling. So much for that.

I closed the door, my heart heavy. I couldn't blame Bethany for her freak-out, especially considering how understanding she'd been about last night. Now in her eyes I was dissing her to attend a clandestine meeting of the cool people—the very people she abhorred. But I was just trying to have a life.

Was that so hard to understand?

After the meeting I was going to go home and study. I swear I was. But then I noticed that Daniel was there and Sage was not. And as much as the angel cried and whined and guilted me from my shoulder, I just could not pass up an opportunity to be with him Sage-free. So I found myself on a mission to steal the West Wind mascot.

It's amazing what love will do to you.

When we arrived at West Wind, everyone gathered around back of the school so Lumberjack Bob/Bobby Goow could hand out assignments. While everyone had seemed on board back at the house, our numbers had definitely dwindled between the safety of the living room and the actual mission at hand.

"Where'd everybody go?" I whispered to Mindy.

"Maybe they didn't want to have arrest records," Mindy replied.

Hold up. Arrest records? We wouldn't actually get arrested for this, would we? It was all in good fun!

"We need a bunch of lookouts," Lumberjack Bob said, surveying us. "Who wants to volunteer?"

Mindy grabbed my hand and shot it into the air together with hers.

"I want to be a lookout?" I asked quietly.

"If we don't actually do the breaking in, we're much better off if we get caught," she explained.

"Wow. You've been watching your *Law and Order*," I replied.

"All right, Mindy, Tom, get the side door by the library. Jaimee and Dave, you take the street. Daniel and Annisa, go around back by the gym and keep an eye on the field," Christopher Healy said.

Daniel and Annisa!? Me and Daniel. Alone behind the school. In the dark. There was no way I could be that lucky.

Daniel and I glanced at each other and he smiled. Every hair on my arms and neck stood on end. He had to feel it too. This weird sort of electrical-current thing that zapped to life whenever we were together. That had to be what that private smile meant.

Sage Barnard, watch your back!

We walked behind West Wind in silence, our eyes trained on the ground. (Great lookout skills, *estúpidos.*) Gravel crunched beneath our feet, growing louder and louder the farther we got away from the rest of the crowd. I didn't even know how they planned to get into the school and find the mascot, but I also didn't care. For once I was glad to be a lowly sophomore. Let the all-powerful seniors take the real risks and do the dirty work. I was getting alone time with Daniel.

"I guess here's good," he said, pausing by the back door to the gym.

"Yep," I replied.

We each leaned back against the wall on either side of the door and looked out across the deserted football field. In the dark, the bright white *SDH* in the grass seemed to float eerily in midair.

"So," he said.

"So," I replied.

"Remember the other day . . . I told you about the whole guitar thing?" he said.

"Yeah?" I replied.

"Well, if the offer still stands . . . I wrote this thing, this song. . . ."

Every inch of my skin tingled with excitement. "You want to play it for me?"

Even in the darkness I could see him blush. "Yeah. I mean, if you want."

"I'd love to!" I said.

"Yeah?" he asked, his eyebrows shooting up.

"Yeah," I replied with a nod. "Just tell me when."

"Whenever," Daniel said. "We'll figure it out."

He looked away and it felt like the bubble of excitement had somehow popped. Just like that.

"Are you . . . I mean, are you okay?" I asked.

"I'm fine," he answered instantly. "Why?"

"No reason. I just . . . you seem . . . out of it," I said. Then I took a deep breath. "Is everything okay with Sage?"

"What do you mean? Did Sage say something?" he asked.

I almost laughed. "To me?" I said. "Nuh-uh."

Daniel sighed and shoved his hands in the pockets of his varsity jacket. "She avoided me all day. She barely said two words to me at lunch," Daniel said. "Something's definitely up."

I chomped on my gum and blew a small bubble, stalling. "Can I ask you something?"

"What?" Daniel said.

I turned so that my shoulder was now resting against the wall, and cracked my gum. "What do you even see in her?"

It sounded catty, the way it came out, but Daniel didn't seem to notice.

"Sage?" he asked. He bumped himself off the wall, then fell back. "I don't know. I mean . . . she's *Sage.* We've been together since eighth grade."

"What does *that* mean?" I blurted.

"I don't know," Daniel said again. "It's just . . . it's me and Sage. It's not always perfect and, I know, she can be a pain sometimes, but we've been together forever. Sometimes I think—"

Don't even say it.

"Sometimes I can't even imagine being without her," he said.

My heart bounced twice on a high dive before plunging right off into a pool of rabid piranhas. Wow. He really cared about her. About *Sage.* The way he was so honest and heart-felt about it only made me like him more.

"You ever have anyone like that?" Daniel asked, turning his deep blue eyes on me. He was right there. I could have taken two steps, stood on my toes and kissed him. I could have reached out and held his hand.

But I wasn't going to do either of those things. Me and my lame-ass shoulder angel both knew it.

"Nope," I replied finally. "Can't say that I have."

Just then, my cell phone beeped, scaring us both into stroke mode. I pulled it out and read the text message.

Jordan: where R U???

"Who's that?" Daniel asked.

"My best friend. She's never been one with the timing," I said as I typed back quickly.

Annisa: on mission. Z U l8r!
Jordan: wait! is cute boy there?
Annisa: yeah. crash & burn.
Jordan: ugh! ☹ he no luv u, he no worth it. call me!

I smiled sadly and turned my phone off. If only Jordan could meet Daniel. Then she'd see how very worth it he was.

• • •

"What's going on?" I asked Mindy and Autumn the next morning after homeroom. The hallway was a bobbing sea of light blue and yellow for School Colors Day and everyone was buzzing with excitement. There had been an announcement that the entire student body was to report to the football field after homeroom, and no one knew why.

"We are so snagged," Mindy replied, looking green.

"I knew I shouldn't have come to school today," Autumn put in, her hundreds of silver bangles jangling as she rubbed her temples. "I did a tarot reading last night and it predicted death, destruction and heartache."

"Death and destruction?" I said. "Come on. It's just a prank war."

"That's just it! Using the word *war* is bad karma!" Autumn exclaimed. "Couldn't we have called it a prank fest?"

We joined the waves of people streaming out the back doors of the school, and made our way to the visiting bleachers. The back of the stands faced the school, and as we came around front to take the stairs, we noticed everyone was staring toward the end zone and the scoreboard.

"Oh . . . my . . . God," Sage said, stopping in her tracks a few people ahead of us.

I followed her gaze and my jaw dropped. It looked as if

139

someone had smashed a picket fence to death all over the end zone. Shards of plywood and splintered boards lay everywhere, covering the blue *SDH*.

"What is it?" I asked.

"It's the Fighting Crab," Mindy said behind me. "They killed the Fighting Crab."

"Death. Destruction. Heartache," Autumn put in, her voice like a funeral dirge.

We slid into an empty row of seats in front of the seniors and juniors from the squad. Tara was quietly seething, her now bruiseless face turning purple with rage. I couldn't tear my eyes from the scoreboard. Where the huge fighting crab used to stand, its clippers raised high, there was nothing but two bare beams—the beams that used to hold him up against the clear blue sky. I eyed the pieces on the ground and was able to pick out half a claw, one big eye, and the *D* from the *SDH* jersey the crab once wore.

It was so very sad.

"I can't believe they did this," Whitney said.

"It's so . . . violent," Felice put in.

"So what if we stole their mascot? It's not like we were never going to give it back," Chandra said.

"Actually, we weren't planning on it," Whitney told her.

"Okay, but still. They didn't have to slaughter the crab."

"Yeah, there's some monster line-crossing going on here," Jaimee put in.

"What do we do now?" Chandra asked. "We can't let them get away with this."

"Bobby and I have a few ideas," Tara said, breaking her silence.

A murmur ran through the crowd, snapping us to attention.

"Buzzkill approaches," Karianna said, lifting her chin toward the field.

Principal Buzzkill had apparently shopped for School Colors Day in the throwback aisle. He was sporting a light blue suit with a white shirt and a light yellow tie with light blue dots. And he actually had the nerve to try to look serious in that outfit.

"Can I have your attention, please?" he called out. He was *loud*—even without a microphone. The entire student body fell instantly silent.

Okay, so maybe he *could* pull off serious in that outfit.

"That Fighting Crab was constructed by the class of 1985 as their graduating gift to this school," Principal Buzzkill said, pointing toward the end zone. "That crab predated your births. It was a symbol of this school's strength, of its spirit, of its tradition. Look at it now."

Hundreds of heads turned to look at the remnants of the Fighting Crab.

"Thanks to this ridiculous prank war, our mascot has been obliterated," Principal Buzzkill continued. "That crab survived hurricanes and tropical storms for twenty years, and now it's gone forever. I don't know how this travesty sits with the rest of you, but I, for one, feel sick."

My stomach turned, poisoned by a sensation that felt a lot like guilt. I could just imagine those poor kids from the class of '85, working their little Duran Duran–loving tails off on that crab, celebrating with a *Miami Vice* party when it was finished. What would they think if they came back to visit the school and saw the fallen crab?

But still, it wasn't like *we'd* destroyed the little guy. Those idiots from West Wind had done it. It wasn't our fault.

Except for the fact that you started the prank war, my little angel whispered to me. *You, you, you, you, you.* Wait a minute. Were angels even allowed to taunt people?

"I thought I had made myself clear when I told certain members of the football team and cheerleading squad to cease and desist, but apparently I did not," Principal Buzzkill continued. "So I've decided to take my message to the entire student body. Now, I want all of you to listen up and listen good. This prank war ends now."

"Whatever," Tara said, shifting in her seat behind me. I saw Bobby and Christopher exchange a look a few rows ahead to my left. *"Yeah, okay, dude,"* Bobby mouthed, then laughed.

"If I hear that anything else has happened at West Wind High, I will have no choice but to forfeit this Saturday's game."

A collective gasp went up over the bleachers. My heart dropped. Forfeit!? To West Wind? This guy *was* a buzzkill!

"He wouldn't," Tara said.

"Believe me when I say that I will not hesitate to do this," Principal Buzzkill continued. "And for those of you who are unclear on what a forfeit means, if we forfeit, we lose. We lose the rivalry game to West Wind High because whoever is committing these pranks refused to take the high road."

He paused and scanned the crowd ever so slowly, seeming to make eye contact with every last student. When his gaze fell on me and the rest of the squad, I could feel the high-beam burn on my face. I looked away guiltily and he moved on.

"You're dismissed," he said finally. "Return to first period."

• • •

"I can't believe this," Whitney ranted as we headed back toward the school in a pack. "He wouldn't actually forfeit, would he?"

"I don't know. I believed him," Mindy replied, hugging her notebooks to her chest.

"But they killed the crab! How can we not retaliate after they killed the crab?" Chandra wailed, her eyes wide.

"You guys, maybe it's all for the best," Tara said.

She was met with stunned silence. Tara Timothy was throwing in the towel? Little Miss Never Say Die? How could she say this was for the best?

"What?" she replied to our confusion. "This will give us more time to practice for regionals. And we need practice. Believe me."

Mindy and I looked at each other, knowing she was talking about us. I couldn't argue her point, however. The routine was complex and everyone else had had months to perfect it. Mindy and I were way behind.

I took a deep breath and let it out slowly. It was kind of a relief to be released from prank-war duty. Now I would also have time to study for the geometry test that was rapidly approaching and catch up in the rest of my classes. Tara was right. Buzzkill's ultimatum was actually a blessing in disguise.

"So, Annisa!" Sage piped up, walking up from the back of the crowd to fall into step with me. "Can I bring anything tomorrow night?"

Once I got over the shock that Sage was actually daring to talk to me, I was able to focus on my bafflement over what she had said.

"Bring anything where?" I asked as we filed back into the school.

"You know. To the big party!" Sage replied, laughing like we were old friends in on some personal joke together. God! Can you say *split personalities*?

I stopped in the middle of the hallway, a skittering sense of foreboding running all over my body. Some of the cheerleaders kept moving, but a few of them hovered around to watch the conversation unfold.

"What big party?" I asked.

"Gabe's big party?" she said, rolling her eyes as if I was some previously unclassified breed of doofus.

"*Gabe* is having a *party*?!" I blurted.

"Wow. You guys really need to work on your communication skills," Sage said, shaking her head. "*Everyone* knows about the party."

Then she walked off, the rest of the squad minus Autumn and Mindy following her. I heard Sage reciting the details all the way down the hall while the others grabbed pens and scratched them into their notebooks.

"Did you guys know my brother was having a party?" I asked, still stunned.

"Sage called me about it last night," Mindy said, biting her lip.

"I already got my mom to lend me her punch bowl," Autumn put in. "Though if I get another negative reading, I'm definitely staying home this time."

I followed them down the hall, my mind reeling. I couldn't believe this. Gabe had *promised* he wouldn't have a party. What was *wrong* with him? The kid needed to join Partyers Anonymous. And where did he get off inviting people from my school? Didn't he have friends of his own?

Some guy I recognized from the meeting the night before grinned at me as I rounded the corner. "Hey, new girl! See you at the party tomorrow night!" he called out. He and his friends slapped hands as they walked on.

My nostrils flared to twice their normal size. I was going to have to lock my brother in a closet somewhere. There was no way in hell I was going to let him throw a party at *my* house tomorrow night. It was time for me to put my size five and a half foot down.

"Omigod! You're Annisa, right? Are you Annisa!?"

I was flattened up against the wall by four freshman cheerleaders wearing matching yellow shirts and blue shorts. There was enough bubbliness among them to pop a champagne cork.

"Yeah . . . ," I said, fearing for my life.

"Omigod! We heard about your party? And we were wondering? Do you think we could come? I mean, are they going to let freshmen in? Because, we're cheerleaders, you know? Do you think we could get in because we're cheerleaders?"

Each one of them had at least one sentence in this verbal diarrhea, but they were so fast, I could never focus on who, exactly, was speaking.

"I don't think it'll be a problem," I said, wondering who the "they" were that might keep these poor girls out of my house.

They all squealed and one of them hugged me harder than I'd ever been hugged before. I had to laugh. Maybe this party wasn't the worst idea. I mean, if it could make people *that* happy . . . Plus, random students had been talking to me all day in the halls—people I'd never spoken to before. It was like I was famous. And not because I had appeared on the school paper with my skirt up.

"Hey, Jersey."

Heart thump.

146

"Daniel!" I said, turning to face him. He was looking much more chipper than he had the night before.

"So, I heard about this party your brother's throwing," he said. "Pretty cool."

"Yeah. I guess," I replied.

"You know, nothing interesting ever happened around here until you came along," he said with a grin.

I felt a rush of euphoria throughout my body. Had anyone ever said anything so totally perfect?

"Well, I gotta get to practice. See you later," he said.

He was gone before I could recover my voice. Okay, so maybe my brother had actually done me a huge favor with this party thing. Maybe it was going to be the most monumental night of my life. I felt a hand on my shoulder and turned around, all smiles, expecting more accolades and appreciation for my hosting of the social event of the year. Instead, I was met with the hard-as-steel eyes of Bethany Goow.

"Thanks for inviting me to your little party," she said.

"It's not my—"

"God! Will you stop at nothing to make them like you?" she blurted, stuffing her hands under her arms.

What? I was no foot-kissing ingratiator! I was a revolutionary, remember?

"Okay, wait a second," I said indignantly. "That's not what this is about."

"Oh, really? Sure looks that way to me," Bethany said. "Suddenly all you care about is hanging out with *them*, sitting at assemblies with *them*, running all over town like a lemming with *them*."

"Bethany, I made a commitment to the team when I tried out," I said, trying to remain patient. "Being on a competition squad takes a lot of work."

"Oh, right. And I'm sure spending every waking hour

147

working on a prank war is right at the top of the squad's official responsibilities," she shot back.

"The prank war was *your* idea!" I practically shouted, drawing a bit of a crowd to our argument. "How can you be mad at me for *that*?"

"Please," she said, throwing up a hand. "If you don't know, then it's not even worth it."

I felt as if she'd actually used that hand to punch me in the stomach. Where did she get off talking to me like that? Like I was supposed to *know* why the prank war made her so mad? I thought she was psyched about it.

"Have fun at your party," she shouted as she walked away.

"It's not my party!" I shouted back, all the frustration of the day going into that one exclamation.

As much as I racked my brain, I couldn't think of a single reason for Bethany to be pissed about the prank war other than the fact that she was jealous—jealous of the time I was spending with the squad. But it was an extracurricular. Those took up time. Bethany spent five hours a night working on her website. She of all people should understand what it means to make a commitment.

"Hey," Mindy said, approaching me. "You okay?"

"Yeah. I'm fine," I said. "Let's go to practice. I feel like I could do about ten million push-ups right about now."

As we headed off for the locker room, I started to wonder if I had been wrong about Bethany all along. Maybe she wasn't as cool as I'd thought she was. Maybe she was just selfish and snobby.

Maybe it was time for me to move on.

• • •

"I can't believe I kicked Felice in the face," I said, my body aching as Mindy and I retreated to the locker room after an exhausting practice. "I'm never going to get all these stunts."

"Yes you will," Mindy said. "You're doing great. You've learned a liberty, a scorpion and a double-base extension in less than two weeks. That's crazy."

"Now, if I could just learn to dismount without maiming my teammates," I joked.

We sat down on a bench to try on the new cheerleading kicks Coach Holmes had ordered for us. My body was bruised, battered and way angry at me, but I couldn't wait to get into those shoes. Somehow just having them made the whole thing seem official.

"They're so white," Mindy said, standing in front of the full-length mirror. "They make my feet look like a couple of cruise ships."

"They're not that bad," I said with a laugh.

I was about to get up and check my own reflection when we heard the door swing open. Mindy and I caught each other's eyes as Tara's voice filled the locker room. I had thought everyone had already gone home.

"Come on, Phoebe, you have to go," Tara said. "It's gonna be fun. Remember fun?"

"Yes, I remember fun," Phoebe's morose voice replied. "I'm just not in the mood for a party right now."

Mindy tiptoed over to me and perched on the bench. We both sat there in rigid silence. Should we make noise and let them know we were there, or eavesdrop like we were already doing? I was too petrified to move, so apparently we were going with option B.

"Pheebs, is there anything we can do?" Whitney's voice chimed in. "If you just want to talk, we could go over to Dolly's, have some ice cream."

"Nah. I think I'm just gonna go home," Phoebe said.

Her voice broke on the word "home." I looked at Mindy. I couldn't take this anymore. So what if she'd told me to stay away from her—repeatedly? She sounded so heartbroken, I had to try to help.

I stood up, bit back my fear of the senior triumvirate and walked around the corner. They were sitting in a huddle on the low bench, and they all looked startled when they saw me there. Phoebe was as pale as a cloud and her eyes were rimmed with red.

"Hey," I said.

"Hey." Whitney was the only one who answered.

"I was just . . . over there and I heard you guys talking, and . . ." I swallowed hard and steeled myself. "Phoebe, I'm really sorry about everything, and if there's ever anything I can do—"

Suddenly Phoebe burst into tears and ran for the bathroom section of the locker room. I heard a stall door slam and convulsing sobs ricocheted off the tile walls. It was beyond awful. Had anyone ever hated me as much as Phoebe Cook did right then?

"Nice one, brain trust," Tara said, getting up and following after her friend.

Whitney gave me a sympathetic look before joining them. I grabbed my stuff and headed out the back door with a quick good-bye to Mindy. It was about time for me and my social ineptitude to call it a day.

• • •

When I walked into my ever-deteriorating house fifteen minutes later, the first thing I heard was a laugh. A girl's laugh. A familiarly cloying girl's laugh.

Sitting in the living room with Gabe, Tucker and Joe was none other than Sage Barnard. She was sipping a soda, twirling her hair around her finger and inching her bare knees closer and closer to my brother's thigh.

Can you say überslut?

Suddenly every positive my brain had recorded about the upcoming party was forgotten. I forgot about how many people had spoken to me that day who had never acknowledged my existence before. I forgot about the chatter-happy cheerleaders. I forgot about Daniel's sentence of perfection. I had had a bad day topped off by a horrendous afternoon and two minutes of concentrated misery in the locker room.

I had to take it out on someone. And at that moment, Gabe-rot was the nearest thing I had to a scapegoat.

"Gabe?" I said, dropping my bags on the floor behind the couch. "Can I talk to you? Alone?"

Gabe and Sage looked over their shoulders at me.

"Baby sis! Take a load off! We're just about to start the *Godfather* marathon," Gabe said.

"No, thanks. I really need to talk to you," I said, pointedly ignoring Sage's presence. "In the kitchen?"

Gabe laughed. "We're all friends here, dude. Whatever you got to say to me, you can say in front of my buds."

"Okay, fine," I said, riding my wave of righteous indignation. I walked around to the front of the couch and lifted my chin. "It's about the party. Thanks to someone's serious lack of subtlety, this thing has turned into an open house."

Gabe blinked. "So?"

"So? You swore—no parties," I said. "Mom and Dad are going to freak."

Now they all laughed. Sage was sitting in my living room, laughing at me.

"Mom and Dad are not going to freak, because Mom and Dad are not going to find out," Gabe said.

"Please! They *always* find out," I said. "Can't we just tone it down a little? Invite a few close friends or something? Does it have to be the party of the century?"

There was a moment of prolonged silence. Gabe looked

151

around at Tucker and Joe and nodded slowly, as if he were mulling it over. For a split second I believed that I had gotten through to him.

Then he cracked up laughing again and the rest of them joined in. "I'm sorry, I just can't keep a straight face," he said. He stood up, cupped my face in his hands and tilted his head condescendingly. "Poor little baby," he said, patting my cheek. "Why don't you go up to your room and I'll come read you a bedtime story in a couple of hours?"

This sent Tucker, Joe and Sage into hysterics. I felt like I was about to burst into tears. My brother had embarrassed me a million times in the past, but how could he humiliate me in front of his friends like that? In front of Sage!

I grabbed my stuff, ran upstairs and slammed my door. Gabe-rot was so going to pay for this. I had no idea how, but I was going to make him pay.

The party was like a scene from a movie. More because I was sitting in the corner, munching on popcorn and watching it happen, than because it was so wild. Bethany hadn't returned my calls, so I was hanging with Mindy. We had taken refuge in the little alcove near the stairs for most of the night, watching as more and more people I didn't know poured in through every available door. The noise level hovered somewhere around the decibel of Times Square, Millennium Eve.

Sage and Gabe were sitting on one end of the couch. Sage's hands were on his chest, her head kept touching his shoulder and Gabe was smiling like heaven had plunked an angel right in his lap.

Barf.

Daniel wasn't there yet, so he hadn't been subjected to this disgusting display. I wasn't sure whether to hope he'd show and see what a bitch Sage was, or whether to hope he *wouldn't* show and therefore not get his heart broken.

It's tough having a conscience.

"I cannot believe her," I said, looking away before the image of Sage twisting one of Gabe's curls around her finger was burned on my brain forever.

"I know. Why doesn't she just break up with Daniel already?" Mindy said.

"Does she *want* to break up with Daniel?" I asked, intrigued.

"Who knows? She kept me on the phone for hours the other night, debating it," Mindy said. " 'Oh, Gabe is *sooo* hot. But Daniel and I have been together *forever*. We have something *sooo* deep,' " Mindy said, fluttering her eyelashes and tilting her head back dramatically. "I was like, 'Spare me! Get a life!' "

"You *said* that?" I asked.

"No! Not really," she replied.

"Well, why not? If that's how you feel. . . ."

"I can't even imagine saying that out loud to her," Mindy said, staring down at the empty soda cup in her hand. She smiled. "You probably think I'm a total loser, right?"

"No!" I said. "Not at all. Sometimes I wish I was *better* at stopping myself before I said things. It can be a good thing, trust me."

"Yeah, well, not all the time," Mindy said. "Don't get me wrong, Sage and I have been friends since kindergarten and she's always been there for me," she said. "There are just some things about her I can't stand."

"Yeah. Me too," I said. *Like everything,* I added silently. "I can't imagine her being there for anyone but herself."

"Believe me, Sage is a good person to have on your side when you need her," Mindy said. "All that energy she puts into being a bitch? Imagine what it's like when she's using it to defend you."

"Why would you need defending?" I asked.

Mindy looked down into her soda and shrugged. "Everyone needs defending at some point, right? Sage was really nice to have around during my awkward phase."

"Oh, yeah. I had one of those," I said, nodding. "Up until

154

about a year ago, my nose was way too big for my face and I had a mouth full of metal."

"Really?" Mindy said, studying me. "For me it was scoliosis and a unibrow."

"Wow," I said. Mindy laughed. She was so beautiful, I couldn't imagine her having an awkward phase, but I guess no one is ever perfectly happy with how they look.

"All right! Let's go! Girl-on-girl Twister!" Tucker shouted. He stepped onto the chair-and-a-half, cupping his hands around his mouth. "Come one, come all!"

Ugh! Was he kidding?

"Kitchen?" I said to Mindy, blanching.

"Kitchen."

We got up and scurried for the relative safety of the kitchen table. The keg and a huge bowl of Skull Punch (I don't know why Gabe's friends called it that) sat on the island in the center of the room. A few people hovered around while a guy with blond curls worked the tap and another, more meaty type sloppily served punch into cups. I stepped into the room, but when I went to lift my foot again, it hesitated a second before peeling off the floor.

"Ew!" I said, looking down. "What *is* that?"

"It's floor film," some guy in a plastic Viking hat—yes, a Viking hat—told me, wrapping his arm around my shoulders. "You know it's a party when you've developed floor film."

"That's great. Can you let go of me now?" I asked, scrunching my nose at the smell of his breath.

Mindy had already slipped around the side of the room and settled in at the chip-and-dip-spattered table, where she was constructing a pyramid out of empty plastic cups. I sat down next to her and sighed.

"Having fun?" I asked.

"Totally," she replied.

"Not much of a party animal, are ya?" I asked.

"I never really thought that drinking until I puked would be much fun," she said as she carefully balanced a clear cup atop two blue ones.

"Have you ever done it?"

"No. You?"

"No."

Mindy smiled. "Then we have that in common." She picked up a half-full cup of punch from the edge of the table and sniffed it. "What is this stuff, anyway?"

"Skull Punch. Apparently it tastes like regular Kool-Aid, but it's about four-billion-proof alcohol," I said. "I'm surprised it's not burning a hole through the cup."

Mindy grimaced and placed the offending mixture as far away from her as possible, as if she were afraid it was going to leap out and slink down her throat of its own volition.

A couple of guys burst in through the side door to the driveway, carrying a huge speaker between them. They struggled under the weight, listed sideways and slammed into the table, knocking Mindy's pyramid down in the process. Plastic cups bounced along the floor and under their feet, but they didn't even notice.

"Whose party is this, anyway?" one of them asked on their way to the living room.

"I don't know. Some brunette babe, I think," the other replied.

Mindy and I looked at each other and cracked up laughing.

"So much for hosting my way to popularity," I said. "This is going to go down in history as 'that party thrown by some brunette chick.' "

"Well, you *are* they only brunette around here, so there's a chance people will know it was you," Mindy said.

"Yeah, what's up with that?" I asked. "Is there something in the water?"

Mindy leaned into the table and tucked her chin. "Let's just say the Drug Fair downtown makes most of its profits off Herbal Essences Amazon Gold."

"I knew it! It couldn't be natural," I said. "Not all of it."

"Well, mine is," Mindy said, lifting one shoulder. "But I have personally been in on many bleach parties."

"Wow. I think this might be the happiest moment of my life," I said, grinning. There was a huge crash in the living room and I winced. "Do you want to get out of here and go to the movies or something?"

Mindy checked her watch. "Actually, I kind of have to get home. My parents are pretty insane about my curfew."

"Okay. Leave me to my misery," I joked. "Maybe I'll just play some Twister."

"Do not do that!" Mindy cried as she got up.

I laughed and walked her to the door, where she surprised me by hugging me good-bye. "See you tomorrow," she said.

I stood in the doorway until she disappeared out of sight, thinking about our conversation. I was glad that she'd started to open up to me about Sage and stuff. It felt like we were on our way to being real friends.

A cheer went up in the living room and I went over to check it out. In the five minutes since I'd left the room, the furniture had been cleared to the walls and the old Twister board had been broken out. A girl from my English class bent backward over another girl to put her right hand on blue while Tucker and his buddies salivated and cheered.

My house had officially become the ninth circle of hell.

"Hey there, Jersey."

Ah! A voice from above! All was not yet lost.

The second after I realized Daniel was standing beside me, my eyes darted toward the couch, which was now flush with the far wall. Sage and Gabe were no longer flirting. They were now trying to swallow each other whole. My heart slammed through my rib cage and I turned and tried to shove Daniel back into the kitchen.

"Hey! Hi! I was just thinking about going to the movies. Wanna come?"

Daniel laughed and stopped moving, his body like a brick wall. "What's up with you?" he said, bending slightly to look me in the eye. "Been hitting the wicked ale?"

"No! I just want to get out of here," I told him as another cheer went up from the living room. "This party is *so* lame."

"Doesn't sound like it," Daniel said. "What's going on in there?"

He sidestepped me and made it to the doorway before I could think of another stupid excuse to stop him. I watched as his face morphed from laughter, to surprise, to total nausea.

"Daniel, I—"

But he was already gone. He crossed the room, stepping on one of the Twister girls' hands and taking their whole knot down in the process.

"Hey! Foul!" Tucker shouted, pointing at Daniel.

Daniel grabbed my brother's shoulder, yanked him off an openmouthed Sage and shoved him right into a big green garbage bag full of cans and cups. The bag exploded and Sage screeched. In his stunned struggle for balance, Gabe took my mom's potted tree down with him and was pinned underneath it.

For a split second no one moved. Then Sage rushed over to Daniel.

"Baby? Let me explain—"

"Save it!" Daniel said, seething.

Is it wrong that I thought he was beyond sexy at that moment?

Sage's mouth snapped shut and Daniel stalked toward me. "I have to get out of here," he said as he brushed by. I could practically feel the angry heat radiating off his skin.

Gabe's friends were helping him up and he seemed fine. A little dirty and ego-bruised, but otherwise fine. And if I knew anything about the male psyche, I was pretty sure that, in 2.5 seconds, twenty surfer dudes were going to go after Daniel like bloodlusting pit bulls. I turned around to make sure Daniel had gotten out of the house okay, but he was standing at the side door, looking at me.

"You coming or what?" he said.

Hell, yeah.

We rushed out and Daniel led me to a black Honda Accord parked down the street.

"You drive?" I said.

"Get in," he replied.

Then we peeled outta there like two outlaws on the run. As my heart pounded and I grabbed the top of the window for balance, I struggled to keep from smiling. Daniel Healy was just full of movie moments.

• • •

Ten minutes later, we were seated across a table from each other at a local hangout called Dolly's. I'd heard it mentioned a few times since I'd started school, but hadn't yet been there. It was basically an old-school beach-bum diner with walls that were open to the elements and a fifteen-item menu

159

that was posted behind the counter with those plastic white letters that slide into little black slots. Dolly was the sun-withered but smiling old lady behind the counter, shouting at a rerun of *Fear Factor* on her mini TV.

"Don't chicken out now, Implant Girl! You survived all that plastic surgery, you can survive a few cockroaches!"

"Nice place," I said.

Daniel stared down at his untouched fries.

"You okay?" I asked.

"I feel like such a moron," he said, suddenly squeezing his eyes closed. "Like two days ago I was telling you how I couldn't imagine my life without her, and now—"

He stopped to bang his head back against the wooden bench. I winced.

"You must think I'm an idiot," he said.

"Not at all. Sage is the idiot," I replied.

"Just to clarify," he said, "I never want to see that freak again."

"Who? Gabe?"

"No. Sage."

"Fine by me," I said.

"I should've broken up with her ages ago," he said, looking out the window.

I blinked. "But wait. I thought you said you couldn't imagine—"

Shut up, *Annisa!*

"Yeah, but that's . . . that's because it's been so long since I've *been* without her," Daniel said, his blue eyes seeming to darken. He sat forward and dipped a french fry into a blob of ketchup. "It's hard to explain. Have you ever been in a long relationship?"

"Um, no," I replied.

"Well, I've been trying to break up with Sage for a year. Or thinking about it, but I just haven't had the guts."

"Are you serious?" I blurted. "What did you think was going to happen? Did you think her head was going to explode?"

"Possibly," he said, looking down. Suddenly he was very focused on dragging another french fry through the ketchup blob. "I don't know. I think I just . . . it sounds lame, but I guess it was just easier to not do it. I mean, I always figured it would be this big drama. . . ."

Which it was.

"I know you probably think I'm a total wuss, but I don't know." He wiped his hands on his jeans and sat back. "I guess I'm not good at change."

"So you thought, Better to stay with Sage and avoid change—"

"Than grow some balls and break up with her."

"Wow," I said.

"Yeah. Wow."

"A year's a long time."

"Tell me about it."

"So that's why you were so upset when she started acting weird," I told him, putting the pieces together. "You thought *she* was going to break up with *you* and you were worried about—"

"Change. Drama. All of it," Daniel finished. "Well, that and nobody likes getting dumped, right?"

I took a long sip of my milk shake. I couldn't believe it. Daniel wasn't helplessly in love with Sage. He had been trying to figure out a way to break up with her for a year. Would it be wrong to get up and do a spontaneous jig on the table?

"I'm sorry I attacked your brother," Daniel said suddenly.

"Please. He had it coming," I said. "Plus, now you've saved me the trouble of getting back at him."

"For what?" Daniel asked.

"Public humiliation," I said.

"Yeah. I think I took care of that."

"So, if you hate change so much, you must really love the way I've bulldozed into town," I said, picking at my nails.

"Are you kidding? What did I tell you the other day?" Daniel said, his face brightening. "Things have gotten a lot more interesting since you've been here. In a good way."

"Really?" I asked, grinning.

"Hey, I participated in a prank war, I've got someone to walk to school with and now I have the perfect excuse for a breakup," Daniel said. "Gimme a break, Jersey, you're like a . . . a . . ."

Guardian angel? Princess? Beautiful, perfect love of my life?

"Well, I don't know, but you're *something*," he said.

"Not much of a poet, are ya?" I said.

"Sorry."

"Hey," I replied with a smile. "I'll take it."

"You're a real wank, you know that?" I told my brother the next morning as I sat at the center island in my cheerleading uniform, eating my Cap'n Crunch. Gabe was attempting to mop the floor, but however wet and soapy he got the mop, it kept sticking in the pockets of film anyway.

"Are you gonna help me or what?" Gabe asked.

"Why don't you get your so-called friends to help you?" I asked, knowing full well that Joe was passed out in a pool chair and Tucker was booting it big-time in the upstairs bathroom for the third time that morning. "Or better yet, get your new *girlfriend* to help you."

"For the ten gazillionth time, I didn't know she had a boyfriend!" Gabe said, mopping vigorously now. "God, Annisa, it's not like I asked the girl to marry me. We were just messing around."

"Gabe, you could've charged for admission," I told him.

He stopped mopping and leaned the handle into the counter. "Why do you care, anyway? I saw the way you followed her man out of here like he was Brad freakin' Pitt. You should be thanking me."

My face flushed faster than you can say *snagged*. I was about to protest when there was a knock on the side door and Mindy and Sage walked in, thereby saving me from lying to my brother.

Was it really that obvious I liked Daniel?

"Ready for the big rivalry match-up?" Mindy asked cheerily.

"Nice power breakfast," Sage said, looking down at my bowl. "But then, I guess you're not hungry, since you were up half the night at Dolly's, chowing down carbs with my boyfriend."

My mouth dropped open. *What? How did she . . . ? Why would he . . . ? When did they . . . ?* My brain couldn't even finish a sentence.

"It's none of your business what I did or didn't do last night," I said, getting up and storming over to the sink, where I noisily deposited my bowl and spoon. God! Did everyone at Sand Dune High think they could tell me where I could go and what I could do? And with whom? I took a deep breath, then whirled on her. "Besides, he's not your boyfriend anymore."

"Yeah? We'll see, *Jersey*," Sage said.

Hearing her say Daniel's nickname for me was like blasphemy.

"Were you or were you not trying to suck my brother's face off last night?" I shot back.

"I think I should go," Gabe said, beating a hasty retreat.

"*That* is none of *your* business," Sage retorted.

"Oh, yes it is! You guys made it the business of everybody at the party!" I replied. "Were you always that much of a ho, or does my brother just bring it out of you?"

Sage looked about ready to rearrange my face and I definitely knew the feeling. Mindy sensed there was about to be a cheer brawl and stepped between us.

"You guys! Stop it!" she said in as loud a voice as I've ever heard her use outside of cheerleading. "We have to get to the game. You can tear each other's hair out later."

I narrowed my eyes as I glared at Sage over Mindy's arm. Tearing her hair out didn't seem like the worst idea. But Mindy was right. We were going to be late.

"Fine," I said finally.

"Fine," Sage replied. She flounced over to the refrigerator and yanked open the door.

"What are you doing?" I asked.

"I'm thirsty," she replied, her back to me.

Who did she think she was? She hadn't even asked if she could have something!

"That's it. I'm going to the field," I said, walking out of my own house and slamming the door behind me. Maybe Sage would slip and fall on the freshly mopped floor and never walk again. Or at least develop a severe limp. Temporarily.

• • •

I've never seen so many people at a high school football game in my life. Fans packed both stands, filling up every available inch of bench space and bursting over onto the grass around the track. One side was a wall of yellow and blue, the other a sea of green and white. At the concession stand, the separate colors avoided each other like they were afraid of catching some horrifying disease by brushing up against the arm of an enemy T-shirt. The tension was so thick, I felt like at any second someone would say something mildly insulting, a punch would be thrown and we'd be smack in the middle of an upper-middle-class riot.

But all in all, the people in the stands were fairly well behaved. It was the cheerleaders who were having problems.

"Tara, you are not my mother. Stop telling me what to do," Phoebe said shakily as I walked by her, Tara and Whitney. They were gathered on the track at the foot of the bleachers, post–football team announcements, pre–hello cheer.

"I'm not telling you what to do," Tara replied. "I'm trying to give you advice. As a friend."

"Is everything okay?" I asked somewhat meekly.

Phoebe groaned. She looked like she was about to explode. "Can't you mind your own business for five seconds?" she asked.

"She's just worried about you, Phoebe. We all are," Whitney put in quietly.

"Well, don't bother. I'm *fine,*" Phoebe said before storming off to stretch by herself. At least she hadn't burst into tears. That was an improvement.

"What's going on with her?" I asked.

"Like she said, it's really none of your business," Tara snapped.

Whitney sighed. "She won't even tell *us* what's going on with her. That's the problem. I think she's doing the whole bottle-it-all-up-until-she-explodes thing."

"Never good," I said, my heart going out to Phoebe.

"Nuh-uh," Whitney replied.

I kind of understood why Phoebe might not want to share her problems with anyone, though. Everyone was already gossiping about her father losing her house. Why fuel the fire? Sometimes people could really suck.

"The captains of the two teams will meet in the center of the field for the coin toss!" the announcer called out over the PA system.

Bobby Goow and Christopher Healy emerged from the line of players in front of us. They didn't even shake hands with the West Wind guys at the center of the field. I was suddenly acutely aware of the void above our scoreboard.

Something bad was going to happen here. I could feel it.

"It's heads! West Wind elects to receive!" the ref called

out. He blew his whistle and the captains jogged back to their sidelines. All the Sand Dune guys huddled up and put their hands in the center of the circle. They bounced up and down on their toes, shouting and grunting.

"Win! Win! Win!" they all called out together. Then they ran to line up for the kickoff and both crowds went totally insane.

"Let's go, Sand Dune!" I shouted out, cheering along with the rest of the squad as we started to take our spots for the hello cheer.

The ball was kicked off. Some guy on the West Wind team caught it and took a dive at the twenty-yard line. We all turned toward the crowd.

"Hello cheer!" Tara shouted.

Please, just let this go okay, please, just let this go okay . . .

"Ready?"

"Okay!"

"We've got the power!"

"To take control!"

Coach Holmes gestured at us manically. She smiled like the Joker and pressed her fingers into her cheeks, pulling her lips up. Apparently we didn't look quite happy enough. Shocker. I grinned as hard as I could as my arms flew through the moves.

"To rock this joint!"

"To go for gold!"

Coach waved her hands in front of her with her eyes wide, the universal signal for "More energy!"

"We welcome you!"

"To our school!"

"Take it from us!"

"Sand Dune rules!"

This time it wasn't me who missed the pyramid count. It was the other side that went down. Not as messily as it had at the pep rally, though. In fact, it seemed like it just never went up. Coach looked as if she were about to have a stroke.

"I missed a mark. *One* mark," Phoebe said to Tara as we dismounted.

"Whatever." Sage hiccuped. "I didn't feel like going up anyway."

"What the heck is *wrong* with you people?" Chandra hissed.

"What's the matter, Chandra? Does everything always *have* to be perfect with you?" Autumn put in.

"Ladies! What are you doing!?" Coach Holmes whisper-shouted from under the bleachers. Her eyes were about to pop free of their sockets. "Call a cheer! *Now!*"

Tara jumped to attention and everyone moved lethargically back to their places. "Defense is hot!" Tara called out. "Ready?"

The "okay" sounded more like a lame "maybe" than a full-hearted agreement. Coach Holmes hung her head. This was going to be an interesting afternoon.

• • •

"When you go out there for your halftime routine, I had better see ten times the energy, ten times the spirit and ten times the precision that I've seen in the first half," Coach Holmes lectured as the marching band finished up their Disney medley. "You look like a bunch of amateurs out there. I'm half tempted to let the freshmen finish the game. Do you want me to bring them in? 'Cause I will."

"No, Coach!" we all said in unison.

Hiccup, giggle, Sage put in, earning an admonishing glance from everyone on the team. She'd been hiccuping for the past ten minutes.

"Good! Now go line up and get ready to go on!" Coach Holmes said.

We turned and jogged toward the sideline. Sage tripped and fell right into Mindy's arms, laughing. What was her problem?

"Oh my God!" Mindy said, helping Sage stand up straight and holding her shoulders. "Are you drunk?" she whispered.

Sage hiccuped and shook her head, her ponytail whacking her in the face. My heart plummeted.

Holy crap.

Skull Punch.

"Mindy! What did she drink back at my house after I left?" I asked, pulling them away from the rest of the squad.

"Just some fruit punch," Mindy told me as Sage giggled at nothing in particular.

"Rooty tooty fruity," Sage said, and laughed.

"Oh my God," Mindy said, finally catching on. "Was there leftover Skull Punch?"

Sage burped. Loudly.

"Apparently," I said.

"And now, your Sand Dune High School varsity cheerleaders!" the voice on the PA shouted out. The crowd cheered.

"What are we gonna do?" Mindy asked, her skin as white as a sheet. "She can't go out there!"

The squad was already jogging onto the field. Coach Holmes waved at us frantically with her clipboard. If we stayed behind, the squad couldn't do the routine. There were too many formation changes. Too many stunts. And if we stayed behind, Sage would get caught and kicked off the squad and we would all be screwed.

"Get her other arm," I said, gripping Sage's biceps tightly.

169

Mindy did as I instructed. I think she was too scared to think for herself. "Let's go."

We jogged out onto the field, Sage between us, and dropped her off in her spot. She stood there, her shoulders slumped forward, her eyes at half-mast. I crossed myself even though I'm not Catholic. We needed all the help we could get.

The music started up, and the rest is a blur. I did the best I could in my first public performance of the routine, but it wasn't me I was worried about. Sage was all over the place, moving right when the rest of us went left, clapping off beat. Phoebe, meanwhile, was so out of it, she was one step behind on everything, if not more. Then, during the last formation change, Chandra actually hip-checked Autumn out of the way to get into place. It was mayhem.

At one point in the routine the whole squad turns around to face the visiting bleachers. When we did, the entire West Wind High cheerleading squad was standing on the sideline, doubled over laughing. I had never felt so utterly humiliated.

Somehow, when the music stopped, all the stunts were up like they were supposed to be. Our fans cheered half-heartedly and I knew they were as appalled as I was. We sprinted off the field, barely able to muster enough energy for a "Whaddup, Sand Dune!"

Coach couldn't even look at us. We were as pathetic as pathetic can be. Then Sage decided to seal the deal by falling flat on her face on her way off the field. Her sister had to pull her up and over to the fence, where she promptly vomited on a pom-pom. A resounding "Ugh!" went up from the crowd.

We were as good as dead.

• • •

"First down! All you need is a first down!" I shouted, half out of my head. "Let's go, Crabs!"

My pulse pounded frenetically as Mindy clutched my hand. In the last few minutes, the squad had lost all semblance of order on the track and Coach Holmes was too wrapped up in the game to care. We all were.

I glanced at the scoreboard as Mindy squeezed my fingers near the breaking point. There were forty-five seconds on the game clock and the team had no time-outs left. The score was 23–19. We had held West Wind scoreless in the second half, but we still needed a touchdown here to win. It looked like it was in the bag if we could just get this first down and if the runner ran out of bounds to stop the clock. Then we'd be on the ten-yard line and have time for a shot at the end zone.

"I can't take it. I'm gonna barf," Mindy said, looking legitimately queasy.

"I think we've seen enough of that for one day," I shouted back.

Sage had been relegated to the first aid station, where she was currently sleeping it off. Coach had yet to deal with her, and I couldn't think about it now. I was too busy having a coronary.

The team lined up. I could just hear Christopher's audible. The ball was hiked and I jumped up and down to see what was going on. He dropped back. He handed it off to . . . Daniel! Daniel cradled the ball and ran for the sideline, gaining one . . . two . . . three yards! Enough for a first down!

"Get out of bounds!" I screamed along with half the crowd. "Get out!"

Some huge defensive end came out of nowhere and smacked Daniel into the ground. You could hear the crack

171

of their helmets for miles. Everyone winced and groaned. Luckily Daniel got right up. Unluckily, he hadn't gotten past the sideline. The clock was ticking away.

Christopher gestured at the team wildly, trying to get them back into position so he could run one last play. Everyone scrambled back to the line. All I could hope was that they had something to call. Something that would get them into the end zone.

The clock was at 20 . . . 19 . . . 18 . . .

Christopher took his place behind the center. 17 . . . 16 . . .

"Hut one! Hut two!"

15—

And then the whistle blew. The ref ran over to the line, waving his arms in the air. He called something out at the top of his lungs that I *had* to have heard wrong.

"That's time! Game over!"

"*WHAT!?!*" (That was me screeching.)

The West Wind High players jumped up and down, hugging each other in celebration. The Sand Dune players gathered around the ref, demanding an explanation. A couple of them ripped off their helmets and got all up in the man's face. Bobby Goow looked like he was possessed, his face purple and his dark hair clinging to his head with sweat. Everyone in the stands was stunned into silence. We looked at the clock. The lights didn't lie. There were still fifteen seconds on it.

The ref blew his whistle manically, trying to get the guys to back off. He hit the button on his belt mic to connect his voice to the PA system. His words rang out over the field like a death knell.

"The clock on the scoreboard . . . the clock on the scoreboard is incorrect," he said.

"What!?"

"He's gotta be kidding!"

"This is bull—"

"The official game clock is kept on the field by the officials," he continued, unperturbed by the thousands of people salivating for his blood. "The official game clock has run down."

The Sand Dune High stands erupted with boos and jeers and cries of disbelieving fury. The West Wind High stands went wild. Their players ran off the field, shouting and screaming, arms raised in victory.

"West Wind has won the game," the official finished, slamming the last nail into the coffin. "West Wind High wins by a score of twenty-three to nineteen!"

Coach Turcott and the assistants rushed the field, lacing into the ref with a few choice words. I heard someone shouting about misinformation. Then something about the bylaws of the league. The players all hovered on the field in disbelief, as if they were waiting to be told to get in that last play even though the Dolphins had long since vacated the line. I had never felt a sensation like this in my stomach before. This must have been what the phrase *gut-wrenching* referred to.

"They were bought off!" someone's dad shouted from the stands. "The refs were bought off!"

"This is not right! It's not fair!" someone else was crying.

Seconds passed . . . then minutes. Finally Coach Turcott grabbed his clipboard and stormed toward the school. Still, no one could believe it. No one could move. How could something like this have happened? And in *this* game, of all games.

Eventually we all came back to consciousness long enough to gather our things and trudge off the field. As we walked by the visitors' bleachers, a bunch of kids leaned over the railings, singing at the top of their lungs.

"Na na na na, na na na na, hey, hey, hey, good-bye!"

Suddenly I saw the support beams under the bleachers give way, collapsing the stands and taking the bevy of bouncing morons down with them. If only I had the power to make my daydreams come true.

• • •

The auxiliary gym was full of colorful banners and signs and some streamers and balloons left over from spirit week, but it may as well have been decorated for a funeral. That was how we all felt as we sat there in front of Coach Holmes. Like someone had just died. It wasn't enough that we had to lose the big rivalry game, but to lose it like that? It just wasn't fair.

"I don't even know what to say to you girls anymore," Coach Holmes told us flatly. Her fed-up detachment was even worse then her shouting. "Whatever is going on with all of you, you had better sort it out before regionals," she said, shaking her head. " 'Cause if you don't, we are just going to get laughed off the mats. And that's the truth."

At that moment Sage, who had rejoined us in a state of semiconsciousness after the game, got up and ran from the room. We could all hear her heaving on the grass. Tara rolled her eyes and sat back on her hands. I kind of felt like ralphing myself.

"Excuse me," Whitney said, quickly following after her sister.

"What the hell is up with Sage?" Coach Holmes demanded of the rest of us. I looked at Mindy and shook my head ever so slightly. Mindy looked at the floor.

"I'm sorry, Coach," Whitney said, rejoining us. She smiled apologetically and bit her lip. "She has some kind of stomach flu. I told her to stay home this morning, but you know

Sage. School spirit all the way." She shrugged innocently, pressing her lips together like, *What else can I say?*

There was a prolonged silence as Coach Holmes took this in and mulled it over, but finally she just raised her hands. "Fine. Whatever you say. Everyone go home and get some rest. Over the weekend I want you to think about what this squad means to you. If you come back on Monday ready to work, I'll be here."

She picked up her bag and walked out. The rest of us slowly got to our feet and followed. Personally, I couldn't wait to get the heck out of there and soak in a nice long bath, provided it wasn't full of beer cans or something.

"What are you doing now?" Mindy asked as we headed for the door.

"I'll probably just chill by the pool this afternoon and try to distract myself with geometry," I told her. "Want to come over and study?"

Mindy opened her mouth to answer, but before she could, we both overheard something that caused us to freeze.

"It's all Gobronski," Tara Timothy said. "The girl is bad luck. Ever since she got here, everything's been falling apart."

That was it. Something inside of me just popped. All Tara Timothy had done since the day I arrived was pick on me and bad-mouth me. I was so tired of her and all her little friends watching me and criticizing every single move I made. Ever since my meltdown at tryouts, I'd kept my mouth shut and tried to fit in, tried to get them all to like and accept me. Well, I was done.

I turned on my heel, stalked up to Tara and the three girls huddled around her and cleared my throat. Tara looked surprised when she saw me there, but not upset that it was obvious I'd overheard.

"You know what, *Captain*?" I said, crossing my arms over

my chest. "Maybe you should stop focusing on *me* and start focusing on the fact that your precious little squad is imploding! If you were any kind of a captain, you would do something about it instead of pinning it all on me!"

She opened her mouth, but nothing came out. It was all I needed to buoy me into a second round.

"Did you ever think about the fact that maybe this is all *your* fault?" I demanded, my adrenaline pushing me forward. "You're supposed to be our leader, right? What kind of leader sits back and watches while things get this bad? Everyone is fighting, no one wants to act like a team and your best friend is a basket case! Maybe you should get off your ass and *lead*!"

Tara was stunned silent. Lindsey, Kimberly and Michelle all stared at the floor.

"And by the way, the name is Gobrowski! *Go. Brow. Ski!* It's not that hard!"

I turned around again, grabbed Mindy's arm and stalked through the doors out into the sunshine. For the first time in days I felt as light as air. I felt free. I felt like the weight that had been pressing in on my chest had been blown to pieces.

I felt like myself again.

"Why do I need to know the sum of the angles of a rhombus?" I asked Jordan that afternoon. "Why? Why, why, why?"

"Honey, no one knows the answer to that one," Jordan replied.

The doorbell rang. "I gotta go, Jor," I said. "Call ya later."

"I'll keep an eye on the news to see if anyone's killed your referees yet," she joked.

"Keep me posted," I told her before hanging up.

I got up and sprinted for the door, grateful for another excuse to avoid geometry and salivating to see who it was. Maybe Bethany had gotten my messages and decided to come over for a make-up talk. Maybe Daniel was stopping by to weep on my shoulder over the injustice of the game. I slid over to the door in my socks and yanked it open. Nothing could have prepared me for the sight of Phoebe Cook standing on my front step, hair falling out of her long ponytail, her face blotchy and caked with dry tears.

"Hey," she said with a sniffle. "I'm running away from home."

Ooooookay. I noticed her one hand was clutching a duffel bag with a pillow shoved through the handles while the other clung to her backpack. Apparently she wasn't kidding. But that didn't explain what she was doing on *my* doorstep. I thought she wanted nothing to do with me.

"Can I come in?" she asked, her voice about to crack.

"Um . . . sure," I said, stepping aside. She walked in and looked around, taking in every detail of her former home. My heart went out to her. Why would she come here, of all places? A house that would undoubtedly bring back a million memories.

"I'm sorry, it's just, I couldn't go to Whitney's or Tara's," Phoebe said, as if reading my mind. "They're driving me crazy. And you said if you could do anything . . ."

God, she looked *really* tired. "Here. Let me take your bag," I said.

"Thanks," she gave up the duffel.

I was unsure of what I was supposed to do. "Can I . . . get you anything?"

Phoebe smiled slightly and I was pretty sure it was the first time I'd ever seen her do it. "Could I just . . . lie down for a while?"

"Sure," I replied. "The living room's kind of a mess. But we could go to my room."

The instant I said it, I regretted it. My room had been her room not so long ago. In her clearly fragile state, walking in there might just push her over the edge. But it was too late. Phoebe was already headed upstairs. She walked right to my room and stepped through the door. I placed her bag down on the floor and pulled her pillow out for her.

"Do you really hate the pink?" she asked.

"I . . . uh . . . pink's not really my color," I said.

"Oh," she said. Then she started to cry.

"We could go to my parents' room," I said quickly. I hated seeing people cry.

"Why are you being nice to me?" she asked, sitting down on my bedspread. She covered her face with both hands.

'Cause you're a blubbering mass of neuroticness? my brain answered.

But she did have a point. Just that morning she had told me to mind my own business, and now I was welcoming her into my house and offering her whatever she wanted. But how could I not? She looked so wan and sick and sad.

"Don't worry about it," I said, handing her the pillow. "Just lay down. You'll feel better if you sleep."

"I haven't slept in days," she said, holding her pillow to her.

I sat down on the edge of my desk chair and bit my bottom lip. "Do you . . . I mean . . . if you want to talk—"

"Did you ever just think your entire family was completely insane?" Phoebe blurted, yanking a tissue out of the box on my bedside table.

"All the time," I replied.

She let out a short laugh and wiped her face dry, then stared down at the crumpled tissue in her fingers. Suddenly I had this vision of Phoebe as a little girl, sitting in this very same room, crying over some grade-school injustice. Maybe she had been a bitch ever since I met her, but she was just another person, really. A person with major problems at the moment.

"Swear to God you'll never tell anybody?" she said, looking up at me.

"I swear," I replied.

"No one knows the whole story. Not even Tara," she said.

"I promise. I have practically no friends to speak of, so who would I tell?" I said.

Phoebe half smiled at the truth of this statement and I pulled my knees up under my chin, ready to be the good listener. I can't say I wasn't intrigued to potentially be the only person who knew Phoebe's sordid story, but that wasn't my motivation. The girl needed a friend and it seemed like, for whatever reason, hers weren't doing the job just then. I wasn't about to turn her away.

"Okay, so, my dad is, like, this compulsive gambler," Phoebe said, playing with the tissue. "He was in Gamblers Anonymous for a while, but he stopped going about a year ago and I thought that meant he was, you know, like, cured."

"Okay," I said.

"So about three months ago, him and my mom have this huge blowout fight and they're saying we're going to lose the house and all this stuff," she continued. "So I come downstairs and ask them what's going on and it turns out my dad's taken out a second mortgage and some other loan on the house, and he's defaulted on all of them."

"Omigod," I said, the air rushing out of me.

"He was betting all our money on dog races!" Phoebe said, laughing bitterly. "Dog races!"

"I didn't even know they actually *had* dog races," I said.

"I know!" Phoebe replied. "And this was going on for ages. Like, while he was in GA," she continued. "So these people come and they take all our stuff. Like, repo guys or whatever, and my mom has to get two jobs and I've been working at the Burger King downtown, which makes me smell like onions *all* the time, and we had to move in with my aunt Gladys, and my father . . . my father has been going to the track instead of his GA meetings, so my mom just kicked him out."

"Phoebe, I'm so sorry," I said. Part of me wanted to get up and hug her, but I held back. We weren't exactly there in our relationship. In fact, we were only about five minutes into our relationship.

"So, still think your family is totally insane?" Phoebe asked.

"Not so much," I said lightly.

She dabbed at her eyes with the tissue and I could tell she was trying to keep from bawling again. I rolled my chair over to the tissue box, pulled out a couple and handed them to her.

"Thanks," she said, sniffling. "I'm sorry I was such a bitch to you when you first moved here. I just . . . I'm *so mad.*" She took a deep breath and clenched and unclenched her fists. "But I know I shouldn't be mad at you."

"It's okay," I told her. "I totally understand."

And I did. I did now.

"I think I'm just gonna lay down," she said, putting her pillow on top of mine. She stretched out and turned on her side, tucking her arm under the pillow, the same way I always did before I went to sleep.

"Okay. I'll just go study downstairs," I said.

I picked up my stuff and shut out the desk light. The sun was just starting to go down and I was glad. It gave the room that comforting, gray feeling. Like bedtime back when I was little.

"Annisa?" she said as I started out the door.

I paused, my heart thumping for some reason. "Yeah?"

Phoebe smiled and yawned. "Thanks for not slamming the door in my face."

I smiled back. "No problem."

• • •

A few hours later, the doorbell broke the silence so suddenly, it almost knocked me out of my chair. I raced to the front door to keep it from ringing again and waking Phoebe. Gabe and his buddies had been out all day and I'd taken the phone off the hook so nothing could disturb her snooze fest and my studying. I'd been at it so long, I got a head rush as I slid to the door once again.

This time I found Tara, Bobby, Christopher and Mindy standing there, all wearing head-to-toe black. Bobby and Christopher had even smudged their faces with black paint, commando style. I didn't like the look of this.

"We've been trying to call you for an hour," Tara said, barely looking at me. "We're going to West Wind."

"For what?" I asked, afraid of the answer.

"That game was a total setup," Bobby replied. "We're going over there to show them who the real winners are."

"Let's go," Christopher Healy said, turning away.

Mindy shot me a helpless look. For the first time I noticed at least a half dozen cars idling in and around my driveway, each packed with people.

"I think you guys are going to have to do this one without me," I said. From the look on Mindy's face, this wasn't anything I wanted to get involved in. Besides, I couldn't leave Phoebe upstairs alone.

Tara reeled on me. I could tell she'd been waiting for just such an opening. "Why don't you put your actions where your mouth is?" she said snottily. (Eloquent she's not.) "Weren't you the one going on about the team this morning?"

"Yeah, but—"

"Well, we're *all* doing this. As a *team*. Either you're in or you're out," Tara said.

"You really think restarting an illegal prank war is going to solve all our problems?" I blurted.

Christopher scoffed and raised his hand to wave me away. "Forget her. Let's go."

"No way," Bobby Goow said unexpectedly. "She started this whole thing. She's gonna help us finish it."

Everybody turned and stared me down. I felt my face heating up as I clutched the doorknob. I could just do what I knew was right and back out. I could close the door in their faces and go down as the loser wuss of the century. Or I could go along and hope for the best. Be a team player.

I stared into Tara Timothy's defiant eyes and noticed the triumphant spark there. She expected me to stay behind. She expected me to wuss out. And that was the only thing I needed to know to do the dumbest thing ever.

"Fine. I'm in," I said. "Give me two seconds."

It's all in good fun. West Wind deserves it after today, I told myself as I jogged back upstairs and changed as quietly as possible. It's amazing the things I can convince myself to do when my competitive side kicks in. I scribbled Phoebe a note and left.

"What are we doing?" I whispered to Mindy on our way to Bobby's truck.

"They won't tell me," she whispered back. "They won't tell any of the underclassmen."

"That can't be good," I said.

"Hey, T! Where's Phoebe?" Whitney called out the passenger side of a gold TrailBlazer.

"Who knows?" Tara said in a fed-up voice. She might as well have said, *"Who cares?"*

"She's here," I said, mostly to shove Tara's face in it. *You don't know where your best friend is, but I do.* Petty, of course, but my ego needed to fight back over being mocked out of the safety of my house and into this escapade.

"What?" Tara snapped, pausing beside the truck.

"She's sleeping. Up in my room," I said.

"What is she doing *here?*" Tara asked.

"Well, let's go get her," Bobby said.

I ran over and got in front of Bobby, stopping his forward

183

progress. He was ten times my size, but I wasn't about to back down. Not on this.

"Leave her alone," I said.

"Whatever, midget," he said, trying to step past me.

I sidestepped in front of him. "She's not coming with us," I said firmly.

Bobby's face grew irate and I wondered if he'd ever shoved a girl. Or a midget.

"Bobby! Forget it!" Tara said. Her expression had completely shifted. She looked concerned and confused. Maybe even a little bit hurt. "Let's just go."

Bobby shot me one last threatening sneer, then gave up on me and got behind the wheel. I guess Tara had realized that if Phoebe was crashing at *my* house, something must be seriously wrong. When I got into the truck next to Mindy, I saw Tara shoot me a curious look in the rearview mirror, but I pretended not to notice.

I wasn't going to be the one to explain what was going on with her so-called best friend. That was something she needed to find out for herself.

Mindy and I stood off to the side in the West Wind parking lot as the other kids piled out of the trucks and started to unpack brown bags from one of the trunks. Some clouds had rolled in since the sun went down, and the sky was pitch-black. No moon, no stars. I shivered even though there wasn't much of a chill in the air. Suddenly I wanted to be anywhere but there.

"Cold?" Mindy asked.

"No. Just freaked," I said.

"I know! Me too!" she whispered.

My heart caught when I saw Daniel walking toward us, his hands stuffed in the pockets of his dark blue jeans.

"Hey, Jersey," he said.

"Hey," I replied. "Do you have any idea what's going on?"

"Not a clue," Daniel admitted.

Sage was helping one of the guys with a bag when the bottom fell right out of it. There was a huge metallic clatter as several cans of spray paint dropped to the asphalt and rolled off in every direction.

"Is that spray paint?" Mindy said.

"Oh, God. It's an *E! True Hollywood Story* moment," I said, swallowing hard.

"What?" Daniel asked.

"Sorry," I said, shaking my head. "My friend Jordan?

Whenever she finds herself in an ethical dilemma, she thinks of whether or not it's something she'd want to have dug up for her *E! True Hollywood Story.*"

"Ah," Daniel said. "Interesting. So this would be a no."

"Basically."

We all watched, our eyes wide, as the seniors walked right over to the side wall of the gym and let loose with the paint. They didn't even hesitate. The second the acrid scent hit my nostrils, I started to back away. Painting the field was one thing—grass grew back. And streamers and balloons could be easily cleaned up. But this was actual vandalism.

"That's it. I'm outta here," I said.

"Me too," Mindy said.

"I'm with you guys. This is insane," Daniel added.

We said nothing to the others and started to walk off. West Wind High was a good twenty-minute drive from the center of Sand Dune, but I didn't care. I'd walk all night if I had to to get away from these maniacs. They didn't even seem to realize what they were doing was wrong.

"Hey! Where are you guys going?" Tara Timothy intercepted us at the edge of the driveway.

"Home," I said. "Somehow I think it's better than jail."

"Fine, whatever," she said. "I should've known you couldn't handle it." She turned to the rest of the crowd who were laughing and running around in the darkness with their cans of paint. "The sophomores are bailing!" she shouted.

A bunch of them jeered and booed and waved their hands at us. My face burned, but I no longer cared about being embarrassed or not being a team player. I wasn't about to become a vandal to impress these people. I had to draw the line somewhere.

"Come on, guys," I said. "Let's go."

Daniel, Mindy and I stepped onto the sidewalk. At that very instant the whoop of a police siren split the night and a red light flashed. Three cop cars zoomed into the West Wind High driveway and screeched to a stop. Everyone scattered, but Daniel, Mindy and I were frozen in place by a flashlight that was directed right at our faces.

"Let's see your hands," the cop behind the flashlight said.

I squinted against the glare and raised my palms. Definitely a movie moment you don't want to have.

"Nobody move," someone said through a megaphone. "You're all under arrest."

• • •

"I'm in a jail cell! A jail cell! I can't be in a jail cell!" Mindy babbled, pacing back and forth in front of me and Daniel.

"Mindy, just try to calm down," I said in a soothing voice. "It's going to be okay."

"No! No, it's not!" Mindy shouted, her eyes wide. "My father is going to kill me! He's going to send me to boarding school. I'm never going to see civilization again!"

"Oh, would you just shut up?" Lumberjack Bob said from across the cell. He'd been banging his head back against the whitewashed wall for about an hour.

"You shut up!" Mindy shouted, surprising us all. She reeled on him and got right in his face. "This is all your fault! It's *your* fault I'm in a jail cell!"

Damn. Go on with your bad self, I thought. Mindy yelling at Bobby was like the island of Bermuda launching an assault on Washington. It just wasn't done.

"She has a point," Tara said. Her arms and legs were crossed tightly and it was the first time she'd spoken since we got there.

"Oh, so this is *my* fault?" Bobby said, turning on her.

"It was your stupid idea!" Tara shouted.

"I didn't see you arguing against it!"

"Yes, I did! I said we should wait! I said it would be too obvious if we did it today!"

"You guys! The cops can hear you!" Felice whisper-shouted, her eyes darting toward the front of the cell. "They can use anything we say against us!"

"Hey! We were all there! We're all at fault!" Whitney said, ignoring her.

"Nuh-uh!" Sage protested. "You guys didn't tell the rest of us what we were there *for!* We were involuntary accomplices. We shouldn't even be here!"

"Give me a break, Sage, I know you were listening on the steps," Whitney said, leaning back. "You knew exactly what we were doing."

"I was not!" Sage said, her mouth dropping open indignantly.

"Please, you so were," Daniel scoffed. "You sit on those stairs and listen in on Whitney twenty-four/seven."

Sage turned purple. "How could you . . . you know that's a secret!"

"Not anymore," Whitney said with a laugh.

"Oh, so what—now that we're broken up, we get to tell everyone all our secrets?" Sage said, sauntering over to us. "What if I told everyone about your cheesy-ass songwriting hobby?"

"My songs aren't cheesy," Daniel said flatly.

"Oh, please," Sage said, looking down her nose at him. "'Thorns of Love'? How is that not cheesy?"

Makes sense if he was with you when he wrote it, I thought.

A couple of the guys laughed and Daniel reddened.

"Tryin' to be the next Justin Timberlake, yo?" Bobby asked.

"It's not idiot pop songs," Daniel said. "It's music. No lyrics."

"Yeah, music with lame titles," Sage said.

Daniel pressed his hands into the bench at his sides and looked Sage right in the eye. I could feel his tension.

"Are you sure you want to keep going down this road?" he asked pointedly. " 'Cause I really don't think you do."

Everyone in the cell held their breath. It was obvious that Daniel had something even worse on Sage than her cheesy-songs dig, and we were all pretty much salivating to know what it was. Sage and Daniel had a stare-off for what felt like an hour before she finally turned away, flounced over to the bench across from us and sat down.

"I have a proposition," Felice said. "How about we don't talk until our parents get here?"

Unfortunately, my parents were in Las Vegas. I didn't tell anyone this, but I wasn't sure I was ever getting out of there. Gabe wasn't home when I left and no one else had the number of my parents' hotel. If Phoebe was still there, she might be able to find it in the kitchen, but she didn't even know my parents were away. This cell could very well be my new home.

Tara and Bobby scowled at each other, then turned their backs on one another. Mindy sat down next to me and put her head on my shoulder. Sage scowled across the cell at her as if touching me was the ultimate betrayal. I looked at Daniel and we both sighed. It was going to be a long night.

• • •

"Where is she? Where's my sister?"

"Gabe! Over here!"

189

I woke up with a sharp pain to the temple. A fluorescent light hovered overhead and my back felt like it had been cracked in ten places. I lifted my head, which was resting on a bunched-up varsity jacket. I blinked at it. The name DANIEL stared up at me in gold lettering on the breast. He'd left me his jacket as a pillow.

"Annisa! Are you okay?"

I sat all the way up and winced in pain. The cell was empty and I had fallen asleep. How the hell had I fallen asleep in this place?

I blinked a few times and saw Gabe and Phoebe standing at the bars at the front of the cell, staring in at me like I was a monkey at the zoo. Gabe and Phoebe. In my half-asleep state it took me a second to process how that had happened. Then relief washed through me. I was saved!

"Hey, guys," I said, standing up. "Are you getting me out?"

"They won't let me 'cause I'm not your guardian," Gabe said, clutching the bars. So much for the relief. He looked around, then lowered his voice. "Annisa, what the hell did you do?"

"Nothing!" I said, walking over to them. "The seniors took us over to West Wind and I knew we were doing a prank, but they never told us what. I swear, Gabe, I had no idea."

"Not surprising," Phoebe said. "No one ever told us what was going on when *we* were sophomores."

"I think that's one tradition we need to do away with," I said, leaning my head against the bars. "Mom and Dad are gonna kill me."

"Yeah, they're not happy campers," Gabe said.

My heart thumped. My parents weren't technically due back until Monday. "Are they coming home early?"

"Yeah. They're somewhere over Texas right about now," he replied, checking his watch. Then he smiled. "I gotta say, of the two of us, I never thought you'd be the first one to end up behind bars."

I laughed bitterly. "No kidding."

"Annisa, thank you so much for leaving me behind," Phoebe said. "I don't think my parents could handle bailing me out of jail on top of everything else."

"No problem," I said, noticing for the first time that she had some color back in her face and was looking a lot less miserable. "I'm glad one member of the squad is record-free. Maybe you can compete solo at regionals."

"Do you think they're gonna keep us out of it?" she asked.

"How could they not?" I said sadly. "But whatever. I'm just glad you were at my house to get the call."

"Yeah, imagine my surprise when I came home to find this beautiful girl waiting for me to tell me that my sister has been picked up by the cops," Gabe said, smiling at Phoebe. I noticed for the first time that he had dropped the surfer-speak. Maybe he forgot it in all the drama.

"Please," Phoebe said, flushing. "I look like death."

"Then death is looking good these days," Gabe said.

"Okay, I don't need nausea on top of everything else," I told them.

"Come on, kids." The officer who had blinded me earlier came into the holding area. "You've been in here long enough."

Gabe rolled his eyes. "We'll be right outside," he told me. He reached through the bars and ruffled my hair like he always did when we were little. "Don't worry. Mom and Dad will be here in a few hours."

Phoebe lifted her hand in a wave and she and Gabe followed the officer out. *Mom and Dad will be here in a few hours . . . to ground me for life,* I thought. *Yeah, that's comforting.*

I walked over to the bench and picked up Daniel's jacket.

He must have put it under my head when I was already sleeping. Just the thought of him carefully lifting my face and slipping it under there . . . *sigh*. It was so perfect, I was sorry I'd missed it.

I unfolded the jacket and slipped my arms into it, savoring the warmth. I wished there was a mirror in the cell so I could see how I looked in it, but no such luck. In the pockets I found one stick of gum—cinnamon—a folded-up five-dollar bill, a Blockbuster card and a guitar pick.

It was so cool. Like a secret little tour of his life. I sat back on the bench to daydream. Maybe Daniel could keep me company for a little while. . . .

• • •

My mother hugged me so tightly when I stepped out of the cell, I thought she was going to crush me. She looked perfect, as always; the only evidence of her worry and the red-eye flight was a conspicuous lack of blush. When I pulled back from her, she placed her hands on either side of my face, looked me in the eye and shook her head.

"Mom, I didn't do anything. I swear," I said.

"Isn't that what everyone says in this situation?" she asked.

"Yeah, but this time it's true," I said, half pleading. "Come on, Mom. I wouldn't do something like this."

She took a deep breath and let it out slowly. "I probably shouldn't believe you, kiddo, but I do."

My entire body uncoiled. As long as my parents were on my side, I was fine.

"Who's Daniel?" she asked, her brow creasing as she looked down at his jacket.

I smiled. "I'll tell you about it tomorrow."

She wrapped her arm around me and walked me out to

the waiting room, where my dad was signing something at the front desk. Gabe and Phoebe rushed over the second they saw me. Phoebe hugged me almost as hard as my mom had.

"You're sprung!" Gabe said, knocking me on the shoulder.

"What's going on over there?" I asked as my mom joined my father.

Phoebe and Gabe pulled me into a little huddle and lowered their voices. "It sounds like West Wind isn't pressing charges," Phoebe said. "Something about the scare of being thrown in jail being enough punishment."

"Please. Like a little jail time is gonna scare *my* sister," Gabe said, grinning.

"Shut up!" I said. "My juvenile delinquency phase is officially over."

"Annisa."

My heart twisted at the strained tone of my father's voice. I turned around and he landed a perfunctory kiss on my forehead. I could tell he was really mad.

"Are you okay?" he asked.

"Yeah, Dad. I'm fine," I said.

"Good. Then let's go."

My heart was pounding as we headed in a group toward the door, wondering what was going to happen when they got me home. A lot of explaining, definitely. A grounding, probably. This was so unfair. I'd already spent a good eight hours behind bars and I hadn't even done anything. Well, except that I left the house when I knew I should have stayed right where I was. Lesson learned.

"Oh, and Mr. Gobrowski?" the officer behind the desk said.

We all paused and turned around. "Yes?" my father said.

The middle-aged man smirked and knocked his pen against the counter, looking at Gabe. "Sorry, I meant the younger Mr. Gobrowski," he said. "I assume you'll be paying that fine by the end of the week."

We all turned to Gabe, who had a sort of kill-me-now look on his face.

"Fine?" my mother said. "What fine?"

"I was going to tell you about this later," Gabe said.

"Tell us about what?" my father asked, his voice shaking.

"Hey! It's just a ticket!" Gabe said. "Annisa's the felon!"

"Hey!" I said, whacking him with the back of my hand.

"Gabriel," my father said. *"What . . . fine?"*

My father never called my brother "Gabriel." It rendered my brother speechless.

"I'm afraid your son was issued a ticket on Friday night for noise violation," the officer supplied helpfully.

What!? I thought. Gabe's party had been shut down by the cops? How did I not know this?

"Noise violation?" my mother said.

"He threw quite a party," the officer said with a grin. "From what I understand, kids are going to be talking about it for years."

His job done, he turned and walked back into the offices, leaving my little family unit (plus Phoebe) in agonizing silence.

"Gabe! *Again!?*" my mother asked, disappointment all over her face.

"In the car," my father added. "Now."

Gabe and I exchanged a look of doom as we led our parents out the doors. We were totally done for.

When I came downstairs on Sunday morning, my parents were fully clothed and sitting in the living room, talking in ominously hushed voices. After dropping a resigned Phoebe back home the night before, they had sent us to bed and said they would deal with us in the morning. I was already sick with anticipation, but my insides took a turn for the worse when I saw that sitting on the coffee table between them was my geometry notebook. And right on top of my notebook was my first and only quiz, the one with a nice, fat D in the top right corner.

I turned to go back to my room, but my father heard me when I tripped up the stairs.

"Come on down, Annisa," he said. "Have a seat."

"Hey," I said tentatively as I padded over to them. I swallowed hard and sat down on the edge of the chair-and-a-half that was caddy-cornered from the couch. There was a huge lump in my throat. Let the sentencing begin. "About the D—"

"Annisa, what is going on with you?" my father interrupted.

"It's just one grade, Dad," I said. "They're way ahead of my class back home. But I have a test this week and if I do well on it, I'll be fine."

"Good. You're going to do well on it," he said, slapping my books into a pile.

"Yeah . . . I am," I said, uncertain in the face of his obvious ire.

"Because you will do nothing but study until the test is taken," my father said, pushing the books toward me. "That means no hanging out with your friends, no cheerleading, no nothing."

I was overcome by sudden and intense panic. "But regionals are this weekend!" I protested. *If they let us compete.*

"In fact, your mother and I are going to have to think long and hard about whether you should be cheering at all anymore," he continued as if I hadn't spoken.

"Dad, come on. You can't do this," I said.

"Annisa, your association with these people landed you in jail."

"But Dad, last night was just—"

"The most horrifying night of our lives!" my father shouted, standing. He walked away from the couch, pushing his fists into the pockets of his slacks. "Do you have any idea what it's like to get a phone call from the police in the middle of the night? Do you have any idea what went through our minds?"

I felt like I was about to cry. I felt awful all over again. I already knew what I had put them through. I had heard all about it on the car ride back from the police station. Did he have to keep rubbing it in?

"David," my mother said. "Is this really necessary?"

Thank you! I thought, with a rush of sheer gratitude.

"Yes, I believe it is!" my father said. "Our daughter was incarcerated."

"Yeah, but Dad, I didn't do anything," I said, standing as well. "Mom believes me!"

"It's not that I don't believe you, Annisa," my father said. "Maybe some kids pressured you into going, maybe you're

196

just trying to fit in. But sweetie, we've moved many times over the years, and I've never seen your behavior take such a radical shift. This isn't like you, Annisa."

The disappointment on his face practically broke my already aching heart. Why does it hurt more when they hit the nail right on the head than when they're accusing me of stuff I didn't do?

"Now, I want you to go up to your room and think about the way you've been behaving since we moved here," my father told me. "We'll discuss the future of your cheerleading career later."

I could tell the conversation was over. And there were so many things running through my mind at that moment, I wasn't sure I could sort out what to say anyway. Instead, I grabbed my books, stormed upstairs and slammed the door as hard as I could. I threw my geometry stuff on the floor and flopped down on my bed.

I was so angry. Angry at my father for not listening to me. Angry at my mother for barely participating. She could have defended me more. She could have said that taking away my cheerleading was punishment above and beyond the crime.

But he's not worried about last night, my more rational side pointed out. *He's worried about you.*

"I'm fine," I protested feebly. So feebly, *I* didn't even believe it.

I rolled over on my side and stared at the red D sticking out the top of my notebook. A D. I'd never gotten a D in my life. And yeah, maybe I'd been behind from day one, but I could've studied. I could've spent time working instead of cheerleading and shopping for Sand Dune–worthy clothes and trying to fit in. My dad was right. This wasn't like me.

I was starting to feel thoroughly depressed.

I sighed and rolled onto my back again, staring at the ceiling. My parents hated me, I was screwing up in my classes, I missed Bethany and hadn't talked to her in two days, I'd spent the night in jail and now I was going to have to tell Coach that I was going to miss two pre-regionals practices and maybe even have to quit the team.

My eyes began to burn and I felt a single tear slip down the side of my face. What the heck was I going to do?

• • •

Monday morning, the vibe in the halls of Sand Dune High was totally erratic. There was a sort of hushed, funereal feel after the travesty of the game, but it was shot through with the excitement of the biggest gossip-worthy story of the year. Anyone who wasn't talking about the evil refs was talking about was the big jock incarceration. As I walked down the hall to my locker, people whispered and shot me curious and awed glances. In one weekend I'd gone from klutzy, brunette nobody to party-throwing criminal. I wasn't sure I preferred the new status.

All you've got to do is get through today, I thought as I twirled my lock distractedly. It wasn't exactly comforting, though. Today was the day I would find out the fate of the squad, *and* tell Coach Holmes that I couldn't practice for two days. Maybe I'd be better off if we were banned from regionals. At least then it wouldn't be as big a deal that I had to bail on my commitment to the squad.

I yanked at the locker door and nothing happened. The little arrow was pointing at the 30. I'd done it again. My old locker combo. I really needed to get my brain back before that geometry test.

"Hey."

It was Bethany. I couldn't have been more shocked if she'd smacked me with an electric cattle prod.

198

"You're talking to me," I said. I carefully dialed in the correct combination.

"Yep," she replied. "Heard about your night in the slammer. You were locked in a ten-by-ten with my brother and his friends for over an hour. That's all kinds of evil. I think you've been punished enough."

I smiled slightly as I yanked open my locker door. "Thanks."

"Bobby told me you were still there when everyone else left. Did your parents go ballistic?" Bethany asked, turning so that her back was up against the wall.

"You could say that," I told her.

"So, when you're allowed to see daylight again, wanna write an article about police brutality for the site?" she asked. "Actually, I guess you don't need daylight for that. I never do. So what do you think, a thousand words by tomorrow?"

She looked so stoked about the idea that I didn't have the heart to tell her that somewhere around 1:00 A.M. the cops had taken pity on my lonely butt and given me donuts and milk.

"Sure," I said as I yanked a few books out of my locker. "But not for tomorrow. Not until after the geometry test and after regionals. If they even happen."

"Hey, if you don't want to do it," she said, putting her hands up.

"Bethany, wait," I said, stopping her before she walked away. She turned and looked at me, her eyebrows raised. "I'm just trying to be honest here. My parents are gonna slaughter me if I don't get at least a B on the geometry test, and regionals are really important to me. I just don't want to make promises I can't keep anymore."

Bethany looked at the toes of her platform Mary Janes

and hooked her thumbs around the strap on her messenger bag. "That's fair, I guess," she said finally.

I let out a sigh. "Good. 'Cause I really want to be friends with you, but if you're gonna freak out every time I have to do something with the squad—"

"Hey, I was just pissed about the prank war," Bethany said.

I blinked and shoved the last few books into my backpack. "Come again?" I asked, slamming my locker door. "I thought you were all *about* the prank war."

"Yeah, until you took the idea and went running off to the blah-rahs with it," she said, as if it were so totally obvious.

My mouth fell open and my gum almost came tumbling out. "*That's* why you're mad? Because you didn't get to participate?" I asked.

"Well, that was why I *was* mad," Bethany clarified. "Until you got your asses arrested. Which, by the way, would never have happened if I had been there."

"Yeah, whatever," I said, rolling my eyes.

"Hey! I'm all kinds of stealth!" she said, looking hurt.

"Bethany! Why didn't you just *tell* me? I would have brought you with us."

"Please! And risk getting sucked into the popular crowd along with you?" she joked.

"Yeah, like you would ever let that happen," I said, starting down the hall.

"Well, I'm over it, anyway," Bethany said, falling into step with me. "I vented all about you on the website. It was very cleansing."

She was starting to sound like Autumn.

"You did? What did you say?" I asked.

"Just how torturous it is to be friends with a cheerleader,"

Bethany said with a shrug. "I titled it *The Devil Wears Pleats.* How kill is that?"

"Very," I said. "So, we are still friends, then?"

Bethany blushed slightly. "Don't get all weepy on me," she said. "I reserve the right to revoke the title if you ever diss me again."

I nodded. "Sounds fair."

"So tell me, did they beat you with a telephone book in there or what?" she asked, walking backward as we turned the corner toward homeroom. "Can you describe any of them? 'Cause I know a guy who's great at composite sketches."

I laughed and opened the classroom door for her. Maybe today wouldn't be *all* bad.

• • •

The entire squad gathered in the gym bleachers after homeroom. The mood was grim. I hadn't been surprised to hear on the morning announcements that Principal Wharton wanted to meet with us, but I had been shocked that he wanted to do it so quickly. I figured it would take him at least a day to figure out our punishment and write an appropriately devastating speech.

"I'm grounded for a month," Mindy told me quietly. "But my parents are still going to let me compete. I mean, if we even are."

"That's good," I said, deciding to keep my own punishment to myself for now.

"What do you think they're gonna do?" Mindy asked.

"I think they're gonna bury us," I replied.

The door to the gym opened and Principal Buzzkill walked in with Coach Holmes at his side. I could practically hear everyone holding their breath. Neither one of the authority figures looked in the least bit happy to be there.

"Ladies, I'm gonna make this short," Principal Buzzkill said.

And sweet? I thought hopefully.

He stood right in front of us, legs spread, arms locked over his broad chest. Coach Holmes looked us over like we were sea slime. We were so very dead.

"We have not yet hammered out the details of the punishment for your behavior on Saturday night, and we'll be meeting with the football team next to tell them the same thing," Principal Wharton continued. "But we wanted to talk to you first because your participation in your regional competition has been called into question."

I heard Tara Timothy blow out her breath. She shifted in her seat and I felt the blade on the guillotine descending.

"After deliberating all day yesterday, talking to a few of your parents and some members of the school board, I have decided . . . to let you compete."

"Really?" someone squeaked.

"Omigod! That's so—"

Principal Wharton held up a hand, silencing us. But Mindy clung to my arm and grinned. We were still going to compete! We were still going to regionals! It was a miracle!

"It's the consensus of the school community that the football team suffered a crushing and unfair loss on Saturday and that keeping you girls out of competition would only compound that," Principal Wharton continued.

I looked over at Whitney and Phoebe, who were both grinning. This was completely and totally unexpected. Even Tara was smiling uncontrollably.

"We will get back to you on your punishment," Principal Wharton said. (I couldn't think of him as Buzzkill anymore.) "In the meantime," he said, "practice hard, and make us proud."

He turned on his heel and walked out of the gym. The second the door slammed behind him, we erupted with screeches and hugs and laughter. We were still going to regionals, which meant, among other things, that we still had a shot at beating West Wind at *something*. I couldn't remember the last time an authority figure had had such a human reaction to a situation like this.

A sharp whistle cut the noise dead and we all turned to find Coach Holmes glaring at us.

"I'm sure you already know how disappointed I am in you, so I'm not even gonna go there," she said. "If it were up to me, you would not be competing. Not after the way you all have been acting. But Principal Wharton and the Board of Education were adamant, so I had to go along."

My heart took a little dive. Coach Holmes was *mad.*

"They're doing you a huge favor here, so you had better be prepared to show them that they're right," she continued. "You will work your little butts off at practice this week and I mean *work.* No coming late, no leaving early. I want one hundred percent from you every second you are out there, you get me?"

My pulse was pounding in my ears. This was it. This was how I was going to die. But there was nothing I could do about it. I had to tell her what was going on.

"Um . . . Coach?" I said, my voice echoing through the gym. "I can't come to practice for the next two days."

"What?" Tara blurted.

"Excuse me, Gobrowski?" Coach Holmes said.

"I'm kind of . . . grounded until tomorrow's geometry test," I said, my mouth dry. "And if I don't ace it, my parents may pull me from the squad."

"I don't believe this," Coach Holmes said, looking at the ground. Her shoulders rose and fell as she sucked in a deep breath. She looked somewhere off to my left. "Timothy, you still the number-one math whiz in this county?"

Huh?

"Um . . . I guess so," Tara said.

"Good. You're tutoring Gobrowski today after practice."

Okay, this was not happening.

"But Coach—"

"You *really* wanna mess with me right now, Timothy?" Coach Holmes demanded. The sheer width of her nostril flare really was quite something. She had such a cute little button nose when she wasn't seething at us.

"No, Coach," Tara said.

"Good. Now all of you get your butts to class," Coach Holmes said. "And please, ladies! Please, for the love of all that is good in this world, do not do anything stupid for at least five days."

By the time Tara showed up that afternoon, I had already been studying for three hours. I'd read the first two acts of *Othello*, answered all my homework questions for Spanish, plodded my way through a chapter of biology and was staring blankly at my history textbook when the doorbell rang. I sighed and went downstairs to welcome the Queen of Torture into my home.

"Hey," I said.

"Hey," she replied. "Practice was pointless without you. We can't do any of the stunts and all the formations are off."

"Nice to see you too. Can I get you anything? Soda . . . water . . . arsenic?"

She rolled her eyes and tromped by me, heading for the stairs. "Let's just get this over with."

This was gonna be fun.

An hour later, after going over three chapters with Tara explaining various concepts to me carefully and slowly, like I was a coma patient, we were both working in tense silence. Tara was doing her calculus homework while I did a few problems for her to check over. She kept sighing every two minutes and each time she did, I tensed up, wondering if she was going to launch another verbal assault.

Finally her arm slapped down on her book and she looked over at me. "What the hell was Phoebe doing here the other night?" she asked.

I took a deep breath and kept writing. "You should really ask her."

"I tried that," Tara said.

Why did Phoebe want to be best friends with a person who was so clueless?

"Look, she's just really sad," I said. "She wanted to get out of her house and I guess she just felt like she couldn't go to . . . her friends."

"But why?" Tara asked, concern lining her face. "It's not like we're not trying. She won't talk to us, she won't let us help her. I just want her to snap out of it already."

"Maybe it's not something she can just snap out of," I said.

Tara sighed again and closed her heavy text with a bang. "Well, now she's basically not talking to me, and Autumn and Chandra are ready to strangle each other over no-one-knows-what, and you and Sage hate each other." She sighed and pushed her hands over her face and through her hair. "I don't know what the hell to do anymore, I really don't."

I sat there through this little speech, dumbfounded. It was not only the first time I'd ever seen Tara act and talk like a human, but it was the first time she had willingly displayed any kind of weakness. Maybe there was something in the air in my room that just got people talking.

"It's gonna be all right," I heard myself saying.

"No, it's not," Tara said. She picked up her pencil and doodled a dark swirl into the top of her notebook page. "Maybe you're right. Maybe I am a sucky captain."

Holy crap. It was a miracle. Had Miss High-and-Mighty really just said that?

"You'll figure it out," I said. But it sounded totally hollow. I really didn't see how we were going to pull it all together by Saturday even if I did somehow manage to ace the geometry test.

"I should've known better," she said, getting up and walking over to the window. "Whenever I really want something . . . like, whenever I think I'm *actually* going to get it, everything just falls apart."

"What do you mean?" I asked.

Tara looked at me as if gauging whether or not to keep talking. Then she sat down on the edge of my bed and leaned her elbows on her knees.

"Okay, first? Last year I had the lead in the school musical. We were doing *Bye Bye Birdie* and I was Rosie, and they *never* give a lead to a junior," she said. "And then, the day before opening night, I get laryngitis. I just lose my voice completely. And I have to sit there for three straight nights, drinking lemon tea while Connie Christiansen, the überbitch of the century, plays the part. Badly, by the way."

"Well, that sucks. But those things happen, right?"

"I'm just getting started!" Tara said, her eyes wide. "*Then,* at the beginning of this year I'm all psyched for select choir."

"You sing?" I asked.

"Hello? I just said I was the lead in the musical!"

"Right. Sorry. My bad."

"So I'm all psyched for select choir. I mean, I've been looking forward to it for *three years.* And when I get my schedule, I'm in concert choir. That's the choir where they throw all the shower singers and tone-deaf freaks," she said.

"Yeah. I'm in that choir," I said.

"Oh. Sorry."

I wasn't sure if she was sorry for insulting me or sorry *for* me because I was stuck in concert choir, but I didn't ask. She was on a roll.

"So I go to Mr. Crouch, the head of the music department, and he says I did get into select, but it doesn't fit in my schedule. It turns out that no matter how they rearrange my classes, they just cannot fit me into sixth-period choir unless I want to drop calc or A.P. English, and I can't do either if I want to go to any kind of decent college. So you wanna know what elective I'm in? Home ec! My first exam was baking brownies—from a mix!"

"That kind of sounds like fun," I said.

"Yeah. If you're brain-dead," Tara told me. "And then! *Then* we finally have a squad that has a shot of beating West Wind at regionals and Kristen and Danielle go and get themselves booted. I mean, what did I do to offend the gods!?" She flopped back on my bed and stared up at the ceiling. "It's my senior year. All I want is for one thing to go right. Just one. Is that so wrong?"

Damn. I had no idea Tara was born under such an unlucky star. Suddenly I could see why winning was so important to—

Wait a minute.

"Did you just say Danielle and Kristen got *themselves* booted?" I asked, my spirits rising.

"Those two boozers were bound to get snagged eventually."

Eureka! I was absolved! "Do you think you could, like, put that in writing and . . . I don't know . . . post it on the bulletin board in the main hallway?"

"Maybe we should just get back to work," Tara said, standing up. "We're screwed if you don't pass geometry anyway, right?"

She pulled my book out from under my nose and opened it up in front of her. "All right, Gobrowski, it's quiz time," she said.

I didn't bother pointing out that she'd just pronounced my name right for the first time ever, but I think we both knew we'd just made some sort of breakthrough. The question was whether or not it was going to hold up. Especially in public, where everyone basically expected me to be her whipping boy.

We were just gonna have to wait and see.

• • •

On Tuesday afternoon, Mindy was waiting for me outside of geometry class. I had that sort of before-the-dentist's-office dread in the pit of my stomach.

"You ready for this?" she asked.

"Who knows?" I replied. "The good news is, my mom convinced my dad to let me go to practice for the rest of the week, so if Loreng takes a while to grade the tests, I'll get to go to regionals no matter what."

"He's gonna grade 'em tonight," Sage said as she passed us by. "He always does."

"I think we should start calling *her* Buzzkill," I told Mindy.

Laughing, Mindy followed Sage into class. Before I could join her, I felt a hand on my back.

"Kick ass, Jersey," Daniel said, his lips practically touching my ear.

Major tingle waves, people. Major.

"I just hope I'm ready," I said. I had told Daniel all about my parents' geometry ultimatum on the way to school that morning.

"You are," he said confidently. "Want some added incentive?"

"What, not having to quit cheerleading isn't enough for you?" I said.

"Forget that. How about if we both pass, we go out and do something crazy Friday night? Something we've never done before," he asked, his eyes sparkling.

Omigod. Was he asking me out on a date? It *felt* like he was asking me out on a date. But it was contingent upon me passing geometry? Talk about pressure! How was I even going to concentrate now?

"Actually, I kind of have to hang with the squad Friday night," I said. "It's a night-before-regionals bonding thing."

"Okay. How about Thursday, then?" Daniel asked. "Is it a deal?"

I smiled slowly, equations and formulas scrolling through my head. I was *so* going to pass this thing. I *had* to.

"It's a deal."

• • •

That afternoon, nothing could flush my good mood. Not even going through the routine for regionals five hundred gazillion times. I was hyper and happy and felt free as I could be. I had worked my butt off for the past two days and had caught up in all my classes. Not only that, but the geometry test had gone well. I could feel it. And if all went according to plan, this Thursday I would be on a date with Daniel and Saturday I'd be at my first cheerleading competition.

"All right, ladies! One more time, then we'll call it a day," Coach Holmes said.

Sweat poured down my face as I got into position. Next to me, Chandra and Autumn were locked in an icy silence. Phoebe was on the other side of the formation, looking like she was about to pass out. Sage had stepped on me at least four times. But at the moment I didn't care. I just wanted to put whatever energy I had left into this last run-through.

Coach Holmes started the music on the portable stereo and we all jumped into action. The routine is only three minutes long, but it is a *loooong* three minutes. In that time I get tossed twice and go up three other times. In between all the climbing and flying there are twelve formation changes, a billion eight counts of high-energy dance moves and one back handspring, back tuck. By the time I went up in my last stunt, a scale, the room was spinning around me.

I came down and threw my arms up to hit the last beat, then lost my balance and tripped sideways a few steps. Oops. Leave it to me to fall over when I'm standing on solid ground.

I flattened my feet again and smiled. The three stunts that were up at the end came down and we all looked at Coach Holmes and waited. I gotta say, she didn't look too pleased.

"Good job, ladies," she said finally. "Definite improvement. Let's hit the showers."

She walked out and everyone collapsed to the mats with a general groan.

"I'm so tired, I can't even remember my name," Felice said to the ceiling.

Erin fought for breath. "I think I'm actually dying over here."

Karianna reached a hand over and dragged her bag toward her by the handle. Without ever picking up her head, she fished through it until she came out with a Gatorade and handed it to Erin, whose head was on her thigh.

"I love you," Erin said.

"You guys, we need to talk about some things," Tara said suddenly.

More groaning. I turned my head and saw her struggling onto her elbows. "I'm totally serious. We can't avoid it any longer. Coach Holmes didn't say it, but I could tell by her face. We're not there yet."

"Yes, we are," Whitney said.

"No. We're not," Tara said. "We're better, but no way are we ready to compete."

"Well, what do you suggest we do about it, oh, Captain, my Captain?" Chandra said sarcastically. "The competition is three days away."

"You don't have to attack her," Autumn said.

"Was I talking to you?" Chandra said.

"This is exactly what I'm talking about!" Tara exclaimed, pushing herself up farther. "We're all biting each other's heads off all the time. Maybe we can hit all our moves and all our stunts. Maybe we can even fake smiles. But if our hearts aren't in it, it's going to show. The judges . . . they're going to know."

"So, like, what're we supposed to do?" Jaimee asked. "We already tried the whole kumbaya thing and, hello? It only got us jailed."

My chest tightened. That stupid prank war. I'd thought it would be something we could all come together over, and it had ended up just splitting us up more. Autumn and Chandra had started fighting during one of the pranks, Sage had met Gabe and started that whole ball of fun rolling, everyone got angrier at Phoebe for not participating, and now we were all in various stages of groundings. Not my finest hour.

"I don't know," Tara said, her voice as heavy as my heart. So much for the nothing-can-bring-me-down giddies. "I don't know what we're supposed to do."

• • •

The next day, things got even worse. Phoebe didn't show up for school, didn't call anyone to say she was sick and didn't answer the phone once in the ten times Tara tried to call her. We had to practice without her, which was near impossible, and everyone was worried. What if Phoebe had really run away this time?

The only good thing that happened all day was something

that actually *didn't* happen. We didn't get our geometry tests back, which meant I was granted one more day's reprieve from having to deal with the consequences of whatever my grade was. Still, it didn't make the whole Phoebe thing any better.

As I walked out of practice that night, I overheard Tara on her cell phone. She was standing right by the door as we all walked out.

"Phoebe? Oh, good! You *are* there!" Tara looked over at the rest of us, relieved. "Yeah. . . . Yeah. . . . No. . . . Okay. Okay, I'll talk to you tomorrow. Okay, bye."

She clicked the phone shut and walked over to the waiting crowd. "She's okay," she said. "She just said she didn't want to talk. But she's going to be in school tomorrow."

Everyone else seemed to take this as good news and headed off for their cars. Whitney and I hung back, however. Tara looked a little shaky. Like Phoebe hadn't been all that convincing.

"She sounded awful," Tara said, shoving her hands through her hair. "I don't know what to do, you guys. Maybe we should just bag the competition."

"What?" Whitney said. "No! No way! We've worked too hard on this."

"Yeah, and it's gotten us nowhere," Tara said, throwing her hands up. "No one is listening to me, we were like the cheering dead in there tonight, we only have two more days of practice, and who knows if Phoebe will even show?"

Whitney and I exchanged a look. When she put it that way, it did sound sort of like a hopeless cause. If only my whole bonding experiment had worked in the first place. Then we would all be bestest buds and Phoebe would be our one and only problem. But as it was, we would have to find a way to heal a half dozen rifts *and* usher the single most depressed person I've ever come across back into the Land of the Happy by this time tomorrow. Forget regionals, this squad was going to need some divine intervention just to stay together.

Tara tipped her head back. "I just wish I knew how to cheer Phoebe up. But she's been like this ever since she moved, and it's just getting worse."

A stab of guilt pierced my heart as I thought of my Room of Pink Shame, but it was followed by an epiphany so brilliant, I barely had time to register the negative. Suddenly my brain was flooded with what I can only call a vision. A vision of all of us working together. A vision of all of us laughing and having fun. A vision of the exactly perfect way to cheer Phoebe up *and* bring the squad together.

To borrow a cheesy but wildly appropriate phrase—it was so crazy, it just might work.

"You guys?" I said, looking from Tara to Whitney. "I think I have an idea."

That night, I found myself crouched in the bushes that lined the park across the street from Phoebe's aunt's house with Felice's backpack sticking into my side and Michelle breathing down my neck. The *Mission: Impossible* vibe of the prank war was back, but this time we were all in crappy T-shirts and shorts instead of black-on-black. We watched as my brother walked Phoebe to his rust-colored Jeep Liberty and opened the passenger-side door for her.

Wait a minute. He did *what?*

"That's your brother?" Karianna asked me.

"At the moment I'm not so sure," I said.

"He is hella fine," Jaimee put in.

"And a gentleman," Felice said.

"Watch it, ladies," Sage snapped. "He's taken."

I looked at Mindy and rolled my eyes. Mindy snickered and hid her mouth behind her hand.

"Then why is he going out with Phoebe right now?" Whitney asked.

"Because we *told* him to," Sage said, starting to fume.

Mindy and I both laughed. We couldn't help it. What did Sage think she and Gabe were, engaged?

"Okay! This is not why we're here!" Tara said, standing up as my brother's car disappeared around the corner. "I want no fighting tonight. Not even between siblings," she added, looking from Whitney to Sage. "We have a lot of work to do, so let's get to it."

We jogged noisily across the street, toting brown bags of supplies. The door opened before we even got there and a woman—who looked just like Phoebe would if she spent the next twenty years in the sun—answered the door.

"Hello, Tara! Girls!" she said, smiling even though her eyes looked sad. "It was so nice of you to offer to do this."

"Just point us in the right direction," I said.

"Phoebe's room is upstairs at the end of the hall," her mother told me as the rest of the squad filed in. "You're Annisa, right?"

"Yeah," I said, surprised.

"I'm Lorraine Cook," Phoebe's mom said with a smile. "Phoebe's told me a lot about you."

Tara and I exchanged a look as the rest of the squad tromped upstairs. I was just as shocked as Tara clearly was that Phoebe had mentioned me at all. But at this point, who knew what went on in that poor girl's head?

"It's nice to meet you," I said. "Thanks for letting us take over the house."

"Well, don't thank me, thank my sister. If she ever comes out of the kitchen. She's making brownies for you all," Mrs. Cook said. "Anyway, you shouldn't have too much trouble clearing out the bedroom. I'm afraid Phoebe hasn't actually unpacked much since we moved here."

When we got upstairs, the rest of the squad was already moving boxes and bags out into the hall. I stepped past Autumn into the small square room and grimaced. The walls were a dirt brown color and the drapes were dark green brocade. But that wasn't the worst of it. The worst of it was the suffocation factor.

"What is that smell?" I asked.

"It's grandma smell," Whitney said, hands on her hips. "Phoebe's mom's mom lived in this room for, like, *ever.*"

"Well, it is way past time to release her spirit," Autumn said. She walked right over to the windows and threw them open, then turned and ripped at the curtains. The curtain rod came down with a huge clatter, taking the big ugly hook it was on with it.

We all froze for a second, and then Autumn cracked up laughing and the rest of us joined her.

"Well," Tara said, slapping her hands together. "Let's do this."

• • •

An hour later, a boom box spun the latest Britney CD and Chandra, Karianna and Erin were dancing around, using paintbrushes as microphones. Autumn and Mindy sat just outside the room in the hallway, making up bowls of potpourri. Whitney held the ladder for Tara, who was using a roller to whiten the ceiling. Felice had taken the rest of the squad into the hall to go through Phoebe's boxes and find her curtains and some other homey things she'd yet to unpack. I was on my hands and aching knees, touching up the edge along the floor molding with paint. A wayward hair fell into my line of vision and I wiped it away, slashing pink paint across my forehead. Almost instantly a rag appeared in front of my face.

"Here."

I looked up, surprised to find that it was Sage offering the rag. "Thanks."

I leaned back on my shins and wiped the paint away.

"How do you *do* that?" Sage asked.

"Do what?" I asked warily, sensing an insult coming.

217

"That," she said, pointing at the floor where I had been working. "It's like a perfectly straight line. If I tried to do that, there would be pink paint blobs all over the wooden stripy part."

"That's molding," I said with a laugh.

"Okay, *molding*. Whatever, *Trading Spaces*," she said. "How do you do that?"

"I don't know," I said. "I guess . . . I've moved a lot of times, so I've painted a lot of rooms. I guess I picked up a few skills along the way."

"You've moved a lot?" Tara asked, coming down from the ladder.

"Yeah. This is the sixth town I've lived in," I said.

Whitney whistled low and long. "Damn. I've never been outta Sand Dune."

"God. That must suck," Sage said to me.

"Not always," I told them with a shrug. "Sometimes it's cool, you know, getting to start over."

"Yeah, except when everyone you meet is a bitch to you," Whitney said. Was it just me, or was she looking pointedly at Sage? And then at Tara?

"What? I'm not *that* bad!" Tara said.

Everyone in hearing distance laughed. I turned bright red and stood up, my knees cracking along the way.

"All right, all right!" Tara said, raising her hands in surrender. "Okay, I am that bad." She looked at me and took a deep breath. "Look, I'm sorry, okay?" she said. "I'm sorry I was such a bitch when you first got here."

And every moment since then? I thought. But I said, "Thanks."

"I'm sorry too," Sage said.

Okay, that nearly knocked me off my feet.

218

"What? I *am*," Sage said indignantly when she saw my dumbfounded expression. She crossed her arms over her stomach and shifted her weight from one foot to the other. "It was just . . . when you first got here, Daniel would not stop talking about you and . . . well . . . it was *really* annoying."

Daniel couldn't stop talking about me? What? Huh? Details! I needed details! But wait a second. Yeah. That had to have sucked for his girlfriend. I suddenly felt kind of sorry for Sage on a girl-solidarity level.

"But Daniel and me . . . we aren't together anymore and . . . we have to be teammates, so . . . for what it's worth . . . I'm sorry. Especially for the whole paint thing," Sage said.

I looked at the floor and bit my bottom lip. I had expected us to bond, but this Dr. Phil moment was a little more than I'd bargained for.

"It's okay, you guys," I said finally, tilting my head. "I . . . uh . . . thanks."

Sage and Tara both smiled and there was an awkward silence broken only by the irritating overproduced sound of bad pop music. I was wondering if any of us were ever going to speak again when Chandra dropped her brush and walked over to the doorway.

"Autumn, I'm sorry I said your thighs were fat."

"It's okay," Autumn said, scrambling to her feet to hug Chandra.

There was a beat of silence, and then Whitney let out a laugh through her nose and everyone cracked up.

"*That's* what you were fighting about?" Tara demanded between gasps. "That's what you've been driving us all crazy over?"

"What?" Autumn said, releasing Chandra. "It wasn't about the comment itself, it was the spirit in which it was said!"

This just made us all laugh harder. We could hear the other girls rolling around in the hallways, and tears streamed down my face. By the time I caught my breath again, my stomach hurt like I'd done a thousand crunches followed by a Pilates chaser.

But even more acute than the muscle pain was the realization that everything was going to be fine. If Sage and Tara and I could make up, and Autumn and Chandra could get past their thigh problem, there was hope for us yet.

• • •

"They're gonna be here in five minutes!" I hissed as we all rushed around the room. "Come on, you guys! Where's the curtains?"

Felice and Lindsey rushed in with one set of white eyelet curtains; Maureen and Michelle brought the others. Felice used the step stool to hang one set while Michelle climbed on the bed and hooked the others into place. Tara and Whitney bunched up the plastic tarps and shoved them into green garbage bags while Autumn and Erin placed bowls of potpourri around the room. We'd already sprayed the place with air freshener to cover up the paint smell, which had eradicated all traces of mothballs and peppermint hours ago.

"They're here!" Mindy whispered, jumping away from the window. I heard the car engine dying outside, the sound of a car door slam.

"Oh, God! The ladder!" Sage cried. We grabbed for it and folded it up together, narrowly missing smooshing my fingers in the process.

"It looks great, you guys," Whitney said. "Let's go! Across the hall!"

We rushed into Phoebe's aunt's room with the ladder and the garbage bags, our hearts pounding. Tara turned off the light and we all stood there, fifteen of us in a huddle, fighting to catch our breath. I heard Phoebe's footsteps on the stairs, then in the hall. I looked at Mindy and we were both grinning. A glance around the twilit room showed me we *all* were.

The door across the hall creaked. I held my breath.

"Oh my God! What the—"

Tara opened the door in front of us and we all came out into the hallway behind Phoebe.

"Surprise!"

Phoebe screamed her head off, turned around and saw us, and burst into tears. But this time, they were good tears. She was smiling as she grabbed Tara up into a crazy-tight hug.

"You guys did this?" she asked, looking around at all of us. "You did this?"

"Yep. We did," Whitney said. "What do you think?"

"I think . . . I think it's amazing," Phoebe said, stepping into her Barbie-pink room. The curtains fluttered in the breeze, kicking up a little of the rose-scented potpourri. "It's exactly the right color. Exactly."

"We took a hunk out of Annisa's wall," Erin said. "The guy at the store matched it."

"Thank you, guys," Phoebe said, turning to hug Erin, then me. "Thank you so much."

As Phoebe went around hugging everyone and we all laughed and beamed and chatted, I realized that this was one of those moments I was going to remember for the rest of my life. It didn't even matter how we did at regionals on Saturday, because at that moment we weren't just a squad. We were friends. Real friends.

Tara found her way over to me in all the mayhem and

knocked my elbow with her own. "You know what, Go-browski?" she said under her breath. "You might not make a bad captain one day."

My grin widened. "Yeah?"

"Yeah," she said. "But only after I'm long, *long* gone."

"You should've seen her face, Gabe. It was classic," I said as we walked into the house that night. "Thank you so much for going out with her."

"It was no problem, trust me," Gabe said, pocketing his keys. "Phoebe is a down girl."

"Oooh. Do I sense some competition for Sage?" I asked, pausing at the bottom of the stairs.

"Shyah. Not on your life. I think I'm done with high school girls," Gabe said. "For now, anyway." He sighed and checked his watch. "I better get back to school. I have an early class. See ya, kid."

"Later," I said.

"Hold it!"

My father's voice sent a chill down my spine. He stepped into the foyer from the kitchen, causing both Gabe and me to freeze in our tracks. You could have heard the collective gulp in the next county.

"I just had a very interesting phone call about you two," my father said, jingling the change in his pocket.

Gabe and I looked at each other, blank but dreading. What had we done now? My father paused between us, prolonging the agony as he cleared his throat and ran his hand over his hair.

"Apparently someone by the name of Lorraine Cook

thinks my children are blessings from heaven," my father said, looking at us with mock suspicion. "What did you two do tonight?"

Gabe cracked a grin and lifted his chin toward me. "I'll let Annisa tell you," he said. "I gotta go start making good on your investment in my future."

"Uh-huh," my dad said as Gabe closed the door. His eyes slid over toward me and he smiled. "I talked to Captain Longo as well. He told me that he's reviewed the officers' statements from the other night and it appears that when they drove up to West Wind High, you and two other kids were leaving the premises."

"I told you!" I said, elated. "As soon as I found out what we were doing there, I—"

"I know, I know," my father said, leaning into the banister. "So based on both these phone calls, your mother and I have decided not to keep you from cheering."

"Yes!" I cheered. I hugged him over the banister and jumped up and down.

"Provided you passed that geometry exam," my father said.

He tried to look all stern, but it didn't work. I could tell he was proud of me over the call from Mrs. Cook. And I could tell he was a little chagrined over the call from Captain Longo. He hadn't entirely believed in my innocence until an authority figure had backed me up, and he felt badly about it. I probably should have been all indignant and tried to milk his guilt, but I was in too good a mood. And it felt kind of good that he cared enough to feel bad.

"Don't worry about the test," I said. "I had good tutoring."

"Good," my father said. He reached out and ruffled my hair. "I love you, kiddo."

"I know," I said, my heart swelling a little. How many good moments could one girl take in a single night? "I love you too."

• • •

Thursday after school, I ran straight to the gym and sprinted over to Tara, who was deep in discussions with Coach Holmes. She saw me coming at the last second and stepped back, but nothing could stop me from barreling right into her side and giving her a huge bear hug.

"I got a ninety!" I exclaimed. "A ninety!"

"Okay, back up," Tara said, extricating herself from my grip. "What are you on?"

"A geometry high," I said. I whipped the folded test out of the back pocket of my jeans and unfolded it, holding it up for both of them to see. The red 90 was visible even through the back of the page.

"Oh . . . my . . . God. I don't believe it," Tara said, taking the test from me. She looked down at the page, slack-jawed. "I am a genius!"

"Apparently you are, 'cause I couldn't have done it without you," I said. "So thanks."

"You're welcome," Tara said. She beamed with satisfaction as she handed the test back to me.

"So, I assume this means you're competing?" Coach Holmes asked.

"I am all yours," I told her, extending my arms.

"Good. Now get your butt changed. Let's get cracking."

• • •

During the final run-through of the routine that afternoon, I knew. I knew like you know for sure that a guy likes you, or that you're kicking butt during an oral exam, or that you're gonna hit the high note that you've never hit before.

225

We . . . were . . . *on!*

When I went up in my second basket toss, I caught so much air, I thought I was never coming down. Coach Holmes clenched her fist and shouted a "Yes!" as I was caught. My grin widened and I slammed into my next move. Our clasps were in perfect unison, the back tucks all stuck at exactly the right beat. I popped up into position for that last scale, then fell back into Chandra and Autumn's arms. The next and last pyramid went up flawlessly. I took my position up front as Sage, Phoebe and Kimberly towered behind me. The music came to its crashing crescendo and we were all perfectly in place. Coach Holmes went wild!

"Yes! Yes! Yes!" she shouted as we all came down, grinning from ear to ear.

I flew into Mindy's arms and hugged Felice and Phoebe. We all jumped up and down, somehow finding our way into a huge huddle in the middle of the gym—one big mass of laughing, sweaty, giddy girls.

"We are so there!" Tara shouted through all the glee. "We are so *there!*"

• • •

"Eyeliner in place . . . all hair curled under . . . no panty line to speak of. . . ." I turned and double-checked my backside in the full-length mirror. One could never be too careful about panty lines. "I think I'm ready," I said to myself, relishing the mixture of nerves and excitement on my face.

My first date with Daniel. The moment I'd been waiting for since the second I'd met him. It was actually going to happen. The doorbell rang and my pulse rushed forward. I grabbed my purse and ran downstairs so I could get to the door before my parents did.

"Whoa! Slow down! You can't compete with a broken leg!" my dad said as I blew by him and Mom.

"Be cool!" I warned them, hand on the doorknob.

"Are we ever anything else?" my mom asked.

I rolled my eyes at her, but smiled, and opened the door.

Daniel had a single white lily. He was wearing a blue short-sleeved button-down and khaki shorts and had some kind of product in his hair. This was definitely a real date.

"Hey," he said. "You look . . . wow."

Chalk one up for the little black dress. "Thanks! You too!"

"Here," he said, holding out the lily. "For you."

"Thanks," I replied, grinning. This was when the parentals decided to make their presence known. They stepped out from behind the door and Daniel's eyes widened.

"Hello, Daniel," my mother said. I could immediately tell she approved.

"Mr. and Mrs. Gobrowski! Nice to meet you," he said.

"You're the young man who gave my daughter his jacket to use as a pillow in the slammer?" my father said.

"Dad!"

"Uh . . . yeah. That was me," Daniel said.

"Well, that was very thoughtful of you," my father said. "I trust neither one of you will be needing a prison pillow this evening?"

"Dad!"

"No, sir," Daniel said. "And we'll be back before curfew."

"Yes, you will."

"Okay! We're going now!" I said. I handed my mom the flower and headed for Daniel's car, only hoping he'd follow before my father could utter another word.

"Bye!" Daniel shouted over his shoulder.

I was already buckling my seat belt when he got in. "So, where're we going?" I asked, the butterflies in my chest having a field day.

"Well, I promised something crazy, so I'm taking you to the craziest place in Sand Dune," he said with that heart-stopping grin. "You ready?"

I grinned back. "You have no idea."

• • •

My eyes were trained on the back of Daniel's head as I slammed my foot on the gas and cut the wheel as hard as I could. The wind stung my eyes and whipped my hair around. My skirt was riding up to precarious points. But I couldn't stop. I had to catch him. It was do or die.

"Hey, Healy!" I shouted out as my go-cart roared up alongside his. "Eat my dust!"

I pressed the pedal all the way to the floor and cut him off on the sharpest turn. For a split second my stomach veered the wrong way and I had a vision of my little park-mobile flipping over and bursting into flames. But I made the turn and hit the finish line yards ahead of my date.

Nothing like a little healthy competition to get the night started right.

Daniel hopped out of his go-cart and stepped up next to mine. "Remind me never to get in a car with you," he said.

"Hey. That's how we drive in Jersey," I said, struggling for a way to get out of the car without exposing my nether regions. Daniel finally offered me both his hands and pulled me up. My foot caught on the side of the go-cart and I fell sideways into him.

Daniel looked down at me. My whole body was pressed into his. And it was *strong*, solid, totally shiver-inducing. What did I expect from a guy who did footballwrestlingandtrack?

"You all right?" Daniel asked with a grin. He tucked some wayward hair behind my ear.

Oh, God. He was going to kiss me. He was going to kiss

me right there on the motor speedway at Cartelli's Family Amusement Park. I hadn't been kissed since the eighth grade when Ronnie Wagner had coaxed me into the basement at his best friend Gareth's birthday party. Did I even remember how to do it?

"Come on," he said, reaching for my hand. "Mini-golf is next. I'll kick your butt at mini-golf."

So much for that.

I relished the warmth of Daniel's hand around mine as we headed for the elaborate, twisty pathways of the mini-golf course. A couple of kids screamed as they chased by us, clutching helium balloons. I laughed and looked up at Daniel.

"How is this the craziest thing we've ever done?" I asked, grabbing a putter.

"Well, it's not crazy for me. I've been here about a thousand times," Daniel said. "But it's the craziest thing Sand Dune has to offer, so this whole thing's for you."

"Well, that's not fair," I said as I dropped my yellow ball on the first putting green. "We were both supposed to get to do something crazy. What about you?"

"My crazy thing comes later," he said with a mischievous grin.

"Oooh. Intriguing," I said. "Naked bungee jumping? Midnight parasailing? Oooh! Are you gonna eat one of those Domino's Philly Cheesesteak Pizzas?"

Daniel looked at me, amused. "You have one weird brain in there," he said.

I smiled and whacked my ball right into a water trap. "I get that a lot."

• • •

"There's one more thing I want to do," Daniel said as he pulled his car into my driveway that night. After go-carts, bumper cars, two rounds of mini-golf, batting cages and a banana split the size of my house, what was left to do? Unless . . .

He killed the engine and I could barely breathe. Was he going to kiss me now? I had thought he was going to do it on the speedway, then I'd thought he was going to do it after his first hole-in-one, then I'd thought he was going to do it over ice cream when he'd practically arm-wrestled me for the cherry.

But now. Now *definitely* seemed like the moment.

Okay, don't panic. Your lips will know what to do. Just like riding a bike. He smiled at me and the air in the car grew insanely warm. My eyes started to flutter closed, I did a mental check of my breath . . . and then the car door opened.

I blinked in surprise. What was going on?

The door let out that bong, bong, bong sound as Daniel popped the front seat forward and reached into the back to pull out . . . his guitar! This was it! He was finally going to play for me! This was even better than a kiss. Well, almost.

"Come on," he said mischievously. He yanked his keys from the ignition and slammed the door. I scrambled out after him and followed him to the backyard.

"Where're we going?" I asked.

"I need someplace to sit," he replied.

I glanced up at my parents' bedroom window as I walked over to turn the pool light on. The window was totally dark. Thank goodness. If Daniel was going to play right here and now, the last thing I needed was Mom and Dad walking in on the moment.

"Okay," Daniel said, sitting down sideways on a lounge chair. He placed his guitar on his knees and blew out a breath. "This is actually my something crazy," he said. "Remember I told you I've never played for anyone before?"

"Yeah," I said, smoothing my dress down under me as I sat.

"Well, besides Mr. Harrison, the guitar teacher at school," he said. "But anyway, you're gonna be my first."

"I'm taking your guitar virginity!" I said. Then wanted to die.

But Daniel laughed. "Something like that. Anyway, I want to try out for the jazz ensemble this winter and I'm kind of freaking out about it."

"Jazz ensemble?" I asked.

"It's, like, this cool ten-piece band the school has," Daniel explained. "They need a new guitarist, so . . ."

Suddenly something clicked into place. "That's why you're not doing wrestling!"

"Yeah . . . wow." Daniel looked mildly disturbed. "How did you remember that?"

I pointed at my temple. "Steel trap," I said. At least it was when it came to random factoids about guys I liked. But he didn't need to know that.

"Well, anyway, you're about to tell me whether or not I should bother risking the wrath of my father and trying out," Daniel said, adjusting one of the strings.

"He wants you to wrestle?" I asked.

"Oh, yeah," Daniel replied. "And he can be pretty psycho about these things, so I'm only doing this if you say I'm really good. No pressure or anything."

I laughed. "No. None at all."

"Okay," Daniel said. He cleared his throat. "Here goes."

Daniel started to play and I was . . . mesmerized. I

231

watched his fingers plucking at the strings, let the notes slip over me like a silky sheet. I didn't recognize the piece, but it was slow and intricate and really, really sad. Daniel shook his head back and forth slightly as he played. He closed his eyes like the music was just taking him over. At the crescendo I actually shivered. It was like the chords were coming from inside of *me*.

This boy could not possibly be any more perfect. For the first time ever, I felt like I really might be falling in love. This had to be what it felt like.

And then he stopped and there was nothing but silence. A breeze rustled the palms above our heads.

"Well?" he said hopefully. "What do you think?"

At that moment I stopped wondering about whether we were ever going to kiss. I leaned forward, knocking our knees together, and kissed him myself, right on the lips.

For a split second he didn't move. He didn't respond in any way. And for a split second I thought I was going to have to kill myself right there.

But then, he slid the guitar away and cupped my face in his hands. It was such a sweet and tender thing to do, it sent everything inside of me racing. He was kissing me back! Daniel was kissing me back!

When we finally broke apart, I was all flushed and my eyelids felt so heavy, they didn't want to open. Daniel's were droopy too, and he looked a little dazed. Like he didn't understand what was happening. But then he broke into a slow, wide grin.

"A girl who makes the first move," he said. "I like it."

I giggled and tried to stop my hands from shaking. I couldn't believe I'd just done that.

"But I get to make the second," he said.

Then, before I knew what was happening, Daniel had pulled me into his lap and was kissing me like I'd never been kissed before.

It was another movie moment. But this one lasted a good forty-five minutes. All PG-rated, of course.

We took a big yellow bus to the competition. A big yellow bus with a caravan of about thirty cars behind it. Parents, students, teachers—all with their cars covered in blue and yellow paint or trailing blue and yellow balloons and streamers—followed us from the Sand Dune High parking lot all the way to Clearwater High, where the competition was being held. I had never seen anything like it.

"This is insane," I said, looking out the window as we made a turn so I could see the trail of cars, my parents' and Gabe's included.

"People take their cheerleading very seriously around here," Whitney shouted.

She had to shout to be heard. The bus was *loud*. Sixteen hyped-up cheerleaders and their coach laughing, gabbing, pretending they weren't scared to death? That translates into deafening. You'd think that after spending half the night gossiping, baking cookies and dancing together in Chandra's living room, we would be totally out of steam, but we weren't. I was more hyped-up than I'd ever been. All morning, I had felt first-day-of-school jitters compounded about twenty times. And also I really had to pee, like, every second. Somehow, shouting and laughing at the top of my lungs made it all feel better. I supposed everyone else was working the same remedy.

I reached into my bag and toyed with Jordan's lucky pen. It had arrived via UPS that morning and I had cried when I opened the package. It was the pen Derek Jeter had signed a baseball with for her two summers ago at Yankee Stadium, and it had been her lucky charm ever since. (Jordan worshipped Derek in a seriously unhealthy way. Like a borderline-stalker way.) So basically it was a big deal that she had let it out of her sight—that she had dared trust it to the United Parcel Service. I wished she was there in person, but having the Derek Jeter pen meant a lot.

We arrived at Clearwater, a one-story structure with a huge WELCOME CHEERLEADERS banner draped across the front door, and clambered out of the bus. A crowd of girls in yellow-and-black warm-up suits, their hair crimped and slicked back into ponytails, rushed inside ahead of us. The second we were through the door, we were assaulted by the spirit cheer from all directions.

"We got spirit, yes we do! We got spirit, how 'bout you!?"

My whole squad instantly took the cheer up without even blinking. Thank God I was toward the back. I was too dumbstruck to process anything that quickly.

"We got spirit, yes we do! We got spirit, how 'bout you!?"

The entire Sand Dune squad, minus me, pointed at the crimped bumblebee girls. Once they did their round, everyone applauded and we were able to move on.

The school lobby was awash with color. A squad of girls in black and green huddled in the corner while their captain gave instructions, her tone intense. As we passed by a hallway, I saw a couple of girls practicing a stunt and nearly taking the climber's head off because the ceiling was too low. Something slammed into my shoulder as a pack of red-and-white girls jogged by me and crowded into the bathroom. No one bothered to apologize, but I didn't blame them. There was too much adrenaline bounding around to think straight.

"How many teams are in this thing, anyway?" I asked, pressing my damp palms into my skirt.

"Twelve in our division. Plus Clearwater will probably do an exhibition performance," Coach Holmes said.

"The hosting team doesn't compete," Phoebe explained.

"Twelve?" I said, my throat going dry. "Isn't that kind of a lot?"

"Don't think about that now," Tara said, grabbing my arm. "We have more important issues to deal with."

"Like what?" I asked.

"Like your hair," Chandra told me.

I knew this was coming. Everyone else on the squad had their blonde tresses pulled back in French braids and tied off with the same blue, yellow and white bow. Everyone except Whitney, who had managed to secure her choppy 'do back with what looked like a year's supply of hairspray and more bobby pins than I knew existed on Earth. Uniformity definitely mattered.

"Okay, let's do this," Tara said, pulling me into a corner with Chandra and Whitney.

"Let's do what, exactly?" I asked as Chandra crouched to the ground and yanked open a duffel bag. "Please tell me you don't have Herbal Essences Amazon Gold in there."

"I wish," Tara said.

"Don't move and this will be painless," Whitney told me.

She lied. First they emptied about half a can of aerosol spray into my hair (good-bye, ozone layer!). My forehead took such a dousing I knew I'd be unclogging my pores until the end of time. Then Whitney smoothed my hair back behind my ears and started shoving bobby pins in along the base of my skull.

"Um . . . ow!" I said.

"Be a woman," Tara said testily.

Chandra clenched one of the SDH bows in her teeth and examined the back of my head. "She's got a little length back here," she said, pulling at my hair so hard, my head snapped back. "I'll see what I can do."

Ten minutes of prodding, yanking and griping later, and I had a My Little Pony–sized ponytail sticking out the back of my head, secured with the approved SDH cheerleader ribbon. My scalp burned and my temples throbbed. Everything felt so tight, I was sure my eyes were pulled into slits.

Tara, Whitney and Chandra stepped back to check their work.

"Not bad," Whitney said with a nod.

"She looks the same from the front," Chandra said. "Well . . . almost."

"You know," Tara said, scrutinizing me. "You really should think about dyeing your hair."

Whitney cracked up laughing and pulled Tara away, protesting. "What? It's just a suggestion!"

"This place is insane!" Mindy said, appearing through the crowd with Sage and Autumn in tow. "I've never seen so much eyeliner in my life."

"What did they do to you?" Sage asked, snorting a laugh.

"They tried to make me one of you," I said.

"Valiant effort," Sage replied.

I wasn't sure if that was a dig, but I let it slide. Our truce was delicate enough as it was and now was not the time to test its strength. I would not be responsible for another pyramid takedown.

"Oh, Goddess," Autumn said. "Look who's here."

My heart thumped hard. The West Wind High cheerleaders, in all their green-and-white glory, filed through the front doors. Their hair was curled up into high ponytails atop their heads and they were all wearing green glitter eye shadow that made them look like Halloween witches. They didn't even wait for the spirit cheer to hit them. They fired the first shot.

"We got spirit, yes we do! We got spirit, how 'bout you!?"

I was so glad they didn't point at us. Our squad was all over the place just then and the four of us trying to answer would have been pathetic. The girls in red and white answered the cheer, and then the West Wind squad moved through the lobby, right toward us. My pulse pounded in my ears. It was like I was ready for a rumble.

They almost walked right by, but then a particularly tall, powerful-looking girl saw us huddled there and paused.

"Hey! Look who it is!" she said with a smile. "I hope you have the timing of your routine down right. Wouldn't want the clock to run out on ya."

Her squad laughed and a couple of them slapped hands.

"Look! It's the AA girl," another West Winder chimed in, looking at Sage with glee. "Did you bring your flask?"

I felt my face burn in sympathy for Sage. I was about to say something when Sage stepped up between me and Mindy and crossed her arms over her chest. Her face was all attitude.

"Well, at least *I* have to be *drunk* to suck," she said with a little tilt of her head.

A burst of a laugh escaped from my lips. A couple of our rivals' mouths dropped open, but no one said a word. It was classic. So *that* was what Mindy was talking about. Sage on your side *was* good!

"Come on, ladies," Sage said.

We all followed her toward the gym where the rest of the

squad was gathering, leaving the West Wind High Dolphins behind to stew over their lack of a comeback.

• • •

"This school is totally substandard," a black-and-gold cheerleader said to her squad as we all gathered outside the gym to wait our turn. "They don't even have a staging area."

"This competition should've never been allowed to happen here," someone replied.

I looked at Phoebe. "Um, what's a staging area?" I asked.

"Like an extra gym or something where we would all wait to go on," Phoebe said. "You don't usually have to stand in a lobby like this."

"We have a practice gym, but it's kind of condemned at the moment?" a girl in dark blue and white said to us. "*Some* other school thought it would be fun to let off about fifty stink bombs in there." She rolled her eyes in the direction of the black-and-gold cheerleaders.

"Prank war?" I said, catching on.

"Oh, yeah," one of her friends replied.

"Trust me, we feel your pain," I said.

Spectators were still streaming in through the front door, and I looked past the girl's shoulder, stunned. I was not really seeing Bethany Goow right then, was I?

"Bethany!" I shouted, louder than was strictly necessary.

She took one look at me and her face clenched like she was sucking one of those Listerine Strips.

"What'd they do to you?" she asked, turning me around to see my pathetic pony.

"Forget that. What the hell are you doing here?" I asked.

"Well, if I'm gonna be a good friend, I figured I had to at least *try* to understand this cult of yours," she said. Then she leaned in and lowered her voice. "Besides, the better I know their tactics, the easier it'll be for me to extricate you when things get dicey."

I laughed and hugged her. "Thanks for coming."

"No prob," she said, actually blushing a bit. "Somebody has to heckle the other squads, right?" She smiled and walked into the gym, looking the West Wind cheerleaders up and down as she went. "What're you guys supposed to be, leprechauns?"

I was still laughing when I felt a tap on my shoulder. I turned around to find Daniel standing there with a smile. But before I could say anything, Sage flew in out of nowhere.

"Danny! I'm *so* glad you came!" she said, hugging him. "I wasn't even sure I could go on without you here."

Daniel looked at me over her shoulder and raised his eyebrows. "Yeah," he said when Sage released him. "Break a leg."

He knocked her on the arm, then leaned down and gave me a lingering kiss on the lips. My knees almost went out from under me. What was I going to do out there without my knees?

"Remember the lessons of the pogo ball," he said quietly.

Then he swept by me into the gym, leaving me hovering about ten feet off the ground.

"Did I just see what I think I just saw?" Sage asked, stunned.

I blinked as I came back down to earth. Sage was visibly paling. I took an instinctive step back, just in case her head decided to actually explode.

"You win some, you lose some," Whitney said, hooking her arm around her sister and leading her away before she could scratch my eyes out. "The only thing you can do now, little sis, is take it out on your performance. . . ."

Whitney turned and winked at me as she walked off and I relaxed against the wall, still feeling the tingle of Daniel's kiss on my lips.

• • •

This was it. We had picked the tenth spot in the lineup. Clearwater High was just finishing up their routine in ninth. We were on deck. It was time. I could barely catch my breath.

"Okay, girls, you can do this," Coach Holmes said, standing between Tara and Whitney in the huddle. "*Stick* those landings, *hit* your moves and, for God's sake, let's see the same enthusiasm out there that I got from you last night." She looked each of us in the eye as the roar of the crowd sounded from the gymnasium, indicating that Clearwater was done. "Now go out there, have fun, kick a little ass and make me proud."

"And now, from Sand Dune High School in Sand Dune, Florida," the announcer said inside, tripling my heart rate to dangerous levels. We all put our hands in the middle of the huddle, clasping them on top of one another. I, for some reason, looked Tara Timothy right in the eye. She smiled. "The mighty Sand Dune Fighting Crabs!"

"Whaddup, Sand Dune!" we all shouted. We flung our hands into the air, and burst through the doors into the gym.

Screams and cheers reverberated off the walls. Blue, white and yellow pom-poms shook throughout the crowd. I threw my arm in the air with a fist and cheered, expending some of my nervous energy as I took my opening position. I had already located my parents in the crowd earlier and I looked right at them and Gabe. My dad winked, my mom shot a picture, my brother pointed at his chest. His white T-shirt read THIS IS WHAT A CHEERLEADER LOOKS LIKE.

I laughed and bent at the waist, bowing my head and slapping my arms down at my sides. I, along with five of the other girls, opened with the back handspring back tuck. *If I stick this, everything will be fine,* I thought. *If I stick this, we're gold.*

The music started. This was it. It was actually happening. I flung myself into the tumble and the whole world went upside down. Seconds later, my feet came down in precise unison with the rest of the tumblers. My grin widened.

Game *on!*

Sage went up in her basket toss and caught so much air, I thought she would brain herself on a ceiling beam. I was too busy dancing to watch her come down, but the whole crowd burst into psychotic cheers, so I knew she'd done something spectacular. Thank you, Daniel. It looked like Sage *was* taking it out on her performance.

Everything was a blur. I hit my scorpion, came down, moved through the next sequence and was up again, spinning through my second basket toss. I grinned as the audience went wild. We were dominating. We had them in the palm of our hands.

I fell back from the last pyramid, walked around and hit my mark. The stunts were up behind me and no one was wavering. The music crashed to a stop and we were still up, still strong. The roar of the crowd was deafening.

"The mighty . . . fighting . . . Sand Dune Crabs!" the announcer shouted. You could tell in his voice that even *he* was impressed.

Everyone dismounted and we cheered and shouted as we ran off the mats. Mindy's arms crushed me as she hugged me out the door. We couldn't stop screaming and jumping up and down. We'd hit everything. We'd given our best performance yet. Phoebe was crying and so were Autumn and Maureen—a mess of eyeliner and mascara, but who cared? It was a moment to remember.

"Yes! Yes! Yes!" Coach Holmes shouted, walking over and slapping our hands. "That's what I'm talking about!"

We all laughed and turned our attention to her as the next squad was announced.

"You really did it, ladies," she said. "I don't know how, but you really did it. Win or lose, you all came together, and I've never been so proud of a squad in my life."

Whitney wrapped her arm around my shoulder and hugged me toward her. Mindy was still clasping my hand. I thought my face would break from all the smiling.

Coach was right. We'd done it. This squad had survived losing two members, last-minute tryouts, the fighting, the pressure of learning the whole routine and getting it together in just a few short weeks. We'd survived it all . . . and we were only stronger for it.

• • •

But I'll be honest here, we wanted to win. We wanted to win so badly that I think we could all feel the trophy in our hands. As we stood along the back wall of the gym half an hour later, flanked by the other squads, everyone was salivating for that towering first-place prize.

Mindy clasped one of my hands, Whitney the other. I couldn't tell whose fingers were whose anymore and there was no circulation left, but who cared? All I could do was stare across the gym at West Wind. They each had their fingers crossed and their heads bent together as the regional director of the competition took the mic to announce the winners.

I held my breath. West Wind had performed last and we'd

watched them through the tiny windows in the doors. From what little I could see through my itty-bitty corner, they had stuck everything as well. But—and I may have been biased here—their routine didn't seem to be as intricate as ours. And their tosses were just unimpressive. Still, they'd snorted at us smugly as they'd traipsed out of the gym, acting for all the world like the whole thing was a lock.

It was quite possible that I wanted them to lose even more than I wanted us to win. That whole school-rivalry thing? It just ain't pretty.

"First of all, I'd like to thank every squad here for treating us to the finest competition I've witnessed in a good many years," the director said, earning an uproarious response from the crowd. "Unfortunately, only three teams can place here today, and it was a difficult decision."

Mindy's grasp on my hand tightened. Behind me, Tara's breathing picked up the pace.

"Without further ado, let's announce the winners, although I think we can all agree that we're *all* winners here today."

More applause.

"Enough with the schmaltz," Tara said, earning nervous, shaking giggles from the rest of the squad and a few others around us.

The director looked down at the index card in her hand. My brain was completely deprived of oxygen. Was I hoping to place here, or hoping to win?

"In third place, the Palm River High Sharks!"

Relief and dread simultaneously filled my chest as the Palm River squad jumped up and down and raced to the center of the mat to claim their trophy. The captain clutched the prize and hugged her teammates, and I smiled. It looked like even third place felt good.

"In second place . . . our champions from last year, the West Wind High Dolphins!"

"Yes!" Tara Timothy said through her teeth.

The crowd cheered, but there was a brief pause before the West Wind squad got their enthusiasm up and headed for center stage. They put up a good front of cheering and screaming as they accepted their trophy, but I could tell they were stunned. They were only in second . . .

And there was only one trophy left.

"Congratulations, West Wind," the director said. "And now, I take great pleasure in introducing to you the new district champions of Southern Florida, the squad that will be heading to nationals next month to represent our region . . ."

Oh, God, just say it. Say it! I thought, gasping for breath. *The Sand Dune Fighting Crabs, the Sand Dune Fighting Crabs, the—*

"The Sand Dune High School Fighting Crabs!"

I launched myself into the air as at least five people tried to simultaneously hug me. I was knocked over, tripped up, and screaming the whole way. By the time I found my footing again, Tara and Phoebe were already hoisting the trophy high above their heads. We all crowded around, clutching each other, laughing, crying. Daniel was on his feet, cheering at the top of his lungs. My dad beamed with pride and my mom held her hand over her mouth to keep from crying. My brother had taken over the camera, crawling over a dozen people to get to the bottom of the stands for a better shot. Even Bethany got into the spirit, leaning into her brother, Bobby, in the stands as they both raised their arms in the air.

Suddenly, in the face of all those screaming Sand Dune fans, it started to really sink in. We had done it! We had won! We were going to nationals!

"Congratulations, Sand Dune High!" the director said, laughing at our mayhem. "Why don't you all gather around your trophy for the official championship photo?"

"Gladly!" Tara said.

She placed the trophy in the middle of the mat and I knelt down next to it with Jaimee and Sage at my sides. The taller girls like Felice, Chandra, Mindy and Autumn stood while the flyers took the floor. I was so giddy, I was barely able to keep my eyes on the camera.

"Why don't you try smiling?" the cameraman joked, earning laughs all around.

Tara reached out and grasped one of the poles on the trophy and Sage did the same. Whitney raised her hand with the classic number-one signal and we all followed suit.

"Now everyone say, 'Nationals!' " the photographer instructed.

"Nationals!" we shouted at the top of our lungs.

As the flash snapped away, I looked around at the rest of the squad and started to feel the pride that Coach Holmes had been talking about back in the hallway again. I was proud that we'd come together and gotten over our differences. Proud that we'd gotten back at those West Wind jerks. But most of all, I was proud of myself for sticking it out, for being myself.

I was a non-blonde cheerleader, and I was at Sand Dune High to stay.

Turn the page for a preview of
the next novel featuring Annisa,

Brunettes STRIKE BACK

"Go! Hey, here we go! Fighting! Crabs! Go!"

I thrust my fist toward the sky and grinned as the cheers of the crowd reverberated through my bones. I was never going to get used to the fact that the fans at Sand Dune High actually cheered along with the cheerleaders. I was never going to get used to the fact that they actually *showed up*. Back at my old school in Jersey, we were lucky if the entire marching band materialized. Even though games were mandatory, they were always finding excuses to skip out on watching our team throw interceptions, run toward the wrong goal and eat mud for four quarters.

"Go! Hey, here we go! Fighting! Crabs! Go!"

I glanced at my friend Mindy McMahon out of the corner of my eye and she smiled back. We were having one of those moments. One of those perfect moments when you just know that everything is coming together. The crowd was totally psyched. The squad was on. Even the weather felt like football. It was a cool night for South Florida—we had topped out at sixty degrees (I know, *shiver*), but because it was chilly by Sand Dune standards, we had finally been allowed to wear our little mock turtlenecks under our cheerleading vests. Honestly, we had been looking forward to this all season.

Meanwhile, on the football field behind us, the Sand

1

Dune High School Fighting Crabs were taking on the West Wind Dolphins in the county championship game. It was the rematch of the century! Well, okay, the decade. Okay, maybe the month. But still, it was huge. You could taste the tension in the air. Or was that just the overboiled hot dog smell coming from West Wind's snack bar?

We finished the cheer and turned to watch the action. Instinctively my eyes darted to the game clock. The last time we had played against the Dolphins, our archrivals, we had lost because of a mess-up by the officials involving the clock. Apparently they didn't know how to tell time. If anything went wrong tonight, this crowd was going to be grilling referee meat on the barbecue and serving it up for breakfast.

Okay, that was gross. But people were really pissed off. Still. Even though that travesty had occurred *weeks* ago. After all, the total injustice of what happened at that game spurred our football players and cheerleaders to go out and *vandalize* West Wind High as a finale to our weeklong prank war— an act that had landed all of us in jail.

Yes. Even me. Even though Mindy, Daniel Healy and I hadn't actually participated in any destruction, and we had been trying to sneak out of there, the Five-O nabbed us and tossed us in the big house.

Sorry. I hardly ever get to use words like that.

But suffice it to say we all wanted to beat West Wind now, fair and square. We all wanted it big-time.

"We have to get the ball back," Chandra Albohm, one of my teammates and friends, said in my ear, her voice as gravelly as ever. Her curly blonde hair danced around her face as a cool wind kicked up around us. "We have to get the ball back *now.*"

She was right. There was a minute left in the game. We were down by three points. The defense had to stop West Wind on the next play or it was over.

I looked down the track at the rest of the squad, lined up like sentries, their little blonde heads all in a row. I, Annisa Gobrowski, was the sole brunette on the Sand Dune High School varsity cheerleading squad. Well, the sole brunette who hadn't fallen victim to the peroxide fetish that abounds around here. Everyone stood with their feet apart, their hands behind their backs, holding their light blue and yellow poms. Everyone looked tense. Especially Tara Timothy, captain of the squad, our "fearless" (air-quote) leader.

Tara was the only cheerleader breaking formation, totally bizarre for a stickler like her, but it had been happening a lot lately. She clutched both poms in one hand behind her back and with her other hand reached up and rubbed the tatty blue ribbon that was wrapped around her long blonde ponytail. Her *lucky* hair ribbon, as she was constantly reminding us. I glanced down at her feet and grimaced. The elastic in her "lucky" socks was all stretched out and the formerly white cotton had taken on a gray tinge. This girl was falling apart.

The whistle blew out on the field. Time-out. I glanced at Chandra and Mindy. Right about now, Tara should be calling a cheer. Instead she was just rubbing her ribbon harder.

"Um, Tara?" Jaimee Mulholland prompted. Jaimee was one of the juniors on the squad and she was next to Tara in the formation.

"What?" Tara snapped, coming out of her trance.

"We should be doing a cheer, right? 'Cause it's a time-out?" Jaimee twirled her thick blonde ponytail nervously. "I mean, if *you* think we should."

3

Tara glanced around as if she was just now realizing where she was. "'Defense Get Tough'!" she shouted, turning toward the crowd. "Ready?"

"Okay!" we all shouted.

We executed the cheer, which ended with me and a couple of other girls up in double base extensions. I shook my poms as the crowd applauded, then dismounted into Mindy, Chandra and Autumn's arms.

"Okay, Miss Tara hasn't changed her socks *or* her hair ribbons since we won regionals," Chandra said under her breath.

"She's become a completely superstitious being," Autumn Ross said, brushing a lock of her white-blonde hair back behind her ear. "It's not healthy. Maybe we should stage an intervention. We could start her on a meditation program to help her de-stress. Oh! Or maybe she could use some acupuncture!"

"Come on, it's not that bad," Mindy said, though she bit her lip when she noticed the socks.

"I just hope she's not doing the same with her underwear," I joked.

"Ew! Annisa!" Mindy wailed. She shoved me with her poms, but she and the others cracked up anyway.

"Okay, if we win this game, then we're going to win at nationals," Tara said, loud enough for all of us to hear. Her two best friends, Whitney Barnard and Phoebe Cook, rolled their eyes behind her back. "No, we'll *place*. We win this game and we'll definitely *place* at nationals," she amended.

Sage Barnard, Whitney's little sister, twirled her finger in a circle at her temple. A couple of the other girls cracked up. I had never liked Sage, but right then she had a point. Tara was making up her *own* superstitions now. The girl was bongo-bonkers.

"Ladies!" Coach Holmes hissed from her spot under the bleachers. "Pay attention to the game, please!"

We instantly did as we were told. Coach brings out the cadet in all of us.

On the field West Wind called a play and Bobby Goow, Tara's boyfriend and the team's star defensive end, burst through the line and slammed the West Wind quarterback into the turf. Sack! It was exactly what we needed. I jumped up and down, screaming with the rest of the fans as Autumn threw her arms around me. West Wind would have to punt. We would get the ball back with fifty-one seconds to go!

My heart pounded as West Wind lined up to punt the ball. At this point, we pretty much lost the will to stay in formation. Mindy, Autumn, Chandra, Jaimee and I huddled together, clutching hands, holding our breath with the rest of the Sand Dune fans. The ball arched through the air, end over end, and came down right in the hands of . . .

Daniel Healy! My boyfriend! *My* boyfriend was going to have the chance to win the game!

Well, my maybe-boyfriend. We hadn't actually said the boyfriend/girlfriend words yet, but we would. Soon. I hoped. In my head he was already my boyfriend. But then, a lot of things go on inside my head.

Anyway, now Daniel was running down the field. He dodged. He weaved. A huge West Wind player came flying toward him and Daniel ducked out of the way and stayed on his feet. The defender sailed right over Daniel and crashed into the ground. It was a total highlight-reel moment. I could just hear the SportsCenter theme music playing in my ear.

5

"Oh my God! Go!" I shouted. "Go, Daniel! Run!"

There was nothing but open field in front of him. Suddenly he was zooming across the fifty . . . the forty . . . the thirty.

"Go! Go! Go!" we screamed, jumping up and down.

There was only one defender anywhere near him. The guy reached out to grab Daniel's jersey just as he crossed into the end zone, but Terrell Truluck appeared out of nowhere and took him out. Crack! A sweet block. And Daniel was in! Touchdown!

"Touchdown, number thirty-two, Daniel Healy!" The announcer called out as the entire team huddled and jumped and thrust their helmets into the air. Daniel and Terrell jumped up and smacked chests, celebrating. I hugged everybody in sight. We were up by three! We could really win this one!

Adam Rider kicked the extra point and now all we had to do was stop West Wind on the next play. They would have one shot for a Hail Mary. One shot to beat us.

Adam kicked the ball off. The entire squad was huddled together. Tara rubbed her ribbon like it was Aladdin's lamp. Some guy on West Wind caught the ball. If he could do what Daniel had just done, West Wind would win. But Bobby wasn't having any of it. He raced upfield and before the returner had taken a step, Bobby smacked into him head-on, drilling him into the ground.

Time ran out. And the world pretty much exploded.

"We won! We won!" Jaimee shouted in my ear.

The entire football team rushed the field. The Sand Dune stands emptied out in a wave of insanity. Everyone was hugging me and screaming and twirling around. The band was playing "Nah nah nah nah! Nah nah nah nah! Hey, hey, hey! Good-bye!" Which was exactly what the West Wind fans had chanted at us when they had beaten us last time. So there.

Flashbulbs popped. Someone was taking a ton of pictures and purple dots floated across my vision. All I could think was, *I have to find Daniel! He's the hero! My maybe-boyfriend is the hero of the county championship!*

I spun around in the crowd and there he was, looking right at me from midfield as his teammates slapped his back and celebrated around him. His hair was matted to his head with sweat and his face was smudged with dirt and grime. My heart stopped and then slammed into my rib cage in total elation. In that split second I imagined the movie moment in my mind. I would jump into his arms. He would lift me off my feet and twirl me around, my cheerleading pleats flying . . . .

"Daniel!"

Out of nowhere, Sage raced across the field and into Daniel's arms. Suddenly I was watching the movie reel exactly as I had imagined it, but I had been bumped from the starring role. Daniel laughed as he hugged Sage and swept her off her feet. Her blonde hair bounced like a shampoo ad as she clutched him in blatant adoration. Daniel wasn't hugging me. He was hugging his evil ex. My heart dried up like a tomato in the sun.

How could he hug her? They were broken up! And she had treated him like dirt, cheating on him with my very own brother in front of a house party full of people! And hello? He was *supposed* to be hugging me!

I had been crushing on Daniel since the moment I met him on my first day of school, and it had almost killed me when I found out he was dating Miss Britney-Clone, Sage Barnard. Okay, that may be overstating it, but still. I had pined from afar until she cheated and they broke up. I was all ready to be a shoulder to cry on for him, but then he admitted to me that he had been thinking about breaking up with her for a while. Eureka! And soon we were becoming maybe-boyfriend-and-girlfriend.

So I ask again, *why* was he hugging *her*?

"Annisa!"

Terrell Truluck—wide receiver, friend of Daniel's, thrower of sick blocks—stepped out of the crowd. He had a white streak of yard-line powder on the dark skin of his forearm and his shaved head was glistening.

"Whooooo! We did it!" he shouted, grabbing me up in a hug. I hugged him back, letting him swing me around, and forced a smile. With his movie-star smile and deep brown eyes, Terrell was pretty much a lock to win best-looking in his class, so if I couldn't hug Daniel, I supposed he wasn't a bad substitute.

"Great game!" I told him as he put me down again.

And then Daniel was there at my side. "Not as great as this playah!" Terrell shouted, slapping hands with Daniel. Daniel grinned and they did the manly, one-armed hug thing before Daniel finally, *finally* stepped up to me and enveloped me in his arms.

He smelled like a gym sock. His jersey was soaked through. Some mud rubbed off on my cheek. Still, I had never felt so relieved.

"You do realize you just won the game," I said to him. "You personally."

Daniel grinned sheepishly. "Nah. It was a team effort."

"Yeah, you just keep telling yourself that," I said. "That was an amazing run."

"Thanks," Daniel said as the celebration continued around us. "The guys are all going back to Crush's house for a party, but I was thinking . . . maybe we could go to Dolly's first? Just you and me? For some victory fries?"

My pulse raced so hard that my body temperature skyrocketed. See? He's totally my boyfriend. He was probably hugging Sage only because she threw herself at him . . . right? One of these days that girl was going to have to start dealing with the fact that Daniel was *my* boyfriend now.

Maybe.

"I'm there," I said.

"Sweet," he replied.

He was just about to kiss me when a bunch of guys emerged from the crowd and lifted him up off his feet, hoisting him over their shoulders. I laughed at Daniel's stunned expression. The mob went wild when they saw the hero of the moment lifted up above their heads. A couple of reporters from the local cable station approached the insanity, gunning for Daniel.

"It could be a while!" Daniel shouted down to me as he was bumped away.

"I'll be here!" I shouted back.

And then I did what any self-respecting cheerleader would do. I leaped into the psychotic throng.

• • •

"Oy. You are just all kinds of barf-worthy right now," Bethany Goow said to me as we walked toward the West Wind High parking lot with the rest of the Sand Dune crowd.

9

"Gee, thanks," I replied with an eye roll. "And did you just say 'oy'? Are you Yiddish all of a sudden?"

"I can 'oy' if I want to 'oy,'" she grumbled.

Actually, Bethany Goow could say pretty much anything and get away with it. She of the black eyeliner, black nail polish and jewelry that could probably double as weaponry was my best friend at Sand Dune High. The antithesis of all my other friends who loved school and loved life, Bethany hated pretty much everything around her. Except me. And her website, sucks-to-be-us.com. She reserved a special place in her bile pit for her brother, Bobby Goow, his girlfriend, Tara Timothy, and all the cheerleaders, football players and pep-squad members at SDH. Again, except for me. She came to the games only to support me—and crack herself up by mocking everybody else.

I so wished I could introduce her to Jordan Trott, my bff from Jersey. The two of them practically shared the same brain from a thousand miles away. Unfortunately, I hadn't even talked to Jordan in days. We were both so busy lately, it seemed like all we had time for was prolonged phone tag. But I would *have* to get her on the phone tonight. Jordan lived for a juicy SDH update and she would know exactly what to say to make me feel better about the whole Daniel and Sage situation.

"Seriously, could you stop blushing for five seconds so I don't have to hurl on Sage Barnard's backpack," she said, glancing up ahead. She frowned thoughtfully. "Actually . . . that could be interesting—"

"Be my guest," I grumbled.

"Sweet," Bethany said, rubbing her hands together.

"No! I'm just kidding!" I cried, grabbing her arm. "I'm not

blushing anymore." While I wouldn't mind seeing Sage's face if someone barfed on her, I wasn't quite jerky enough to let it happen.

"Okay, so, I really want you to do an exposé on this whole nationals thing for the site," Bethany said, unwrapping a Tootsie Pop and shoving it in her mouth. "You could go around and ask all the cheerleaders which is their preferred eating disorder of the moment and—"

"Bethany!" I said with a groan. "I thought we were working on our stereotypes!"

Her dark eyes widened. "I am! I just—"

There went that flashbulb again, going off like a strobe light in my face. I squinted and instinctively raised my hands. Before I knew what was happening, I heard a scuffle, and when I was able to focus again, Bethany had a tall, skinny guy in a blue polo shirt pinned up against the chain-link fence that ran all around the football field. He looked vaguely familiar, but I couldn't place him. Maybe it was the look of terror in his eyes that was throwing me off.

"Bethany!" Jaimee gasped, jogging up from behind us.

"Somebody's been working out," the kid said.

Bethany ripped the camera out of his hand and let his neck go. "Ever hear of personal space?" she asked.

He looked and smirked. "Ever hear of small claims court? 'Cause if you break my camera, that's where we'll be."

"No need to sue," I said. "Bethany, give the nice boy his camera back."

Bethany narrowed her eyes and offered up the digital camera. The kid checked it over quickly, making sure nothing was broken. He looked at me and sort of half smiled, and suddenly I knew why I knew him. This was the guy. The guy who had taken the most humiliating picture of my life. I *hated* this guy.

A few weeks back, during my very first pep rally at Sand Dune High, I had gotten overzealous and missed the foot placement on one of our pyramids. Thanks to my supreme klutziness, the whole stunt had gone down and this kid had snapped a picture of me with my skirt up and my briefs on display. As if that wasn't bad enough, he had slapped it on the front page of the school newspaper, the *Weekly Catch*, for all the world to see and save.

"Annisa, this is Steven Schwinn," Jaimee said with her ever-present bright smile. "Steven is one of my best friends. We've known each other since we were about five years old and he knocked on my door and asked my parents if he could swim in our pool. He already had his swimmies on and a mask and everything. And he was, like, breathing through a snorkel. I thought he was going to faint. It was so cute. So anyway, when he said he wanted to meet you, I told him I would introduce you, natch. You don't mind, do you?"

Did I mention that Jaimee is a natural babbler? And she asks permission for basically everything. I wonder if her parents are really strict.

"It's a pleasure, milady," Steven said. He lifted his camera and snapped a picture of my undoubtedly ill-looking face.

"Did you just call her 'milady'?" Bethany said, amused.

"You have a problem with chivalry?" Steven asked, arching an eyebrow.

"Yeah, it was very chivalrous when you took a picture of me with my skirt over my head and published it for the entire school to enjoy," I said flatly.

"That was one of my favorite shots of all time," Steven

said proudly. He looked into his viewfinder and adjusted some knob or other. "I have it blown-up on the bulletin board in the *Weekly Catch* office. You know, you should autograph it for us!"

Unbelievable. I looked at Bethany. "Him, you can barf on."

"Annisa!" Jaimee said, wide-eyed. She looked at Bethany like she thought Bethany was actually going to stick her finger down her throat.

Steven lifted his free hand. "I was just doing my job!"

"You have to take that picture down," I told him. "I'll beg if you want me to."

"*Real*-ly?" he said with a kind of suggestive grin.

"Okay, you don't know me well enough to look at me like that," I said.

"You're right. I'm sorry," Steven said. "Consider me shamed."

"I'd like to consider you invisible," Bethany said, rolling her eyes.

"I second that."

Bethany and I shook our heads and rejoined the crowd. I couldn't believe Jaimee was friends with this nutcase. But then again, Jaimee was one of those super-nice people who could be friends with anyone. You had to love that about her.

I noticed that Sage, Whitney, Tara, Bobby and Christopher had stopped up ahead to chat. I had no idea where Daniel had disappeared to, but my guess was he was being interviewed by those reporters who had corralled him after the game. My maybe-boyfriend the celebrity.

"You're going to have to get used to me, Annisa," Steven said, failing to take our not-so-subtle hints. He fell into step with me. "I'm going to be covering all of the squad's events from now until nationals. You know, following you all on your road to glory."

"He's doing a retrospectacle," Jaimee said.

"I think you mean retrospective," Felice put in, walking up behind us.

"Yeah, right," Jaimee said, blushing slightly. "Anyway, he's even coming on the bus with us and everything. Coach Holmes said it was okay."

"Great. Maybe you can get a shot of me snoring with drool coming out of my mouth," I told him.

"Funny," he said. He whipped out a digital planner and powered it up. "So I want to schedule a time to meet with you one day this week. What's good for you? I'm free Tuesday."

"Why do you want to meet with me?" I asked.

"To interview you for my piece," he said, like it was obvious.

"Again, the question 'why me?' comes to mind."

"Yeah, why her?" Sage added, jumping into the conversation as we passed her by. I saw Bethany's fingers curl into fists. Sage's very voice sent Bethany's undies into a twist. Mine too, actually.

What was *really* irritating about her was that I had *thought* we were starting to become friends—or at least calling a truce. I mean, she had apologized to me for all the crappy stuff she had done to me in my first weeks on the squad. I had thought that meant something. But ever since regionals when Daniel had kissed me for luck instead of her, she had been back to her super-bitchy ways.

"Well, you're the new girl on the squad," Steven said,

addressing me and ignoring Sage. Nice. Maybe I *did* like this guy. "You're from New Jersey and I heard you never competed before. You're the perfect human-interest piece."

"Please! Her?" Sage said, pulling a disgusted face. "She's *so* unphotogenic!"

How this girl is in honors English with me, I have no idea.

"Sage!" Jaimee scolded.

"I'm not sure that's a word," Felice said.

"Whatever, I'm just trying to be honest!" Sage replied. "Really, Annisa, your hair is, like, ripped from *I Love the 90s.*"

"You *sure* you don't want me to barf on her?" Bethany asked.

"Ew! What are you even doing here?" Sage said to Bethany. "Shouldn't you be under a rock somewhere?"

"And shouldn't you be off getting your lip waxed?" Bethany shot back.

Sage gasped, brought her hand to her lip and scurried off. Good riddance.

"Does she really need a lip wax?" I asked.

"Please! Haven't you ever seen her in natural light?" Bethany asked. "It's like Chewbacca molted up there."

"So, about the article," Steven said.

"Look, I got dibs on Annisa's story for my website," Bethany told him, looping her arm around my shoulders. "So you can just take your little camera and go interview the water boy or something."

"You can't have an exclusive on her!" Steven replied, his jaw dropping. "I work for the official SDH newspaper. We take priority over your underground web crap."

"Web crap? Oh, you are so dead!"

Omigod. The press was arguing over me.

"You guys!" I said, stopping in my tracks. "This isn't about me! It's about the squad!"

I was no different from anyone else on my team. Well, unless you counted the short brown hair and the occasional—*occasional*—pyramid-obliterating clumsiness. Besides, my relationship with most of my team was sketchy enough as it was. After all, I had made the squad only when two other members had been tossed over getting caught drinking—an event most of the team blamed me for, thinking that I had tattled on their fallen teammates. (Not true, but people believe what they want to believe.) The last thing I needed was for any of them to think I was trying to steal the spotlight or hog the glory.

"If anyone's doing a story on nationals, it should be about the team," I said firmly.

"That's just it. I'm doing a bunch of pieces, so I need a lot of different angles," Steven told me.

"That's why they call it a retrospective," Felice put in.

"Exactly," Steven said. "You'll just be one angle of many."

"Come on, Annisa, you should totally do it," Jaimee said. "I mean, if you want to," she added with a shrug. "You don't want to turn down your fifteen minutes, do you? I mean, unless you do."

"If you don't do an interview, I'm going to do the piece anyway," Steven said. "I'll just have to talk to your teammates instead. Sage Barnard seemed like she might have a lot to say . . . "

"You wouldn't," I said.

"Try me," he replied.

Bethany stuck her finger in her mouth and tilted her head toward him suggestively.

"Come on, Annisa! You should do it! Free press!" Felice said.

I sighed in resignation. "All right, fine. I'll do the interview," I said, my shoulders slumping as I started walking again.

"Freakin' mainstream press," Bethany grumbled under her breath.

I smirked and kicked at a soda cup in my path. Maybe Jaimee was right. Maybe it was time for my fifteen minutes. Well, at least my fifteen minutes with my skirt on properly.

17